A VORACIOUS GRIEF

LINDSEY LAMH

A Voracious Grief

©2023 Lindsey Lamh

THE POEMS OF EMILY DICKINSON: READING EDITION, edited by Ralph. W. Franklin, Cambridge, Mass.: The Belknap Press of Harvard University Press, Copyright ©1998, 1999 by the President and Fellows of Harvard College. Copyright ©1951, 1955 by the President and Fellows of Harvard College. Copyright © renewed 1979, 1983 by the President and Fellows of Harvard College. Copyright ©1914, 1918, 1919, 1924, 1929, 1930, 1932, 1935, 1937, 1942 by Martha Dickinson Bianchi. Copyright ©1952, 1957 1958, 1963, 1965 by Mary L. Hampson. Used by permission. All rights reserved.

Published by Lamh Books LLC

First edition, 2023

Library of Congress Control Number: 2023908282

www.LindseyLamh.com

Dedicated to firstborns everywhere —
you're so worth it

CONTENTS

CHAPTER 1

The Feet, mechanical, go round —
A Wooden way
Of Ground, or Air, or Ought —
Regardless grown,
A Quartz contentment, like a stone.

— EMILY DICKINSON

W hat place is fitting to hang the portrait of the man who caused us much misery? This one decision proves more of a conundrum than I anticipated. At the manor house, Grandfather's portrait hung in the formal parlor, where guests too important or not intimate enough to be shown to his personal sitting room were received. In either case, the life-sized replica of Lord Henry's heavy gray brows was sure to impress or intimidate. Now, our patriarch's face leans against the foyer wall at Norwich House, scowling at my long black dress shoes and our housekeeper's narrow brown ones.

Tothill makes yet another suggestion, her hands folded neatly over the waist of her apron. "You could put it over the fireplace in the library."

Picturing my grandfather's aged jowls and piercing glare hovering above my favorite pair of armchairs, I shake my head. "No, that won't do at all."

"The stairway, then?" Her tone holds the barest hint of exasperation.

I tilt my head to one side and study her. The woman couldn't peer over my shoulder even on tiptoe. Despite her red hair and foxfire eyes, she's an even-tempered, gentle old soul.

"Would *you* like to think of Grandfather stuffed into some dim corner while folk pass him by without a glance?"

Tothill shivers. "I ain't superstitious, you know. But I suppose doin' such a thing may well cause his lordship to haunt me."

"Indeed." I sigh. But there truly is no comfortable place here at Norwich House. Not in the dining room, where his scowl would banish all cheerful conversation. The library is full of fond memories in which he played no role. A bedroom is unthinkable. In each, his thin, tightly closed lips would be too pointed a reminder of the lectures we endured when he was alive.

"The sitting room," I say at last.

Tothill follows me to the adjoining room, a very long space divided into several groupings of settees and armchairs. It is meant for entertaining, with a pianoforte tucked in a sunny back corner. There is not one mantle over which to place my grandfather's portrait, but two.

"Which one?" Tothill asks, turning round and round in the middle of the room, attempting to examine both fireplaces at once. "And what will you hang over the other?"

"Did my father never ...?"

But it is pointless to ask. I know Francis Bancroft was only ever lord in name, not in practice. Having his portrait painted would never have crossed his mind.

I run my fingers along the neck of my cravat, loosening it. "I really don't know."

"Perhaps Miss Bancroft could paint something fitting," Tothill suggests. "I'll have his lordship put over the nearer fireplace, if that suits?"

"That will do just fine, Tothill."

I go up to my study. It's a small space off my bedroom, with only a desk and a mountain of crates I've yet to unpack. Books, mostly, and all the legal documents and records from Linwood, which I've brought to London to go over with the assistance of my solicitor, Monsieur Belot.

Leaving the door open, I pull the lid off the nearest crate and breathe in the sweet, pungent scent of old books. A fat, leather-bound volume lies near the top, and I tug at it, chuckling at its weight. The spine is worn, the fabric cover softened with age, but the faded gold lettering is as familiar as my own name. Dr. Gustavo Haenel's *Librorum Manuscriptorum*, my old Latin textbook. The next volume is the first of twenty-eight worn, dog-eared encyclopedias, which I had pored over as a child. I place them on a pair of shelves to the left of my desk at a comfortable height, then I step back and appreciate the effect.

A light rap on the door brings me out of my quiet, dust-mote world. I turn to see Donnie peering round the doorframe. "May I bring in the last of 'em, Lord Bancroft?"

"More?" I say, surveying the cramped space.

"Yes, sir." Donnie heaves in a box stuffed in haphazard fashion with leather-bound journals. "There was this, which Tothill was instructed by his lordship—that is, Lord Francis—to present to you when you might—that is, when it seemed fitting."

Casting his eyes about the room, Donnie shoves the box into a corner and steps quickly across the threshold as if to take his leave of me.

"Wait a moment," I call after him.

He's our driver and stable keeper, but he's also Tothill's adopted son and, therefore, a long-term member of the household. When we were children, he was sometimes permitted to play with my siblings and me during school holidays. After so many years, I recognize the blotched red on his face as a sign of discomfort.

"You said my father asked her to give it to me? *Me*, in particular? Not the Bancroft heir?"

Donnie's eyes shift to the crate. He wrings a tan wool cap in his broad, calloused hands. "Are you not the heir, m'lord?"

"I am now."

This interchange serves to unsettle poor Donnie further. He shuffles his feet, keen to be going.

"Do you know what these are?" I press him, picking out one of the journals. The script is unfamiliar. Not my father's. I look to Donnie for an explanation.

He's taller than I, though his deferential hunch masks it. His broad shoulders have no trouble handling four rowdy horses and a carriage, but in company or upstairs, next to the private chambers of his employers, he is out of his element.

"She weren't given any further explanation, sir. Only that you should have the box when the time came. It happened when his lordship were on his sickbed."

This last tidbit is worth digging for, though I have no idea what it means.

"That's all, on my honor," Donnie adds, clapping his hands, muffled by the hat, and giving me a perfunctory grin.

"Very good." I release him at last. I hear his boots clomp down the nearby servant stairs.

I find I've lost interest in unpacking my old books. The mysterious new box is waiting in a dark corner. It proves too heavy for me to lift. Looking sheepishly out the door, I'm relieved no one witnessed my futile attempt. Instead, I take half a dozen of the journals to my desk. I turn my chair to put the window at my back so the afternoon sun falls across the page and begin to read.

There's nothing quite as soporific as perusing the spidery script of an unfamiliar hand, especially when the entries turn out to be rather mundane. When I sit up again some time later, the afternoon light is dimming to evening. Snapping the journal shut, I stack it and its fellows along one side of my desk and cross the hall to Mattie's bedroom. My sister will not join me for tea, but I never fail to ask.

"Mattie, aren't you coming down? It's five o'clock." I rap lightly a third time.

She replies in a muffled, annoyed tone, and something lands against the other side of the door. A pillow. Most likely, my sister has yet to emerge from her bed.

"Very well." Running my hand down the wood, I add with a prolonged sigh, "Oh, Mattie ..."

The next day is Sunday, and I attend Mass at St. Barnabas. In a twisted sort of way, I am aware of how this place lacks painful reminders. I do not feel my late brother's absence as I enter the vast, painted nave amid thundering organ arpeggios. Bennett was an Anglican. I have never visited his church in London, though he came once to St. Barnabas to hear a traveling boys' choir.

"Very pretty," he said, with that far-off look of his, which meant he was lost in some train of thought having to do with *why*.

This morning, I'm a nameless gentleman in a sea of satin dresses and silk suits. I'm a single tenor in a thousand-voice choir, lifting up the tune of a hymn three hundred years old. When we sit again, surrounded by the dying vibrations of the song, the Latin words of the liturgy pour over my ears as soothing as the play of a brook. Like water, the power of these words is ancient, molding stone and turning aside the hearts of men. I sit under them willingly.

"Amen," rings the last word. Then I'm moving, smiling a stiff stranger's smile, heading outside in a throng of Londoners.

"Lord Bancroft!" A mature woman's voice catches my attention as I'm descending the church stoop. "Yes, it is him. Come, my dear! Come and greet Lord Bancroft!"

They are Mrs. and Miss Amity, the elder being a well-respected hostess of popular soirees, the younger her unwed daughter. Mrs. Amity's interest in renewing our acquaintance is obvious.

"Lord Ambrose Bancroft, may I present Miss Catherine Amity," she says, and they sink into elegant curtsies.

"Ah, Miss Amity! I do believe we met last autumn when you were a debutante. How could I forget it?" The young woman blushes and looks down at her folded gloves. But before her mother's hopes can soar too high, I turn upon them a most somber frown and add, "Indeed, I cannot soon forget that night. You might recall my brother and I leaving the ballroom in something of a hurry? That night marked the beginning of Bennett's illness. He was coughing blood, you see. I've not been back to London since his death."

Mrs. Amity clutches her daughter's arm, a gasp escaping behind her raised handkerchief. "Oh, that's right! I'd nearly forgotten you've only just emerged from mourning. Beg your pardon, good sir."

Inching away from me, Mrs. Amity and her daughter fling apologies and condolences behind them like an exorcist flinging holy water. Feeling a small twinge of guilt at misusing my brother's memory, I make my way out from under the shadow of St. Barnabas.

This close to the Thames, London is fog-cloaked. I amble under maples half-dressed for autumn, eventually turning onto the wide, chaotic Pall Mall. Returning on foot to St. James's Square after church was a ritual of mine when I lived at Norwich House with Grandfather. Despite being a walk of over a mile, I undertook the journey in all kinds of weather, thankful for a long respite from the oppressive air of Lord Henry's domain.

"Ah, Norwich," I say, pausing at the iron fence to look over the house. Fourteen cobalt-shuttered windows stand at attention under the steep slate roof and a quartet of chimneys. The lawn is clipped short, the cream stone walls kept bare of creeping ivy. The only gesture at softening the militaristic exterior of the place is a pair of topiaries which flank the front door. It suited my grandfather.

When we lived here together, I trodded carefully, keeping to my room and never daring to invite callers of my own set. But Bennett would draw me out. He fled the Oxford dons rather frequently. The two of us would cloister ourselves in the cramped upstairs library, our wing-backed armchairs pulled close as we spoke in low voices.

"You look older," I tell the old house as I push open the iron gate. It whines at me.

"Gate needs oil," I tell the butler. Only, it's Grandfather's voice I hear grinding out of my lips. But the Norwich butler was hired recently. He nods and hurries off for the oil, mistaking the flush of my face for impatience instead of embarrassment.

The maid, arranging hydrangeas on the foyer side table, pauses in her task to pull a string-bound packet of letters from her apron pocket and curtsies. "The post, sir."

I take them upstairs with me, shuffling through the first three in quick succession. The fourth is an expensive invitation. The wax seal bears one of the most recognizable family crests in London society—the rampant eagle of the Lawrences.

Breaking open the envelope, I hurry along the narrow hall to stand outside my sister's bedroom door. There are hydrangeas in this hall too, and the dark mahogany floorboards are freshly oiled, but the wallpaper still smells of tobacco. Rapping on the door to Mattie's bedroom, I listen for her muffled response. But I hear nothing at all.

With incredulous anticipation, I turn to the door of her sitting room and crack it open.

"Good God, Mattie, you're out of bed!"

She startles at the sound of my voice, hiding something under her skirt. "Ambrose! Did you just break a commandment? On the Lord's day, no less."

Looking at her, it's obvious my sister is the sort of woman who suffers bouts of severe melancholia and fevers. Her frail shoulders are slumped, wrinkling her dress and giving her a sullen air. She still wears black, despite our being well past the proper period of mourning. The dark clothes and near-blackness of her hair exaggerates the ghostly paleness of her complexion. Her large gray eyes study me, unblinking, as I cross to sit next to her on the settee. At least her hair is curled and pinned up, as befits a lady of Matilda Bancroft's station.

I take her hands. They're too cold.

"Forgive the exclamation. I'm merely relieved. Do you feel well?"

"My body suffers only the vagaries of a troubled mind," Mattie says, lifting a sardonic brow. "I got up because I wanted to look through the things Father left you. Tothill mentioned she'd sent Donnie to your office with a box of journals. I was quite curious."

"Ah, yes. Those were ..." I search for a word, wondering again why Father bequeathed such a strange collection to me in particular and without a bit of explanation.

"They were boring." Mattie groans. "And now I've endured an hour of being made presentable for no reason at all."

"Then make it more worthwhile. Let's walk the square." I stand to pull at her hand. A ribbon of yellow afternoon sun slips between the sitting room curtains. But Mattie doesn't rise.

"What's that?" she asks, dropping her gaze to the stack of letters in my hand.

"An invitation." I hand it to her. "I've already received the new dresses Madame Bouline made for you. Will you try them on? You might enjoy it now we've a soiree to attend."

Mattie glares at the gold lettering, then lets it drop to the floor. "No need. I won't be going."

"What do you mean? This is the whole reason we've come to London."

Mattie squeezes her hands in her lap, two large tear drops falling over her white knuckles. "I'm not ready. Not by far, Ambrose."

Sitting again, I place my hand on her trembling shoulder. "We've spent six months in mourning, as is proper. We must reenter society before it's too late. All of our departed—Bennett especially—would want to see you happily settled and our lives return to normal. You and I have so much left to do, Mattie."

This speech brings to mind a vision of things as they should be: Mattie no longer cloistered in her darkened bedroom, no longer in a state of near-insanity, unable to speak a word to anyone. I picture myself too, sitting behind my father's desk, settling accounts, overseeing some sort of charitable enterprise counterbalanced by various prudent investments suggested by my solicitor. Sitting under an awning on the village green, sponsoring a picnic, perhaps. The village folk would come up in groups of twos and threes to compliment me on how Mattie and I are getting on, to express their gratitude that I'm not like my grandfather.

I'm satisfied with such a vision.

But Mattie wrings her hands, stumbling to her feet. "Ambrose, give me a little longer. I'm not ready to go back into society. It'll be a disaster!"

I stand, taking her damp hands. "You'll have to come out again sooner or later. Why not get it over with? We'll do it together."

Mattie shakes her head, pulling away, and crosses to her bedroom door. Her footsteps are too soft to be heard; her movement hardly stirs the air. I'm left standing in the middle of the room, feeling foolish, as though I was talking to myself. Stooping, I take the invitation and look at the date inscribed on it: *Tuesday, October 12th.*

"There's time yet," I tell myself.

It will take a lot of coaxing to bring my sister to the place I envision. But for as long as I can remember, I've been looking after Mattie. A good brother cares for his little sister, doesn't he? I only want what's best for her—to see her settled somewhere other than our empty manor, away from this sterile townhouse. Someday, I hope to see Mattie happy again.

CHAPTER 2

*There's been a Death, in the Opposite House
As lately as Today—
I know it, by the numb look
Such Houses have—alway—*

— EMILY DICKINSON

"She's feverish," Tothill tells me, emerging from my sister's bedroom the morning of the twelfth. "It makes no sense. She was quite well yesterday."

"These fevers come and go," I say, rubbing my beard. "Though it seems they come on at the least convenient times."

Tothill nods. "Shall I send for Dr. Brooks?"

"No, it's only a fever."

Tothill passes me by, heading for the servant stairs, and a wave of memory knocks me over. Spinning in its undertow, I reach out toward her. "Wait!"

She turns. Her expression softens, though she doesn't speak until I've managed to choke out the rest of what I want to say.

"It wouldn't hurt to have Dr. Brooks look in on her, does it?"

Tothill doesn't shame me. She doesn't say, "If you'd called for him *that time*, maybe Abigail would be the one procuring Mattie's gowns, tempting her with healthful broths, and coaxing her to emerge from her shell of sorrow. *Abigail* would've been far more adept at all these things, you know."

Instead, Tothill dabs at her eyes with the corner of her apron. "It never hurts, sir."

When she's gone away, I come back to myself, gulping air like a drowned man. My feet sink into the sitting room carpet, and my hands feel the heat of the fireplace behind me. I can smell the dried lavender Tothill uses to scent my suits. The cracked window lets in a whiff of a rain-washed street, and I hear the distant bell of St. Paul's Cathedral.

"Right." I exhale. "I've plenty of time before I must dress."

The study is just as I left it. I run my fingers across the *Librorum* as I pass the bookshelf. I still need to make a thorough examination of the journals. But the task will have to wait until I've more time. Sinking into the leather chair, I take out the stack of mail and fumble in a drawer for my ebony letter opener. The pile of leather journals is sitting just as I left them. I feel the cool, smooth bone inside the drawer.

"Strange," I say aloud, pulling it open further. Last time I dug through here, it rattled. "Is something missing?"

The ebony opener makes short work of the envelopes. I open up the estate account book, pile the business correspondence neatly to one side, and dip my pen in the inkwell. With the steel nib hovering over the page, a droplet evaporating slow as glacial ice, I remember the boyish glee with which Father used to settle the accounts. Even now, if I turn back two pages, I can see where his last entries come to an abrupt halt and mine begin, his handwriting as familiar as my own. It makes the identity of the journals' author all the more mysterious.

"Drat it all." I plunk the pen down in the inkwell again. "Whatever did you leave me these journals for, Father?"

I shuffle back through page after page of the account book, questing for a clue. Father wrote notes of a strange sort in the margins surrounding his tidy bookkeeping. They're written in red ink, perhaps for distinction. But skimming them sheds no light upon the matter.

Pushing back in my chair, I snatch one of the journals, and the whole pile clatters over. They're strange shapes, stuffed full of pages, each bound by a thick leather strap to keep from bursting open. I recall Mattie mentioning she was curious enough about these journals to rise from bed.

"But if she *did* look through them, they ought to have tumbled down then as well," I say to myself.

Unfastening the strap on the journal in my hand, I open to the first entry. It's obvious at once this is the same journal I read and then placed on the top of the pile. My frustration mounting, I tidy the desk again, returning everything to its usual place. "Why would she lie to me?"

Then the cause of the missing rattle comes to me. The

laudanum bottle rolling and bumping about. It was packed among my things after Bennett's funeral, though I am no longer his sickbed nurse, nor do I intend to begin dosing myself to sleep. But now the drawer holds only extra paper and slides out smoothly.

"What's she done now?" I huff, slamming the drawer shut.

I march downstairs and meet Tothill coming in from sending the telegram for Dr. Brooks.

She plucks nervously at the ribbons under her chin, dislodging her hat. "She's not taken a turn for the worse, has she?"

"Not unless you mean her moral character," I say, snappish and green. "Tothill, is it possible my sister is faking this illness? You know how reluctant she is to attend the soiree."

Tothill is not an imposing figure. Her tiny feet can wear her daughter's handed-down school shoes. Her spindly hands and pile of wispy red hair atop her prim head make her look like a fairy. As a boy, I often wondered whether the heavy, clinking chain she wore round her waist, with all the accoutrements of housekeeping suspended from it, was the only reason she didn't blow away when she stepped outside.

At my suggestion that Mattie might not be ill, that she might be behaving like a petulant child at the expense of our nerves, Tothill's back grows straight as a broomstick.

She fixes her cat's eyes on me, worrying her lip. "Dr. Brooks will be here in a few hours. I'll send for you at the Lawrences' if he's concerned about her condition. Other than that, Lord Bancroft, I have nothing to say."

❦

Attending Sir Remington Lawrence's October soiree is something of a custom for London gentry. Lady Lawrence's opening of the autumn season sets a tone for the other hostesses, though her guest list is infamous for being a collection of oddities and sensations. I know quite well my inclusion is due to my status of *recently bereaved* and *wealthy widower.* Mattie is most likely pegged as *artist approaching spinsterhood,* an insupportable prick at her pride.

"No wonder she's willing to fake an illness to avoid this evening," I grumble.

Lady Lawrence and Lord Remy greet me in the colonnaded entryway, standing atop the first three steps of the winged stair like imperials receiving their court. Lady Lawrence's blue gown, specked with egg-shaped emeralds, will be the talk of the season, no doubt. I give my bow and the stiff greeting, sweat gathering along the top of my cravat, aware of nothing in the room but how her sharp, bird-like eyes glitter at me over the dark feathers of her fan as she speaks.

"We were longing for a peek at Miss Bancroft." She sighs, fluttering the feathers before her mouth. "She's not taken *ill?* Your family does have a certain *frailty,* you know."

"My sister will be speechless when I tell her about your soiree, Lady Lawrence. The grandeur of your new town house has me enraptured. I'll have little else to speak of to Miss Bancroft for some time."

Lady Lawrence's nasal tittering reminds me of the royal peacocks at Buckingham, a comparison which will amuse Mattie far more than a house. Lord Remy, thankfully, proves more private with his thoughts than his wife. He offers a laconic wish for me to visit his club—a social formality I'm certain he doesn't mean for me to accept—then dismisses me with a curt nod. Free at last, I abandon the fawners and minglers and squeeze past two pot-bellied lords obstructing the door to the parlor.

"You'd think there was a plague afoot," one of them snorts, "judging by the number of blackweeds in company."

The other man digs for a handkerchief, shrinking from me. "Indeed!"

Heat flushes my face, having nothing to do with the closeness of the crowded room. I glance down. There on my arm lies the telltale black band. Wearing this sign of mourning has become such a habit, I'd completely forgotten to remove it before leaving Norwich House.

I feel an urge to rip it off and stuff it in my pocket, to whirl round and explain that the season of mourning is past for me, that I've fulfilled my six months for a brother, year for a parent, and more. I want to swear that even though I'll never stop wearing my wife's name over my heart, I put away the black band for her remembrance five years ago.

I'm no plague to society. At least they would have forgotten about my family being so intimate with death had I remembered to leave Bennett's band at home.

I suffer more embarrassment at dinner. My name card waits at the far end of the dining room. Lady Lawrence has placed me across from a woman wearing widow's weeds. The rest of the company steals glances in our direction throughout the meal, as though enjoying a private joke with our hostess. I don't doubt the Lawrences are hoping to take credit should we end the season as a couple.

The first two courses come and go, ornate enough they give me some trouble with how to eat them, and I almost lose myself in the distant hum of the other diners. But then I raise my eyes to look for my goblet, reaching vaguely forward, and my fingers bump against the widow's. Our eyes meet as my flinching hand nearly upsets my wine. She smiles a little, laughing at me, though her blue eyes have a softness to them which keeps her mirth from being mistaken as mockery.

"Will you make an alliance with me, sir?" she says, watching me hide my flushed face.

I return to my plate, holding my utensils at stiff, odd angles.

"How do you mean"—I glance at her name card—"Miss Anna Holm?"

"A pleasure, Lord Bancroft. The alliance I suggest is this: We agree neither of us are in danger of falling in love. Perhaps then we may enjoy ordinary conversation and confound the gossips at their game."

Her bluntness earns her my attention. I take a closer look at the woman. Her expression holds the openness of a child, though perhaps a child haunted by ghosts. Faint creases grace where smiles and grimaces alike have marked her. A light accent is the only clue to her foreign origins. She wears an austere mourning dress made of inexpensive fabric and lacking any ornamentation. Even her gray-blond hair is arranged without pretension in a plain knot atop her head. She's made a preposterous suggestion. Yet, taking her as a whole, I'm inclined to believe she means every word.

"I will happily make such a pledge, madam. You might say, quashing gossip is something of a pastime for me," I say, saluting her with my glass.

Hers clinks against mine across the table, and her smile relaxes as she takes me in too. I return to my lamb, feeling a little heat in my face. "Tell me, do you come from Stockholm? Your accent ..."

"I'm from Bergen, though I lived in the countryside of that region with my late husband."

"I'm sorry for your loss," I say, mimicking hundreds of leaden condolences I've despised hearing ever since Abigail died.

"Is your estate in the country, Lord Bancroft?"

"Yes, my grandfather's manor is near Eaton."

"Ah, forgive me," Miss Holm says, her thin eyebrows rising. "I was told you held the title."

It takes me a moment to understand. Then I pass a hand over my eyes, exhaling. "No, the error was mine. My grandfather *was* Lord Henry but passed several years ago. It's difficult to remember how everything's changed since he was living."

"Yes," she says, and I hear many things in that single word: Empathy. Comradeship. Regret.

A course of lobster is brought, and I take a moment to glance round. It seems our pact has convinced everyone within earshot we aren't the least bit interesting. Anna Holm picks at her food, blushing when I catch her puckering over the fishy smell. She lays aside her fork and knife.

"My Lucia would love this. More's the pity I can't bear fish."

"Your daughter?" I ask. It's not an implausibility. Miss Holm looks old enough to have a nearly grown daughter waiting up at home.

"No, my younger sister," she replies.

I sit up straighter, furrowing my brow. "Is she not present this evening? It's not like Lady Lawrence to overlook members of the household."

"Lucia is someone I alone take pains to look after. I don't expect Lady Lawrence to manage such a feat." Miss Holm smiles to herself a little as she sips her wine. Then a shadow passes over her face. "I wonder, Lord Bancroft, have you ever known someone you feel you *must* protect at all costs? Would you besmirch your reputation for family? Could you kill for them?"

Despite the air of sorrow clinging to Miss Holm, this turn in conversation takes me off guard. Leaning forward, I look a question I cannot form with words. Miss Holm's eyes refocus, and she taps the top of my hand in reassurance.

"Not that I'm confessing my crimes to you, good sir! Nothing of the kind. But when you spoke of your dead grandfather, I felt a kinship with you. Perhaps I'm mistaken, and your past is a far less interesting one than mine. Tell me, are you alone in the world?"

"No, but nearly so." I pick through her insinuations in my

mind. "I have a younger sister, like you. She gives me a great deal of trouble, actually." I laugh, trying to shrug off my growing discomfort. "But I don't think it shall become necessary to kill for Mattie."

Anna Holm dabs her mouth and sits back in her chair, fixing her blue eyes on me without a hint of merriment. "Tell me about her," she says. "What worries do you carry on her behalf?"

It's the first time anyone's asked me something in this vein. A constricting in my throat makes me press my fist against tightly closed lips.

"She's ... Mattie takes the losses poorly, you see. Ever since Mother died, she's not been herself, unable to undertake ordinary routines, often keeping to her bed with illness. It falls on me to draw her out, and I fail miserably. Mattie refuses to make an effort."

"Make an effort?" Lines deepen in her brow. "Toward what end?"

"Why," I cough, incredulous, "toward her well-being. Toward living as a functional member of society." The sentiment isn't reaching Miss Holm. There's a coldness in her gaze. I'm moved to dig deeper. There's another wish I bear, something I've not even whispered to Mattie. Lowering my eyes to my balled fist on the tablecloth, I whisper, "Unlike those we've lost, I want my sister to have a future."

"Yes." There are fathoms in that word. I can hear her tears without raising my eyes.

Dabbing my mouth with my napkin, I sneak a swipe of the cloth at my own eyes before laying it aside. When I can lift my head again and breathe more easily, I notice Miss Holm's eyes flit, nervous and haunted, toward the head of the table. The Lawrences' gaze is upon us.

"Will you be staying in London long?" I ask, returning to safer waters.

Miss Holm sniffs. "Yes. That is, we've moved here indefinitely. Sometimes I wonder why socialites like Lady Lawrence bother with me. My sister and I are a perpetual enigma to society—we must work and, therefore, ought to be thought common, but we are fallen gentry involved with charity, making us a most uncommon case."

"A nine days' wonder, to be sure," I say, shaking my head. "As someone whose family name rose from obscurity in the recent century, I commiserate with your tenuous social standing. If I may ask, what is the nature of your employment?"

"I'm a teacher, but at the moment, I've been given charge of a children's home in the south river slum." Miss Holm's pronouncement takes me by surprise. While I can picture her as a schoolteacher, the image of a tidy, sunlit schoolhouse doesn't harmonize with what I know of the narrow, dank tenements of south London. Before I can form a response, however, she's turned the question back upon me, as seems her wont. "And you, Lord Bancroft? What brings you and Miss Bancroft to London?"

"We are only recently emerged from mourning, but I hope to reestablish my sister among her peers. Of course, I have personal ambitions as well, but my primary concern is to see Mattie settled and comfortable."

"You mean to marry her off?" Her voice holds the slightest edge of censure.

"Not right away, I assure you." My laugh is less carefree than I mean it to be. "There'll be months of parties and soirees such as this one, afternoon calls and small gatherings hosted at our London house. All in all, we shall reacquaint ourselves with the gentry we once knew. Perhaps matrimony will work itself out for Mattie, perhaps not. In any case, she's studying at the Royal Academy of Art. She'll never want for companionship, if she has an open mind. But she's stubborn."

"Did she so hate leaving the country?" Miss Holm says,

accepting the servant's offer to remove our place settings. Tea will be arriving shortly with dessert.

"Mattie has no particular attachment to Linwood."

"Then is it marriage she dreads?"

I shake my head, tapping the empty table before me. "No, nothing of the sort. I'm quite puzzled by her behavior of late. In truth, I expected Mattie to rely upon me to guide us toward our new life in London. She used to consult me for everything, great and small. She would ask me to check her spelling while writing letters. She'd ask whether a blue or white ribbon ought to be put into her hair. It was like we were sisters." I chuckle, remembering dozens more odd little instances only we two shared. Many of them I'd forgotten, until the Mattie who once sought me out abruptly vanished.

"She doesn't want your help now?" Miss Holm presses, then sighs, sitting back in her chair as the tea is served. "I'm sorry, I shouldn't pry."

"No, I feel you are someone who can advise me," I assure her. "You have a sister of your own."

"Lucia is quite different from your Mattie, from any sister you might imagine for me," Miss Holm says, with the ghost of a smile. "But if you will take my advice—and take it lightly on account of my not being acquainted with your sister—please, do your best to listen to her."

"Listen?"

Miss Holm nods, lifting her teacup. "There are many, many ills which can be thwarted by a careful listener."

We take our tea in silence then, Miss Holm spooning her pudding with the fastidious delight of someone for whom it is a rare treat. I mull over her words, knowing them to be worth considering, but lack any inkling of how I might better listen to someone who would be hard-pressed to put three words together.

When the dinner breaks up, I bid Miss Holm a good night

with much fervor, taking her hand over the table. She feels like an old friend, though we've just met.

"Please, call on us at Norwich House," I tell her. It doesn't occur to me until later that she may not know whether my invitation is a nicety or truly meant.

CHAPTER 3

When I have lost, you'll know by this—
A Bonnet black—A dusk surplice—
A little tremor in my voice
Like this!

— EMILY DICKINSON

On the evening of the Sutton's harvest ball, I rap on my sister's door. The new maid, Penny, opens the sitting room for me. "Lord Bancroft, miss," she tells my sister and then slips out to give us a moment alone.

"You've come to drag me away, then?" Mattie mumbles, slumped in an apathetic heap against the arm of her chair. She's not pretending to be sick this time. Penny has put her in the dress I've chosen for this evening, and Mattie's hair is arranged in two fashionable coils behind her ears, curls dangling with strings of pearls and small white flowers. My sister couldn't look lovelier—or more miserable. Kneeling, I draw out a white rose I had Tothill affix to a black ribbon.

"This is a ribbon I cut from Father's suit the day of his funeral, when you couldn't be there. The rose is for Mother, of course. The color of the ribbon, our own private rebellion in memory of Bennett. Black's inappropriate for a harvest ball, just as weeping is inappropriate when one reenters society. This will be our secret, Mattie. We've returned, but we're not as alone as people think we are. Let this little reminder be your strength tonight."

Mattie's eyes widen. She sits upright, holding out her wrist, and allows me to tie it on. I take her hand and pull her to her feet. We stand face-to-face without a word while tears run to her chin and drop unchecked to the floor. I offer my handkerchief and freeze. I've forgotten to exchange my black one for the colored silks. Mattie's eyebrows lift, her expression one of pity and relief.

"I suppose you'll be bringing your own little reminder too," she gasps through a sob. "I'll try to keep a hold of myself and not make you use it."

She dabs her eyes, then returns it to me.

"Are you ready?" I ask her.

"I'll never be ready. But I'm dressed, and I'm not alone." She tucks her hand inside my elbow, casting the train of her gown behind her with an angry flick of her wrist. At the threshold, she pauses and adds, almost in an undertone, "You didn't tell me I look pretty."

I pat her white glove. "You are. But I recall compliments make you uncomfortable."

"Thank you," she whispers.

We go together, too tense for conversation until we've been deposited by Donnie on the street outside the Sutton mansion. It is ablaze with lights, vibrating with music, and brimming with nobility. Mattie clings a little tighter to my arm, and we squeeze our way through the foyer and the hall, the dining room, and then the doors of the ballroom. A small pocket of open space near the glass door to the conservatory harbors us from the bustle and press of the party guests. Mattie seems torn between a desire to remain stuck to my side and the beckoning seclusion of a nearby potted palm. We're not left to ourselves for long.

"Why, it's little Matilda Bancroft! I thought not to see you in London for some time. And a good evening to you as well, young sir." A gentleman with shrew-like whiskers nods to me, then, recollecting himself, adds, "That is, *Lord Bancroft*."

I keep my voice level, but the smallest feeling of triumph blooms in my breast as I return his greeting. "Lord Wessex."

"Have you been back long?" he asks my sister, angling his broad, rounded shoulders so that we may be easily interrupted. The proprietary necessity of calling me by my title has given him too heady a whiff of death for his liking; I do not expect him to linger here long. We exchange the smallest tidbits of news with the earl, hardly having anything to say ourselves after spending over a year in the countryside. He warms a bit to the gossip but is drawn away before telling us anything of real interest, his wife beckoning wildly with her fan and a glare in their son's direction.

"The Honorable Lloyd Wessex has entangled himself with someone of whom Lady Wessex doesn't approve," I tell Mattie, watching their ensuing ambush of the young man with amusement.

"I feel dizzy," she replies, steadying herself on my arm. "It was a mistake to come. I've not been around so many people in such a great while!"

"Will you have some punch?" I ask her.

Mattie shakes her head hard enough to dislodge one of the flowers nestled in her hair. "Don't leave me! Can't we go somewhere out of sight and just sit?"

Shielding her from the other guests, I lean close to Mattie's ear and speak in a calm tone. "You and I must dance with at least one other person. It's only proper. I promise to lead you out for the first, but beyond that—"

"Is that you, Bancroft?"

Glancing over my shoulder, I'm surprised to see a friend from university and his wife standing behind us. The woman's brown doe eyes peer above her fan in thinly veiled fascination at us. She sidles around me to stand next to Mattie, snaps her fan closed, and offers my sister a lace-gloved hand. "How do you do? I believe we've never met."

Mattie takes the offering, mumbling her name too softly to be heard.

"Miss Bancroft," I say for her and move to Mattie's other side. "Mattie, this is an old friend of mine and his wife, Lord and Lady Stewart. How have you been, Your Grace?"

The duchess monopolizes my sister, twining her hand through Mattie's arm and leaning close enough to hear her half-hearted replies. I engage His Grace with light, humorous reminiscences of our time together at university. But all the while, there's a flutter of unease in my belly.

Stealing glances at Mattie intensifies my fear for her. If there is anything my sister hates, it is the sort of female who pretends an intimacy predicated on intrigue or the telling of secrets. I am grateful when the musicians cast out tendrils of their special magic, drawing dozens of couples to the dance floor.

"If I may be so bold," Lady Stewart gasps, nudging Mattie forward, "will you take the first turn with dear Mattie, my love? You know how shy a young girl can be the first time she comes into society."

Mattie drops her eyes to the floor, but not before I see tears gathering in them. She's red all the way to the tips of her ears, unable to voice a bit of protest. I lead Lady Stewart out, almost forgetting the correct stance in my preoccupation with my sister. At the edge of my vision, I watch the duke bow deep enough to mollify any amount of my sister's annoyance. They step into the ring of dancers just as the music swells, and I sigh in relief.

But as I make a full circuit of the room, sinking into the familiar long and short steps of the waltz, a strange feeling comes over me. The figures surrounding us take on a hazy quality, while the polished floor reflects the light too sharply. I see myself dancing with someone else, someone much more present, more alive than myself. A personality more vibrant than the rich wine-red of her dress.

Had I waltzed with my sister, I'd doubtless feel the same pull of nostalgia. Lady Stewart remains unaware. Perhaps Mattie would've seen the sparkle of salt in the corner of my eye as I turn sharp, then sharper. Step out far, then farther. Turning on the ball of my heel fast enough to throw my partner's head back, I whirl faster, drawn back almost a decade to another ballroom. I'm holding the familiar, bony fingers of Abigail's hand, watching her dark curls stream over her shoulder turn after turn. I hear her laugh, startlingly loud. I'd blushed in embarrassment while she'd only let herself go more, inviting me to forget myself in the moment.

"Mr. Bancroft!" The duchess's rebuke pulls me up short as we near the edge of the room. She breaks away from me like a woman whose reputation has been impugned. "Really!"

Stunned, I mutter an apology, though for what I couldn't say. But Lady Stewart has already disappeared through the double doors of the foyer. Turning to survey the remaining couples, I spot Mattie. Lord Stewart has passed care of my sister on to some other gentleman, a tall young man with blond whiskers creeping down either side of his jaw, like some playful, pale raccoon. He stoops over her, speaking while they trot to and fro. When his back turns toward me, I'm unable to catch sight of Mattie's face because of his height, but I doubt she looks as carefree as he.

"Excuse me," I tell someone who's just approached me and slip round to the further end of the room, toward the place my sister will be when the music winds down.

"I feel sick," Mattie growls, almost running to my side as soon as she sees me. Her partner freezes a moment, left alone before the song has ended. But he quickly recovers his wits and closes the distance.

"Lord Bancroft, allow me to introduce myself. I must beg your pardon, His Grace insisted I take his place after the waltz." He offers me a genial smile and a bow. "Lord Hathaway, at your service."

"I'm going to be sick," Mattie repeats, tugging at my arm, her back rudely turned upon her dance partner. I study her face. Though pale, there's no alarming sign of illness, and I'm inclined to believe she's putting on an act to avoid enduring the remainder of the ball. Taking her elbow, I firmly draw her to one side, allowing Hathaway to join our circle. Then I proceed to introduce myself and engage him in a rather lengthy conversation about his family and social status, ignoring Mattie all the while.

"If I may, I'd like to ask your permission to call on Miss Bancroft," he says at last, eyeing my sister sidelong.

"We're honored, I'm sure," she replies, sardonic enough for my detection, though I hope Lord Hathaway remains unaware of her true feelings.

"Indeed, you are most welcome at Norwich House," I add, bowing in farewell.

When the man has gone triumphantly away, his whiskers close to standing on end with glee, I turn a reproachful look upon my sister. But Mattie preempts my lecture by buckling and falling against me. I am forced to half-carry her from the room amid a flurry of whispers.

"Call for our carriage," I hiss at the valet standing in the hall.

Setting Mattie on a bench near a half-open window, I touch her brow and hands. Neither are over-warm, and the way her eyelids flutter is hardly natural. "Come now, Matilda Anne, this is no way to behave in public!" I snarl, giving the back of her hand a smart tap.

She stirs, bringing her reddened hand to her mouth with a frown. "How dare you!"

"How dare *you* make a scene!" I'm pacing in front of her. The hallway outside the ballroom is blessedly empty of occupants after the musicians struck up a popular French gavotte, and I thank them for it. "We'll return to Norwich House at once, but this sort of thing will *not* happen again."

The valet returns with my coat, hat, and Mattie's cloak. When we're once again in the privacy of our carriage, I'm surprised to feel the night air stinging my cheeks. I brush at my face, incredulous that my gloves come away damp.

"Now who needs the handkerchief?" Mattie's eyes gleam in the dark. She reaches for my hand. "Oh, Ambrose, you're crying. What is it?"

"Nothing," I snap.

Mattie shrinks back into the dark corner of the carriage. We rattle along the London streets, lamplight casting about through the windows, failing to reveal either of our faces. I see Mattie's hand folded over the rose on her wrist, crumpling it to pieces.

"You didn't dance with me, after all," she says, when our carriage pauses amid a press of cabs and oxcarts. "Lady Stewart was abominable to you, wasn't she?"

"She was mortifying you, or so I thought. Would you have preferred me to drag you away, decorum be damned? I suppose then you could've made a scene during the *third* dance of the evening instead of the second. Our reputation would've been slightly less sullied."

"Ambrose!" Mattie yelps, ripping the ribbon from her wrist, tossing my present back in my face. "You haven't changed a bit, have you? I thought you'd remembered how kind you used to be, how you used to look after me when I was little. Now I see you were just ingratiating yourself before dragging me to that horrid ball!"

"That was not my intention in the least," I counter, squeezing the edge of the carriage seat. "Furthermore, what was wrong with the ball? I thought it was going quite well, all things considered. It's not uncommon for a spinster and widower of the lower peerage to be shamefully overlooked, especially after a prolonged absence. But Lord Hathaway paid you quite the compliment. Even Wessex took notice of us."

"Oh, I see! Because you were able to hold your own with Grandfather's crony, the pompous Earl of Wessex, you felt things were *going well!*"

"Mattie, dear, calm yourself."

"Why? Because a trollop might overhear and look down her nose at us?"

The suggestion is so ludicrous I can hardly form a response. But then I realize it isn't mirth choking me, but a fiercer ire than

I've felt in a long while. Stirred by a deep sense of injustice, I stammer, "Y-you know that has nothing to do with why we're at odds. I'm trying to help you, sister."

"Really?" Mattie huffs, restless in her seat. "Because you always want something when you call me *sister*. I see now, the great truth of tonight is you are quite eager to be rid of me. Nothing could make you happier than to marry me off to the first man who shows interest and be done with it."

Her overreaction suddenly makes sense. It's just like Mattie to read into a situation, imagining the worst result on the least bit of evidence. Feeling vindicated, I take a moment to fill my lungs and try reasoning with her in a more patient tone.

"I won't deny it would be a fortunate turn of events should an opportunity of marriage be presented, Mattie. But there's no need to rush anything. We may take as much time as we need, working toward a secure future. Not just for you, dear sister, but for me as well. I bear a heavy responsibility to steward what remains of our family name and the estate. Consider how your actions will reflect on those who've gone before us. The Bancroft name has yet to pass into oblivion. You and I remain to make it so."

Mattie waits, as though expecting more. When I fail to add anything further, she leans back with a heavy sigh, covering her dark hair with a hand the streetlamp paints pale yellow.

"What a fine speech. Grandfather would be proud of you, for once."

CHAPTER 4

"Because I could not stop for Death—
He kindly stopped for me—
The Carriage held but just Ourselves—
And Immortality"

— EMILY DICKINSON

After the debacle, we receive fewer invitations. Mattie takes petty satisfaction in asking each morning whether any have arrived in the post. She's begun to come down for breakfast, though she wears a bathrobe over her nightgown and refuses to let Penny put up her hair. The lack of variety in our day-to-day begins to wear on me once I've concluded the unpacking at Norwich. Donnie and the horses see very little use in London, where most everything is a brisk walk up or down the Pall Mall. Early one afternoon, I send for him on a whim.

"Let's take the carriage out today, Donnie. I've a mind to drop in on an old friend in Oxford."

Donnie brightens. "Very good, sir!"

The weather is fine for a November day. The gray road to Oxford is wide and well kept, dotted by brown autumn leaves where it winds through an occasional maple copse. London's outer suburbs are making the best of a sunny day, airing out cottage bedrooms and hanging long strings of bleached linens from eave to fence. We clatter past rumbling carts of apples and pumpkins, scatter herds of wool-heavy ewes, and ford creeks bursting their banks after the recent rains. The blue sky and whitewashed houses are mirrored in the water as our road runs along the Thames, approaching Oxford.

"Where to, sir?" Donnie asks when we reach a crossroad. But it's been so long I can't recall the address.

"I think you take this turn here, and then there will be a little lane with flowers climbing over a wall. Only, it's not the season for them, I suppose ..."

It's not much to go on, but Donnie pulls up at the right house before long. I give him a bit of coin for his drink and dinner. Then I'm left alone before a wicket gate in a low stone wall.

The place is a tenement but a respectable one. The two

stories are home to bachelors and university dons, the sort who eat supper at a pub and amble home, smoking their evening tobacco. I was invited here once with Bennett, when I'd earned a rare holiday from keeping Grandfather company at Norwich. I'm only a few years older, but a nosy neighbor watching me fumble my way through introductions that spring morning wouldn't recognize the man standing at the wicket gate tonight.

I lift the latch and walk through the tidy little garden. The bell echoes in the big, empty house. I assume it's empty because all the windows are closed on such a rare afternoon. I wonder whether it was a mistake to call on my friend unannounced. But then the yellow-painted door swings inward, and a familiar face peers round it.

Godfrey Foxe looks like an overgrown cherub. His placid, green Irish eyes are set in a childlike face rimmed with gold-red curls. His cassock would only add to the impression, if he were wearing it. With his usual quick warmth, he invites me inside for a cuppa.

"I'm shocked to see you, Ambrose," he confesses, bustling through to the kitchen and returning with an already hot teapot and a tray of sandwiches. "But your timing is impeccable. I'd lost all motivation for teatime. It takes a great deal of verve to cook for yourself day after day. Now I'll just remind myself visitors can drop in at any moment, and I'll never be sorry I was prepared."

I thank him, taking the armchair with an embroidered dust cover. Godfrey sits across from me and pours tea, sets two sandwiches each on the chipped plates. I decline cream and sugar, not wanting to put him out on my account.

For a long moment, Godfrey and I sip our tea and look at the objects in the room. They're relics of another time, left to gather dust on the mantel and the corner cabinet. Through the window, the distant sunset paints the moving waters of the Thames. Soft golds fade into ochre and then die out as grays dipping into inky blue. Still, not a word passes between us. Godfrey gets up to light a few candles.

"Did you come for anything in particular?" he asks me, setting the last sandwich on my plate.

"I came to see you, see how you're getting on."

"Ah," Godfrey says. He leans back against the settee and folds his hands over his chest, very clerical and sage. "I'm still leasing my room here, despite having requested a church appointment over a year ago. I gave the diocese a nudge last month and was told I must be patient. But what they mean is, I have no connections. There's no benefit to the bishop in appointing me a vicarage."

"I'm sorry."

I scowl at the cold hearth. Godfrey doesn't put it in so many words, but things were different when he was a close friend of the Honorable Bennett Bancroft. While they'd both been studying at Oxford, promises had evidently been hinted at. Promises which were no longer in effect.

"Have you been busy?" he says after a while. "I sent a note to Linwood several months ago. I heard you and your sister have gone to London since."

"Yes, I came from Norwich House this afternoon," I say, rummaging through my recollection of the last few months. I must have lost track of Godfrey's note in the chaos of the move. "I thought it best to bring Mattie back into society. Actually, I am in need of a change myself. I'm going to establish a charitable beneficiary, you see. As there's no one to succeed me, the title will return to the Crown. I want our estate and its proceeds to be put to better use."

"That's a noble sentiment," Godfrey says. He looks closely at me, perhaps for the first time since my arrival. "Though it's also a sad conclusion to your story, my friend. You truly feel there's no hope for remarrying?"

"There's no danger of my ever falling in love again. Not after Abigail."

"What if you adopted a child and brought him up as your heir? Such things are not unheard of today."

It's preposterous, but I smile at the thought. This conundrum would've strained Grandfather's values to their breaking point. Is it better to lose the title altogether or pass it to a person of doubtful heritage who could never build the prestigious reputation Grandfather wanted?

"No, thank you. But the idea of sponsoring a children's home has occurred on more than one occasion. What do you think?"

"To my mind, taking your sister on a long holiday abroad would do greater good than adopting a pet project, Ambrose."

I scrutinize him, frowning. "You're the last person I would expect to advise something as selfish and frivolous as a holiday."

"For someone like you, and for Mattie, it would not be selfish. It'd be a change for the better. Leave behind reminders of the past and take time to learn afresh who you are. You're never the same once you lose someone. Six months isn't enough time to find out what's left of you."

I shrug, discounting the idea of a trip at once. "You're right about Linwood, of course. One feels that ghosts are around every corner in that old place. In London, Mattie and I have so much else to do and think of, we can't possibly wallow."

"Mattie may not know Norwich, but *you* lived there for years with Lord Henry. Even for me, Norwich holds many painful reminders of Bennett. Do you remember how he'd tramp through the house, road-dirty, with his tousled hair standing on end, and drag you out of bed to go to his club? He'd drag me on those jaunts too."

I shake my head, grinning. There was never any point in saying no to Bennett. He always got his way by charming and cajoling. "He vowed Grandfather wouldn't hear of it, and yet Grandfather always knew we'd been out. He didn't say a word, so long as it was Bennett's idea."

Godfrey nods, patting his vest front with his wide, calloused hands. "Lord Henry had a soft spot for him."

"A very calculated one," I counter. "Anyhow, I hope you'll come to London and visit us. Bennett would want you and I to get on, even though you were *his* friend at the start."

Godfrey Foxe stares at me as the church bells chime five o'clock. "I always considered you as much a friend as your brother, Ambrose. I'm rather disappointed you don't think of it that way."

His rebuke is softened by his smile, but I sense a heavy truth behind his words. "Well, you will come and visit us— often—won't you?"

"I'm afraid I can't," he says, rather abruptly. Godfrey gets up and shuffles over to the fireplace. He takes down a flint from the mantelpiece and begins to lay kindling and logs on the hearth.

Watching him, I wonder to myself, why did I come here tonight? Was it really to see an old friend or get a priest's advice on charity? A cold feeling creeps through my chest and makes even my fingers and toes numb. What do I actually know of Godfrey Foxe? On many occasions, I sat beside him, both of us leaning forward in our seats, listening to my brother talk long into the night. We were like two moons revolving around one sun. But now that sky is dark, and we're left reeling through a black unknown.

Godfrey returns to his place, folding his hands over his knees. His right foot bounces under his laced fingers like the leg of a flea-bitten hound. Grimacing, he drags a palm across his forehead, then jumps back to his feet, pacing in front of his armchair. Looking like a man enduring intense pain, his green eyes meet mine and hold my gaze.

At last, he says, "I love your sister."

Before I can answer, he grinds out more words, his voice hoarse with tears. "I've loved Mattie and watched her bloom into such a beautiful, beautiful soul. She was so gentle, then. Kind. Considerate of others' feelings to a fault. When Bennett brought me to Linwood that Christmas, I felt it would kill me to leave again without something to tie me to her, some promise to bridge the vast chasm which separates us socially and geographically. That's why"—Godfrey's eyes drop, and his voice sinks to a whisper—"I asked Mattie to marry me."

I think back to that night, recalling the modest Christmas Eve dinner and the small family dance in the ballroom. It was the first and last time Bennett brought his university fellow to the manor. Mother had made Mattie wear a new dress, one she'd thrown a tantrum about all afternoon until Mother promised to let her act the adult and have port with her dinner. Mattie had never looked so dazzling. Everyone was wild that night. Something was in the air, a turning we sensed in our blood, making us careless and sprightly. Grandfather sat in a chair by the hearth at one end of the ballroom, watching the dancers. He'd been very quiet that night.

"When?" I ask Godfrey, clenching my hands. "When did you ask her?"

"While we danced," he whispers, reddening. "I know it was a ridiculous notion."

"That was the night," I say, picturing it in my mind, "we became so occupied with family affairs, we forgot we had a guest."

"Yes, it was the night Lord Henry died."

"And we left you to your own devices for days on end."

"I didn't mind."

"But she didn't say anything. Did Mattie not remember your proposal?" I ask him.

"Oh, no. She refused me at once!" Godfrey's laugh rings too bright in the dim room.

"She refused you?" I repeat, incredulous.

"She banished me."

My jaw slackens, and I recollect myself only when I see my own shock mirrored in Godfrey's eyes.

"I have come round to my point, you see," he continues. "When I proposed to Mattie, I never for a moment thought she would turn me down. I've had some time to reflect on my behavior since. I now realize I'd assumed that because Mattie was soft-spoken and hated to displease anyone, she'd agree to the match to make everyone happy. Fool that I was, I didn't doubt my ability to provide anything she might want or need. I thought love itself would fill any gaps in my personality, and that if Mattie didn't love me then, she would in time."

He grins sheepishly. "You're surprised? I was too. Mattie proved more scornful and derisive than I thought possible for one so sweetly disposed. Reeling from that shock made it difficult to navigate the upheaval caused by Lord Henry's death. And so, I was content to hide myself away in the guest room and be forgotten."

"What do you mean, she banished you?"

Godfrey leans back, scratching his curls absently. "She made me vow, on my friendship with Bennett, never to return to Linwood and, further, that I'd never speak to her again."

"Mattie?"

"Why, is she so compliant you can hardly believe it of her?"

I look askance, reminded of the scene Mattie had caused at the harvest ball. "Well, no …"

Godfrey sighs heavily. "After Lord Henry died, I began to observe your family more carefully. I learned something. None of you Bancrofts are what you seem. Mattie might've *seemed* delicate when I proposed, but she's no more delicate than a rose with two-inch thorns."

The logs pop in the fireplace, and the view from the window now shows black night and a dim reflection of flickering candlelight. Somewhere in the back of the house, a door opens, and a man's footsteps tread the creaking stair. The various pieces of Godfrey's story come home to me. He won't visit Norwich because of a promise. Looking at him, his eyes like green pinpricks of light in a wan face, I recognize the truth.

"You love her still," I say.

Godfrey frowns, reproachful.

"You love her still!" I lean forward, my voice rising. "How can you love her and stay away? All this time, I've been failing at everything with Mattie—I can't get her to eat, she won't rise from bed, she never dresses, she's unkempt, all bones and rat's nests. And here you sit with the golden key, doing nothing."

Godfrey shakes his head. "You're wrong, Ambrose."

"God dammit, I'm never wrong about Mattie! Who knows her better than I? Was Bennett the one she confided in? Was he there for her to cry on when people snubbed her and Grandfather made biting remarks?"

"Ambrose—"

But Godfrey's voice can't reach me now. He doesn't know how Mattie's wasting away pains me. Every month, she grows more frail and sickly, as though she only waits to follow the others. I jump to my feet, wrestling against the fate I dread.

"Godfrey, if you love my sister, fight for her. Make her listen to you! Come to Norwich House and remind her there are things she wants. She has a *future* with you."

Godfrey's on his feet already, braced against my pleas. His hunched shoulders spell my defeat. "Ambrose, you're wrong. No one knows Mattie but she herself. She hasn't let you in, so don't claim to own her heart."

"I don't claim to own anything but what was freely given," I retort, clenching my fists. "Mattie's *my* sister. I love her far more than you can comprehend. Evidently, the love of a suitor is nothing compared to a brother because I'd do anything to keep Mattie safe—"

"Anything?" Godfrey interrupts, his voice low and pregnant with meaning. It reminds me of the preposterous things which escaped the lips of Anna Holm. *Would you besmirch your reputation for family? Could you kill for them?*

"Of course not! Not *anything*. But you know what I mean. A brother ought to care for his sister, and I am nothing if not a dutiful brother."

Godfrey looks at my arm. I'm no longer wearing the black silk band of mourning for Bennett. He says nothing, but his look stings.

"I've overstayed my welcome," I say, more tersely than I intend. "I'll bid you good night."

Godfrey crosses the small room, wrapping me in an unexpected embrace. "Come again. I mean it."

Then we shuffle out into the garden. I reach the gate and turn to see him still standing in the shadowed doorway. I walk away, unaware of how much further I'll be altered before we see each other again.

⚜

When Donnie brings me home, it's late enough the lights are extinguished. Norwich House is like an empty body, waiting for someone to stir it to life. But there's not enough vitality remaining in me. After my argument with Godfrey, I feel as though I only possess venomous words, a double-edged sword wounding me as it leaves my mouth.

My knock is answered by the Norwich butler, a young man whose name I've yet to put to memory. He takes my jacket and hat, hiding a yawn.

"This house is full of ghosts, you know," I tell him, unaccountably malicious.

He hurries off to store my things. My feet carry me up the carpeted stairs, till I'm standing in the library, between the matching winged chairs that used to hold Bennett and I—a pair of slight men dressed in fine clothes, with dashing brown hair and matching mustaches. His gray eyes would twinkle, full of thoughts and ideas. His lips were always spilling over with them, words strung together in the effortless elegance I'd envied.

I reach inside my vest and pull out an oval, jet-black locket. It clicks open in my hand, and I stare down at the single curl of brown hair encased in the glass. I brush the smooth surface with my thumb and look at the photograph opposite. *Bennett.* I may no longer wear the black mourning band, but I carry him with me always.

One evening not long ago, I sat across from Bennett beside a darkening fire in this room. That night, Bennett asked me a question. It led to a lengthy discussion, a thought exercise. Such things were his arena of prowess. He'd become something of a philosopher while at university. Grandfather insisted Bennett study law, but alongside his formal studies, he read a great deal and developed a mind for poetry, iconography, and the mysterious workings of the human mind. I was interested in none of those things. But as his older brother by two years, I was required to always have an opinion. If it weren't for his everlasting wondering, some of the things we talked about would never have occurred to me.

"At the risk of repeating myself too much, I wonder if this isn't all connected, Ambrose," he'd said, pressing his fingertips together, alert even after sitting for hours in the dying light.

Trying my best to concentrate, I'd asked, "How do you mean?"

"Well, you say, 'God made man for work,' and at the same time—to put it bluntly—you're a nobleman. You're inheriting a title and an estate, both of which you've done nothing at all to earn, which will be given to you because of the actions and ambitions of our grandfather."

"I'm afraid I don't see a connection between my status and your hypothetical. Perhaps I'm getting too tired to think, little brother." I yawned.

Bennett laughed, clapping me on the shoulder. "Old man, seems I'll have to run it by you again when you've had breakfast."

"Do that," I said, rising to go. "Or better yet, ask Godfrey Foxe when he comes."

"Oh, but I already know what Foxe will say." Bennett chuckled. He banked the fire and propped the grate in front of it to keep the coals from rolling out.

"And what's that?" I asked.

"He'll say, 'God made man for work, and the people's work is prayer.' Which, I suppose, has something to do with what England is becoming after the Emancipation Act. Catholics and Anglicans alike tend to pray *in church*. What they do *outside* of it ... That's what I want to know about."

We had gone our separate ways. I lived in London with Grandfather, developing my social connections in expectation of becoming the next Lord Bancroft of Linwood Manor. I didn't see Bennett again for some weeks. He and Godfrey were always out and about. University students in their third year, they were full of busy importance and magnanimous ideas of the world.

On nights like this one, in the wake of my argument with Godfrey, I feel Bennett's absence intensely. He would've advised me how to make things up. He always knew instinctively what people needed to hear. Now, I wonder what we might've talked about if I'd been willing to engage with Bennett's deep questions. I wonder what he would've said if I'd been honest about feelings I've yet to put to words.

"What do I do now, Bennett? Tell me ... I'll do anything. Anything at all."

The jet locket slips from my fingers into the seat of his chair. It lies there, with my dead brother's face gazing in contagious, incongruous joy from its little window. I'm leaning forward against the back of the chair, unable to breathe, as though someone's knocked the life out of me. Hiding my face in the crook of my elbow, I shed tears for the first time since his funeral. If I keep on like this, my sobs will turn into an ocean of bitter grief. I'll drown.

Dragging in breath after ragged breath, I reach down and snap the locket closed. I tuck it away. Turning my back, I leave the library and its memories behind.

"I've got Mattie still," I remind myself. As I said to the butler, Norwich House is full of ghosts, ghosts of memory. "I've got to get out of this place," I say, gritting my teeth. I descend the stairs and throw open the front door, plunging into the teeming night life of London.

By the time I'm standing in the club foyer, hatless, coatless, and rubbing my numb hands, my pulse has settled. I resolve not to let the unpleasant events of the day get to me. I hand the reception clerk my calling card and turn to enter the dining room. Just then, a group of university students flock in through the brass-gilded doors of the club. Their raucous energy fills the room as they laugh and shed coats with the enthusiasm of a murder of crows. They bustle past me, preening and joshing one another. My chest tightens as I watch them, my hands clenching. A rebuke is spelled out in their well-cut figures, boasting the prime of manhood, brimful of life. Bennett laughs back at me from every face.

CHAPTER 5

One need not be a Chamber—to be Haunted
One need not be a House—
The Brain has Corridors—surpassing
Material Place—
Far safer, of a midnight meeting
External Ghost
Than it's interior confronting—
That cooler Host—
Far safer, through an Abbey gallop,
The Stones a'chase—
Than unarmed, one's a'self encounter—
In lonesome Place—
Ourself behind ourself, concealed—
Should startle most—

— EMILY DICKINSON

I can hardly think of Bennett's university days without thinking of Godfrey Foxe as well. In the midst of my repulsion, I wonder whether Godfrey inwardly recoiled from me standing on his doorstep. Did he endure unspeakable torture as we sat for hours in that small room, reminding each other of the one thing we have in common—my dead brother? Perhaps this nausea I feel, watching the young men pass me by, is my just reward.

The club represents Bennett's realm. He was the gregarious boy my grandfather took under his wing and schooled in political niceties. Here, he was in his element. No wonder Grandfather passed me over, the eldest and the heir, in favor of Bennett.

The moment of my eclipse remains vivid in my memory. On that afternoon, Mattie and I had stood in the passage outside Grandfather's sitting room. The walls rumbled, reverberating deep voices. He'd warned me the summons would come when he esteemed me ready to join the grown-ups. Sixteen might be old enough in his estimation, but I felt unprepared for this first step into adult territory. I told myself excitement was the cause of the pounding, rushing blood in my ears. My face was hot.

Stuffing my hands into my pockets, I was aware of eight-year-old Mattie watching me, hovering at arm's length like a second shadow. I'd glared at her briefly, wondering what she wanted. Her large, gray eyes took me in all at once. I knew how perceptive she was at reading my moods.

"I'm not afraid, so don't make a scene. You know Grandfather hates children being a nuisance. Run along and play with Bennett."

I could hear our brother's laughter ringing through the house. Despite being too old for such things at fourteen, he was playing "chess pieces" with Donnie on the black-and-white foyer tiles. Mattie didn't budge. I stepped forward, trying to ignore her. My fingers had curled around the doorknob looked so small. Their childishness irritated me. The one thing I wanted was to be confident and self-assured, like Grandfather and all his set.

Pushing the door open, I entered the sitting room. Cigar smoke choked the light from the low fire and single window. I stifled an urge to cough. As I closed the door behind me, I was met by falling silence. A dozen thick-lidded eyes rested on my small person hovering near the door.

I made a short bow. Shifting from one foot to the other, I wondered whether I ought to move further inside. Grandfather had sat near the marble hearth in his oak smoking chair. He inhaled slowly and tossed the butt of his cigar into the flames. His voice broke the tense expectancy of the room. "This is the heir, my eldest grandson."

A gentleman in a yellow brocade vest harrumphed, lounging within a cloud of smoke on one end of a settee. The Earl of Wessex. At the further end, a gentleman with dark hair reaching toward the ceiling snickered with ill-disguised mockery. There were two or three others about the room, but I was too unsettled to look at them. I returned to the familiar austerity of Grandfather's face.

"Young lord," sneered Wessex from the couch, "perhaps you can settle this matter for us. When Kant said that happiness depends on one's belief in God, did he mean a Catholic's belief or an Anglican's?"

"Or an Orthodox's belief?" The young nobleman on the couch snorted.

Grandfather made no comment, but there was something in his eyes which I mistrusted.

He'd been arguing with these men, I gathered. Several moments passed before I was able to open my mouth. Not because I didn't know what to say—my tutor, Master Humphries, had introduced me to philosophy long ago, and

Father and Grandfather often engaged my verbal rumination on the various subjects which arose from my studies. But in this situation, I had a distinct feeling there was a right answer and a very wrong one. Did these men want my opinion? Did Grandfather want me to impress them? What should I say?

When I did speak, the words jumbled together, awkward and sticky in my mouth. The dampness on my palms became unbearable, but I refrained from wiping them on my trousers. "Kant is famous for his skepticism of religion—no matter what religion—so I don't suppose he was thinking of either Catholics or Anglicans."

This was not at all what I'd intended to say. It was neither impressive nor eloquent. It gave no inkling of my thoughts on the matter. Lord Wessex shot me a derisive look and turned to Grandfather.

"You're not wrong, Bancroft. The younger generation *are* foppish idiots, no matter their rank. But you could at least teach your grandson to recognize when he's speaking to nobility. Really, you go too far in making your point."

The tips of my ears burned. My face flushed red. *I should've said "my lord," or at least "sir"!*

Grandfather chuckled and rearranged his arms across his torso. He didn't appear perturbed by Lord Wessex's derision, but he avoided looking at me. Decorum demanded I remain in the room until dismissed, but Grandfather didn't invite me to sit. Neither did anyone else pay attention to me. Their wager had been settled by my idiotic remark. I'd become peripheral.

"I don't think Kant was antireligious, though!" I blurted the words, railing against my uselessness, and instantly regretted it.

Their insipid attention returned to me, and I longed to disappear among the jungle vines of the wallpaper. Grandfather coughed, a warning. But it wasn't needed. I'd no more desire to impress these men. What did I have to say, after all? I was only furthering Grandfather's point, embarrassing him and my family at the same time. Even if I could've reigned in my nerves and made a cohesive argument, I doubt he'd have been pleased.

I bit my tongue instead, making a lame recovery. "At least, that's what I read, my lord."

"True British pigheadedness," laughed Lord Wessex. "My son would say the same, you're thinking, Bancroft. But I say, Lloyd's savvy enough to know when to keep his trap shut."

The laughter of the half-dozen men rumbled about the room like thunder. Grandfather sniffed, unamused. I wondered what game he was playing with these nobles. He'd bought his title, and they knew it. I felt myself shrinking, becoming smaller inside myself. No one looked at me. I kept my stiff face polite. But the weight of failure crushed me into a compact grain of sand, wearing me down. A few minutes more and I might've cried. Surely, Grandfather intended to keep me there for hours, to impress on my mind the shame of public humiliation.

Before the laughter died down, the sitting room door burst open and smacked against the wall, bounding back on its hinges. Bennett rushed in and slammed the door closed behind him. He was a miniature of myself—the same wavy brown hair and gray eyes, same black suit and smart shoes—but there were two years between us. Two years that felt like an eon when sixteen meant I was almost grown and fourteen meant Bennett still wore knickers and had yet to hit his growth spurt. He clambered into Grandfather's lap in the blink of an eye.

"Lollies, Grandfather!" Bennett laughed, digging into Grandfather's jacket pockets.

I was frozen in place, horrified. But the nobles didn't mock my little brother. In a matter of moments, he had them enthralled. Standing on the side table next to the settee, Bennett held a lolly between his teeth and buried a hand in his coat pocket, imitating Grandfather smoking a cigar.

"When I was in A'rica, there weren't no el'phants at all!" Bennett puffed on the imaginary cigar, scowling.

The men laughed again, and this time their mirth lacked oppressiveness. Bennett was making a fool of himself in an appropriately genteel way, it would seem.

"Pst," someone said behind me.

I turned to see Mattie beckoning from the cracked door. Without hesitation, I backed out of the room, fleeing Grandfather's sitting room politics.

My sister tried to take my hand. "It was awful, wasn't it, Ambrose? I knew it would be when you went in."

"I'm fine," I insisted, crossing my arms. I went to the library and buried my shame in familiar, uncomplicated things, like Latin and Mathematics. I didn't know what was wrong with me exactly. Maybe sixteen wasn't old enough to be what Grandfather expected of the Bancroft heir.

I was angry with Bennett at the time. Recalling the incident as an adult, I'm free of the old bitterness. From that day onward, Grandfather drew Bennett into the realm of the grown-ups more and more, while I was left to my own devices. Eventually I realized Grandfather had chosen my younger brother as his favorite instead of me. I felt relieved.

Now I can't even go to my club without associating its smoke-scented dining hall with painful memories. The thought of dinner makes me sick. I leave the club without a word of explanation to the clerk.

A mist of freezing rain descends on London as I cross the street, bareheaded and shivering without my coat. Turning a dark corner, I stumble over someone and catch myself by clutching the wall. I scuff my palms against the rough stones. As I turn, a flashing glint of metal thrusts toward my stomach.

"Yer money or yer life!"

My heart leaps to my throat, and I shield my torso from the knife's gleaming threat. But it's wielded by a child who can barely hold still for shivering. I relax my wary stance and look at the boy more closely. He's not dressed for winter, wearing an oversized shirt and knickers which barely touch his knees. His matted hair might be blond or brown, depending on how much of it is colored by mud. The poor fellow stands no higher than my ribcage and could be seven or eight.

I pat my vest, feeling for my wallet, but I've left it at home in my coat.

"I've nothing on me," I tell him. "What would you have done with it, had I given you a whole ten pounds?"

The boy's eyes widen. He stashes his weapon in his belt and wrings his small, mud-smeared hands. "Gor' a'mighty! Wouldn't Joe be happy with me then! Are you gonna give it to me?"

"Why give it to this Joe person? Why not buy something to eat, lad?"

He eyes me with suspicion. "Joe would know, wouldn't 'e? Besides, Joe gives me food."

I wonder if the child is being taken advantage of by some older vagabond with a troop of children in his thrall. "Is Joe your father? Your brother?"

The boy cackles, clutching his ribs. "Is 'e?"

"Then you're an orphan?"

Growing suddenly suspicious, the waif skitters backward a few steps. "What's it to you?"

I know nothing at all of children, but ever since speaking to Anna Holm, I've learned that a growing number of orphans fill the London streets. Their bodies are often found frozen to death in winter. I am reluctant to leave this boy in Joe's keeping. Everything I own will one day pass to strangers—why not ensure it goes to care for needy children whose only protection is someone else's charity?

I kneel, showing the boy my empty hands. "I don't have anything to give you, but if you're really a destitute orphan, perhaps I ought to give you a gold watch I've no more use for. It belonged to my grandfather. He and I didn't get along. Would you like it?"

"Like it? Truly?" The boy creeps closer, his eyes shining.

"You'd have to follow me home to fetch it," I warn him.

"A'right," he says, grinning with a cunning I'm sure he's picked up from the company he keeps.

"Come along, then."

Once we've left the alleyway, I have trouble getting my bearings in the misting rain. The boy leads the way as soon as I tell him we're headed for St. James's Square. He enters the Norwich gate boldly, marching into the house like a regular lord, much to Tothill's astonishment. She's answered my knock in her nightgown, a candle in one hand and a frilly nightcap holding back her volumes of wispy red hair.

"You've a child with you?" she exclaims. "Pray tell, who are you, little lad? For I know my Lord Bancroft hasn't thought to ask your name, has he?"

The child beams up at her. Who could fear a brogue-ish grandmother in a nightcap?

"It's Tom!" he declares.

"Right then, Tom. I'll get you sorted. You need a hot meal, I can tell."

Tom follows Tothill through the hall toward the back of the house, but before leaving, he turns round and shouts back at me, "Don't forget the gold watch!"

"I won't." I smile and wave him off.

In the morning, Tothill has her hands full with restraining poor Tom. After waking in an unfamiliar room, he'd rushed out into the passage, opening and slamming doors in search of an escape route. When Cook and Tothill, with the help of Donnie, finally cornered the boy in the kitchen, he'd crumpled into a ball of tears, insisting they were kidnappers and pirates. Cook lured him out of his tantrum with some raspberry jam spread on fresh-baked biscuits, while Tothill hurried upstairs to wake me.

The hour is earlier than I'm used to, the sky an azure not yet diluted by daylight. I throw on my dressing gown and slippers and descend to the kitchen, the warm realm of servants and small children, mouth-watering scents and the sound of pots bubbling. Tom is sitting atop a stool, his grimy face smeared with jam and cheeks stuffed with biscuit. He glares at me until his mouth is empty.

"You lied!" he squeals at last, pointing an accusatory finger.

"Now, now, young man!" Cook tuts, grabbing a rag and pinching his cheeks between her finger and thumb. "That's no way to speak to a lord."

Tom's eyes widen. Sounds squeeze out of his lips, but his face is too squashed to make sense of them. While Cook hunts with the cloth for every last speck of dirt, Tothill takes a silver comb from her chatelaine and works out the knots in his hair.

"Master Tom," I begin, pulling up a stool to sit across the kitchen table from him. "I beg your pardon for the confused state of your rising this morning. But I am in no way attempting to mislead or imprison you. I promised you a gold watch, did I not?"

Tothill suppresses a gasp, exchanging a look with Cook over the boy's head. But Donnie, ever helpful, leans forward and pats the boy's shoulder without hesitation. The four of them make a charming picture.

"See here, Tommy," Donnie says, "I've worked for Lord

Bancroft all my life. Grew up with the Bancrofts, you see. He's a man of his word, you can be sure."

"Thank you, Donnie." I smile. "Now, let Tothill and Cook get you cleaned up and clothed properly, have your breakfast and some coffee, and then you may come up to my study, and we'll have our chat."

"Very good, sir," Tom says, bold as brass.

Tothill follows me out of the kitchen. "If you please, m'lord, what do you intend to do?"

I'd an idea of reasoning with the child and convincing him to abandon his predatory master, Joe. But staring into Tothill's earnest eyes, I realize such a plan will not satisfy her. I've never thought myself good with children, and Tom may not be relied upon to make the best choice.

"Why, what would you suggest?" I whisper.

"It's a little late to be makin' suggestions, don't you think?" she snaps back at me, smiling despite her exasperation. "Lord knows, you're not prepared to take care of him yourself."

"Honestly, the thought had never occurred to me," I say, smarting a bit at the suggestion. Godfrey too had proposed I find an orphan child to raise as my heir, like a misfit sock stuffed into a fine shoe, merely on the principle of not wearing shoes barefoot.

"What about an orphanage?" Tothill adds.

This reminds me that Miss Holm never came to call after the Lawrence dinner. Though I've often thought of our strange conversation since, it also never occurred to me to seek her out. Here is a perfect excuse to do so.

"In fact, I recently met a principled woman who's the matron at a children's home in London. I've no idea where, but perhaps Donnie might ferret out the place. Send him up to my study, and I'll write out what I know of the establishment."

Tothill nods and hurries back, much to the chagrin of Tom, who fears her silver comb.

All three of them come up to the study a short while later, Tothill with her hands on the shoulders of a small, unrecognizable boy with blond hair sticking flat to the top of his head and a broad grin. He's been stuffed into a pair of trousers and a vest, with a too-large shirt tucked in at the waist and the sleeves rolled up. Donnie's lent him a red kerchief to wear as a tie and stands beaming down at him like a proud uncle.

Tom enters my study on bare feet, one hand stuffed into his vest pocket as though he can already feel the weight of a gold watch there.

"Where's my watch?" He leans over the desk to look for it among the objects piled everywhere.

"Here," I say, removing it from a drawer. "But before I let you have it, we need to have a talk."

Tom squints at me, growing suspicious again.

"This watch belonged to my grandfather, and it's a family heirloom." I open the gold casing and show Tom the glass face. "I may want it back someday. Now, you also may change your mind about things one day. Today, you look up to Joe and want to be like him, isn't that right?"

Tom remains silent, too cautious to agree.

"Well, someday, I hope you'll realize Joe isn't looking out for anybody but himself. Then you'd be sorry you gave your gold watch to him. Besides, wouldn't it be much more fun to wear it yourself?"

Tom's eyes widen at the thought, and tears prick at their corners. Slowly, his chin lowers and his gaze drops to the floor.

"You're a smart lad, Tom. I think you already knew what sort of fellow Joe is. Now, I've an idea which should make everyone happy. I'm going to send Donnie here to look in on a lady I met recently. Her name is Miss Holm, and she keeps house for children like you, boys and girls without parents to care for them."

Tom shifts on his feet, glancing over his shoulder at the two adults standing in the doorway. He swallows hard, looking at me with those world-wise eyes of his.

"I know you may not like to stay at a home after having the run of London," I say gently. "It's far less adventurous, to be sure. But your gold watch won't be safe on the streets. In five minutes flat, you'd have it taken off you."

He nods. "Yessir."

"Well then, here's the deal—if you'll stay at the orphanage and mind Miss Holm, you can keep my grandfather's watch as long as you like."

To his credit, Tom gives my proposal a long moment of thought, glancing from the watch to my face and back again. He seems to understand what's at stake. Despite being quite young, he must have seen a good many things beyond what is proper for a child, educating him on the prudence of wariness and circumspection. At last, he throws his hand across my desk, fingers splayed.

"I so swear," he says, mimicking someone in a witness stand.

Chuckling, I hand him the gold watch, enjoying the care he takes in fixing the chain to his buttonhole. Tom turns it over and over in his hand, admiring all sides of the engraved metal.

"Gor' a'mighty," he breathes.

Tothill squeaks in surprise at his language, but over little Tom's head, she and I share a satisfied smile. Our little conquest was a success.

⁂

Donnie stops the carriage in a narrow street outside a tenement that towers over the rough cobbles like a hunching witch in shabby gray clothing, ragged and stitched together with ill intent. As I step out, my shoes squelch in the slimy, putrid rivulets of waste water trickling downhill toward the Thames.

Tom hops down next to me. Bringing my sleeve to my nose, I tell Donnie to take the horses to a park and wait an hour before returning for me. I don't want him loitering alone in this place, tempting pickpockets and worse.

"Right you are, sir," he says and flicks the reigns.

I turn to the door with "38" painted in sloppy white just above the letter box. There's no bell pull, but my knock is answered almost at once. The hinges whine as we are let into a cramped passageway by a young man wearing too-large trousers and no shoes.

"Lord Bancroft, here to see Miss Holm," I tell him, though I'd sent Donnie ahead with a message and the explanation is hardly necessary.

"Yessir." The lad shuffles ahead in the dark without a backward glance.

Tom looks to me. I hear him shifting on his feet but can barely make out his silhouette. Our guide's disappeared into a square of dim light at the end of the passage.

"Come along," I tell Tom, my voice lighter than I feel.

Tom follows me through the dim, carpetless hallway and round a corner. There we find a long stairway going straight up into the ceiling, a single, papered-over window from which emanates a soft light, and another door standing half open. I recognize the voice of Miss Holm speaking in a stern tone.

"And what do we do in company?"

"Listen!" Another speaker giggles.

"And what do we *not* do in company, dear?"

"Embraces and naughty faces" is the answer, followed by a creak of the floorboards. "May I go and fetch them now? Please!"

Permission must have been granted, for the door flies back in the hand of the last person I might've imagined belonging to the laughing, childish voice. A vibrant young woman of twenty-odd years fills the doorway in openmouthed awe. Her blond curls are pulled back from her face with a sky-blue ribbon, but in all other respects, she's dressed in the modest clothing of an unwed lady. A delighted grin breaks over her face, and she steps back with a flourish of her hand to announce us.

"Presenting Lord Bancroft and a little boy!"

"Tom, as you please," he tells her, recovering his surprise faster than I.

Following Tom into a bare sitting room, I'm relieved to see Miss Anna Holm looking much the same as on the occasion of our meeting. She comes forward to curtsy and intertwine her arm with the young woman's.

"Lord Bancroft, it's wonderful to see you. Allow me to introduce my sister, Miss Lucia. And the young man there is Finn."

The barefoot lad who answered our knock hovers in a dim corner near the door. He dips his head to us and then slips out, quiet as he came. Miss Holm pulls Lucia along with her to a wooden bench, leaving the only settee in the room for us to occupy.

"Please, sit. Finn will bring along tea in a moment," Miss Holm says, while Lucia waggles her fingers at Tom with a playful smile. "I was quite surprised to receive your driver this morning, Lord Bancroft. I didn't expect our paths to cross again after the Lawrences' dinner."

Lucia nods hard enough to shake her curls, shifting in her seat. "The dinner wasn't too nice, was it?"

"Oh, it was as to be expected, dear," Miss Holm says, gently laying a hand over her sister's fidgeting knee. "Would you like to go into the kitchen and help Finn bring the tea things?"

"No," Lucia states. "I want to see the guests."

Miss Holm gives me a tight smile, her cheeks tinged with pink. I realize I've been staring at Miss Lucia in poorly disguised shock ever since our arrival. I angle my knees toward Miss Holm and place a hand on Tom's shaggy, gold head.

"Although Tom and I are only recently acquainted, he and I

have come to an agreement. I've asked him to leave behind his life on the London streets and live with you, if he may."

"He gave me this!" Tom declares, shooting to his feet and producing the gold watch.

Lucia gasps, clapping her hands.

Tom gives Miss Lucia a closer look at his prize, her obvious interest drawing him to her side. The odd little bargain seems somewhat foolish now, in the presence of Miss Holm and a house full of orphans just like Tom who've never been given anything as fine. My face feels hot, and I cough a little, turning to practical matters.

"I understand that children here are sponsored by various nobility in town. An excellent notion, to be sure. I'll gladly take up Tom's sponsorship. You can have the name of my solicitor and settle everything through his office in—"

Cutting across my speech, Miss Lucia says, "Annie, what's a *slister*? Is it a kind of machinery?"

"No, dear," Miss Holm says, her voice verging on reproachful.

"Good, 'cause if it were, you couldn't afford it. Isn't that right?" Lucia says, sighing. "*Where* will we be getting our supper from if the nobility won't pay?"

Miss Lucia's pronouncement is the epitome of impropriety, stated without a hint of misgiving, and I'm flummoxed by it. Anna Holm rises slowly to her feet, her face draining of color.

"I beg your pardon, Lord Bancroft. Here I am, negligent of the time, and you've surely many matters to attend to." She moves past me to the door and glances out into the passage. "It seems tea has proven too much for poor Finn to manage alone."

Rising, I follow her out. "Please send word should any need arise for Tom."

"Of course, Lord Bancroft."

"Indeed, Miss Holm," I say, looking backward into the room

where Tom and Lucia are joking together without paying the two of us any mind. "I'm sure you're quite capable of managing any number of children, with the practiced care your sister requires."

I meant it as a compliment. But her pale, frozen expression pulls me up short. My smile recedes, though I don't know where exactly I went wrong. "Miss Holm?"

"Let me fetch a candle. The passage is far too dark," she says, turning her back to me. She goes to a cupboard in the base of the stair, producing a match and candlestick. Preceded by a halo of light, Miss Holm leads me to the door. She bids me good day on the front step, with a curtsy and contempt in her piercing blue eyes.

CHAPTER 6

There is a Languor of the Life
More imminent than Pain—
'Tis Pain's Successor—When the Soul
Has suffered all it can—

— EMILY DICKINSON

Octber draws to a close, and I fail to convince Mattie to return to the Royal Academy. She's missed the entire first term. Over breakfast one November morning, I remind her of the first time I escorted her to a lecture at the famous school of art. She'd been hesitant to brave the sea of men on her own—women artists are rare in London —but she'd been cautiously excited as well.

"Well, things are different now, aren't they?" she retorts, stirring her coffee and leaving the pastries and porridge untouched.

"Of course they are." Both of us used to laugh on those walks, finally out from under the sobering cumulonimbus that was Grandfather's presence. "But it's still worth returning to things we enjoyed before."

Mattie raises her eyebrows at me. "I don't see you reading much of late. Or did you only mean for *me* to pursue old occupations?"

These snide comments are nothing unusual. Mattie's barbs come out after a funeral. And while I wouldn't call her terse conversation an improvement, Mattie's behavior is gradually returning to normal. She leaves her bed at an acceptable hour and allows Penny to dress her each day, though still all in black. I press my lips together, biting back a reproach. I'll let my sister toss her head at me, if she likes. In the end, she'll come round.

"You'll never believe who I saw at my club yesterday evening. Lord Hathaway bought me a cigar and asked after you, sister. Perhaps I'll invite him to dinner, seeing as how he's not forgotten you after so many weeks."

Mattie's eyes widen. "Don't you dare, Ambrose!"

"Oh? You *don't* want me to invite Lord Hathaway?" I say, a little too forced. "Then perhaps you'll go to art class after all. When you've no better options, pick the lesser of two evils, as Grandfather used to say." I shrug, returning to my meal.

"Fine," Mattie hisses, shoving back her chair. "I'll go. But it's not like you to play games, Ambrose. You'd better make damn sure you've a stomach for it."

I look up from my poached egg. But Mattie's already gone.

An hour later, we leave Norwich House and walk the Pall Mall arm in arm. I remind her of the praise she received during her first year at the Academy, when her skill as an artist caught the attention of peers and teachers alike. We share dozens of memories from that brief spring term we spent in London, before Mother's illness took Mattie home again.

None of my efforts at reminiscing draw my sister out of her cold, silent shell. She used to love her art classes. She'd beg Grandfather to allow me to accompany her. Now I'm the one dragging her along.

When we moved from Linwood Manor to London, Mattie tried to leave her paints and easel behind. Her tools are in bad repair, her last work half-finished. It's a small canvas covered in greens and yellows, palest blue and bright specks of red. The subject is Mother's rose garden and two figures—our old gardener and Mother herself, wearing a maroon shawl over her hunched shoulders. The shawl Father gave her, which she wore every moment until she was taken from her bed to be buried. I know why Mattie couldn't finish the painting.

Two years after Father's death, Mother also died, and our bleak autumn deepened into a dark and depressing winter. During the months that followed, we watched Bennett fade too, leaving us further behind each passing day. He died on the 2nd of April. His passing was like a gong that ended a long, dark winter. Spring burst forth, and the land came alive again.

But without Mother to tend her rose garden, and without Bennett to liven the house, spring happened to other people. Its touch has yet to sink into our skin. Mattie and I are waiting to be brought to life as the land was. She, far more than I, is at risk of dwelling in eternal winter, as though she's paused on the doorstep to another world. The faintest nudge will pull her out of this one, beyond my reach. I'll be left alone. It's no use trying to convince Mattie of these things. She sees a wall of grief before her, and nothing beyond. It's my responsibility to carry her onward. To keep both of us moving forward.

The familiar walk to Trafalgar is not far, but Mattie hangs heavily on my arm as we pass the familiar white stone buildings. Their stately entryways drop behind us one by one, marking our progress toward the National Gallery. We emerge at last from the bustling street into the fountain square. England's center of the arts towers above us, crowned with a spire-wielding dome, its formal entrance guarded by twelve white pillars.

We enter by a smaller doorway and move along hushed passages. Tiled halls wind and crisscross inside the belly of the building, bringing us at last to a lecture hall. Mattie and I settle in at the back of the auditorium, she with her notebook and I with the *Morning Post*. I keep an eye on her throughout the lecture, watching her pencil draw idle circles across the page. She's shown no sign of her earlier rebellion, but her lip is bitten raw from her nervous chewing at it.

After an hour, we move on to a painting studio. It's on one of the upper floors, where the natural light is strongest, reflected off white walls. A dozen easels line the room. Without a word, Mattie goes to one of them in the back corner furthest from the door. I stand at a window, not sure if I'm welcome. I feel relief seeing my sister unfasten the buttons on her cuffs and roll up her sleeves, preparing to participate in earnest. Her mouth is set in a firm line, and she's ignoring me.

I whisper to the instructor, "Should Miss Bancroft ask, I'll return after lunch."

He gives a curt nod, then launches into his introductory remarks. As I leave, I see a robed male model coming up the passage. Perhaps it's for the best I don't sit in on this part of

Mattie's artistic education. I'm not sure I'd be able to stomach it.

I nod to him stiffly as we pass each other.

When I return, a secretary is waiting for me in the passage. She escorts me to an austere sitting room and serves me coffee. I'm confused at first. But she talks a good deal about the awkwardness of women artists being accommodated in an establishment originally designed to educate male students. I gather from her monologue she's been tasked with hosting me until my sister's class adjourns for the day.

I hear the bells of St. Paul's chiming outside. "Miss Hamel, it's now four o'clock. Will the class break for dinner?"

"Master Crowe will be here any minute, I expect."

As she speaks, the door swings open. I jump up, looking for Mattie. Master Crowe motions for Miss Hamel to take her leave, closing the door behind her. I shake Crowe's extended hand.

"It's an honor to make your acquaintance, Lord Bancroft," he says as we sit. "Our studio session has concluded, and the students are tidying their workspaces. But I wanted to speak to you in private first."

My pulse quickens. Something's wrong.

Master Crowe regards me with a furrowed brow and twiddling thumbs. "There's no easy way to say this, Lord Bancroft. It pains me to say it. In fact, if there were any other way of looking at the matter, I'd be willing to turn a blind eye. But as things stand—"

"Good God, man, just tell me what's happened!"

"Of course, my lord. I understand you and Miss Bancroft are recently bereaved. In such times, a morose perspective naturally bubbles to the surface. Art is the baring of the artist's soul, to some extent. However, I've never seen such brutal, violent depictions of human anatomy in all my years of teaching. Your sister ..." Master Crowe avoids my eye. "Your sister's not fit to be in public, sir."

"What do you mean?" I demand, rising to my feet.

"Come now, Lord Bancroft, calm yourself. Nothing untoward has happened. We're all just a bit shocked by the nature of her painting. I'm putting her readmission on hold, though not due to any shortcomings of Miss Bancroft herself, understand."

"You'll not allow her to attend class?"

Master Crowe stands, placing a hand on my shoulder. A gesture of empathy which infuriates me. "Believe me, it's for the best. Miss Bancroft is in no condition to be out in society."

"I'll be the judge of that," I bark, striding from the room.

Mattie's in her corner, tucking a sheaf of sketches inside a leather portfolio. The other students try to hide their stares, but as I confront her, I'm acutely aware our conversation is not private. She fastens the buttons on her cuffs, avoiding my eye.

"Did he tell you I've gone mad?" she asks, loud enough for everyone to overhear.

I glance round, reading shock on their faces. And then it catches my eye. The canvas on her easel, oozing black and red and moldy green. A pale, naked corpse lies across a tangle of wild rose bushes, their thorns tearing shreds of skin from the body. In the center of his bare chest, someone's plunged a jewel-crusted dagger, and across his belly is smeared a bloody handprint. My stomach flops over at the sickening sight.

"You did this on purpose," I whisper through gritted teeth.

Mattie meets my eye, her unflinching, stubborn rage confronting my defeated fury. It seems we, at last, understand one another.

Mattie doesn't come to dinner. After she's gone to bed, I find a brief note left on my desk.

I'm returning to Linwood tomorrow.

I can't let her go alone. Despite her rejection of me, despite how humiliated she makes me feel, I'll never abandon my sister.

"Oh, Mattie." I crumple the note and cast it into the corner.

Sinking into the leather chair, I bury my fingers in my hair, massaging my aching temple. This is most certainly a rout from which it will be almost impossible to recover. Spending more time at Linwood, out of sight of the gentry, while gossip from the Academy spreads like Greek fire in our wake—

"Idiot," I groan, realizing how stupid it was to threaten her. Bennett would've known better. He'd have heard the warning in Mattie's voice at breakfast. In every way, my brother would've been a far better companion for our sister to rely upon after losing everyone else. Why couldn't *he* have been the one to survive?

"It's not fair." Angry tears threaten to fall. "Even Grandfather thought Bennett would've been a better lord. Why does everything have to be so backward? Why can't I be the little brother nobody needs, the little brother who dies young?"

I push to my feet and try to barrel out of the room in search of some sort of distraction. I've a vague notion of purchasing liquor and returning home to nurse both it and my ridiculous, petty rage. But the toe of my house slipper catches on the chair leg. Stumbling forward, I stub my toe hard against the base of the desk. The roaring curse that rips from my throat might have woken the dead, not to mention the ghosts of memory after memory. Those same words emanated from Grandfather's red-faced, spittle-splaying visage on more than one occasion.

Utter defeat and inescapable despair follow. Brought to my knees, I shove papers and books off the edge of the desk and lie over its side, weeping with abandon. As the mysterious journals Father left me slide heavily to the floor, one of them falls open, the thin leather cord binding it having snapped in two.

My frustration quickly subsides. I'm not one for wallowing, though I don't remember the last time I felt this discouraged. Thinking of Tothill, I begin to pick up the mess I've made, unwilling to cause her worry by leaving evidence of my coming undone.

"What's this?" I take up the open journal.

Its pages have fallen open to a place near the middle of the book where someone covered the entire leaf with the captivating sketch of a man's portrait. He's a young, handsome fellow with Norman eyes that are both mischievous and aloof. His good looks are of a devilish sort, his mouth twisting into a smile full of meaning. The portrait is at once enthralling and enigmatic. "Who *is* this man?"

On impulse, I take the journal to my bedroom and stow it in my trunk. I refuse to move us back to Linwood permanently, but after today, I expect Mattie will induce me to spend several weeks in the countryside. I've yet to uncover the mystery Father's left me in these strange journals, but their author dedicated hours of careful study to preserving this man's image, and that fact makes me certain this volume, out of all the journals, may hold the key to unlocking their secrets.

CHAPTER 7

"It was not Death, for I stood up,
And all the Dead, lie down—
It was not Night, for all the Bells
Put out their Tongues, for Noon.
It was not Frost, for on my Flesh
I felt Siroccos—crawl—
Nor Fire—for just my marble feet
Could keep a Chancel, cool—
And yet, it tasted, like them all,
The Figures I have seen
Set orderly, for Burial
Reminded me, of mine . . .
But most, like Chaos—Stopless—cool—
Without a Chance, or spar—
Or even a Report of Land—
To justify—Despair."

— EMILY DICKINSON

On our return journey, I endure wordless hours. Never in my life have I felt such deep bitterness toward another person. Never have I been so misunderstood, ill-used, and mistrusted as I have been by the one person I'm trying to help. There are no niceties capable of mending the yawning chasm separating Mattie and me. What ought to be done eludes me. All I do comprehend is my recoiling anger, simmering undiminished, in the wake of this betrayal.

The drive to Linwood Manor from the Eaton Village train station is mere miles. Donnie and the other servants came ahead of us with the carriage. He loads our trunks with the help of the station porter. Although it's November, I've removed my gloves, hat, and cravat. Opening the carriage window does nothing to relieve me in this unseasonable heat.

Clouds pool over the hilltops like soap bubbles, gray pushing blue back toward the horizon. A humid shadow blankets the countryside. Ewes gather at a pasture fence, bleating bloody murder, as their shepherd comes to fetch them to their shed. Late-in-the-year thunderstorms topple trees and wash away footbridges. Not even an animal will want to be outside today.

I look to Mattie, who refuses to wear anything but black and is stubborn enough to have put on her heaviest veil this morning. She's still ignoring me, the breeze through the window tearing at the dark gauze hiding her face. Donnie drives the horses at a sharp clip, hurrying to avoid the gathering storm.

A deeper cast of gray falls over the carriage. We've reached the line of linden trees flanking the road. Grandfather planted them when he bought the estate, before I was born. I stick my head out the window, letting the breeze sop sweat from my brow. The carriage clips up the rise. By design, the manor reveals itself gradually, hiding the full extent of its size until one has mounted the rise.

My grandfather's house sprawls atop the hill, teeming with ebony-windowed rooms. Its towers, gables, and pinnacles are crowned with spires that might have suggested a congenial family home if I were approaching anywhere other than the hollow manse that is Linwood Manor. Even when we were children, we barely stirred the air in its vast rooms and halls. But it never felt empty when we were together. Now that I'm almost the only Bancroft remaining, I feel like the lone mouse in a haunted castle. I wish, not for the last time, Mattie would leave this place behind for good. That she'd be content to live with me in London.

The carriage slows around the circle drive, passing Mother's miniature rose garden and coming to a halt under the marble portico. The double doors swing wide and a travel-weary Tothill comes out to greet us as Donnie opens the carriage and hands Mattie down. She enters the house and goes upstairs without a backward glance.

I motion to our housekeeper. She follows me into Father's study, and I close the pocket doors, going to pour myself a glass of brandy. When I down it in one gulp, Tothill's eyebrow flits ever so lightly upward. She waits, her eyes holding a dozen questions.

I sit behind the desk, clasping my hands around the empty glass, uncertain how to put into words what transpired yesterday. I'd forgone explaining our sudden departure from town, requesting the staff pack our things right after breakfast.

"Something's happened, Tothill. You know how Mattie can be. It's just, this time, I almost believe she *is* going mad."

Tothill goes ashen, and she crosses herself. "Merciful Lord! You don't really think so, do you, sir?"

I pour her a glass of brandy and myself a second. "I'll send for a neurologist, if I must."

Tothill sips at her spirit. She smiles, sad and sweet, seeing everything there is to see without my having to say any of it. Dear Tothill has known me for longer than I can remember. She's done more for us Bancrofts than we'll ever repay.

"You'll weather this too, m'lord," she says at last. "By all that's good and right in this world, you and your sister aren't alone. You'll be all right. Give it time."

It's only faith. But her presence and her tone is enough. I feel calmer. "Thank you, Tothill."

She takes my empty glass and gives me a little nod. Then she's off to work her magic. I don't doubt she's already overseen the old house's needs from cellar to attic. All that remains is teasing out what will best help Mattie. Meanwhile, I can do no more than lean back into my chair with one hand over my eyes, trying not to feed this seething anger.

Mattie doesn't appear for tea, nor does she come to the dining room for supper. I eat alone, scraping my silver against the china because my distraction's reached a fever pitch. She's not been well of late. Still, I thought once I'd capitulated and returned her to Linwood, she would want to gloat, not vanish. Tothill clears the supper dishes, admonishing me not to worry.

"She's probably just tired," she tells me with a parting pat.

But her words go unheeded. If I retire now, I'll just end up lying awake, wondering what's become of my sister. Passing from the dining room, I climb the front stairway to the family gallery. It reminds me we've left Grandfather at Norwich House. With a guilty smile, I turn down the east wing, passing empty room after empty room. First, Bennett's old quarters, which I've left untouched. Then the bedroom Abigail and I shared—the one with the adjoining nursery we never had use for and all the fine furnishings my wife selected.

At last, I come to my old retreat, my boyhood room and the smallest and least prominent in the entire manor. Across the hall are Mattie's bedroom and the sitting room where we used to sit up together—me with my book, Mattie with her sketchbook propped up against one knee. I'm not shocked when she doesn't answer my rapping. When I enter the sitting room, I find her bedroom door standing open and her trunk left untouched at the foot of the bed. The sitting room fire is lit, but there's no sign of my sister's having been here.

"Where's she gone now?" I say aloud, swallowing panic.

Lighting a lantern, I search the house. I start with the attic, working my way down the back stair and through the formal rooms that have fallen into disuse. My route leads past the library and my tutor's old rooms. I've spent many happy hours in this part of the house. Before Grandfather took me to London, study was my passion. It was my escape when I felt out of place in my own family.

I peer inside the dark little room and am greeted with the comforting scents of paper and dusty book covers and the sight of the ancient, moth-eaten rug. I know I won't find my sister in here, but nostalgia pulls me forward to the small desk that sits in front of bookcases bearing Latin textbooks and histories, and a newer set of the *Encyclopedia Britannica*, which my father purchased when my old set had lost its luster. It's remained here ever since, a reminder that while my father cared for his children, he never quite understood me.

I run my fingers along the smooth, dust-lined wood of my old desk. Its familiar grooves take me back to one day in particular. I was thirteen years old on a rare, warm February afternoon. While listing the Tudor kings and the dates of their reigns, I heard Master Humphries chuckling. He was standing at the window with his hands folded behind his back, a smile on his face.

"Your sisters appear to be enjoying themselves, Master

Ambrose," he said, turning to me. "It's too fine a day for study. Go outside and join them."

"But sir, the exam—"

"It's only a mock exam, after all. Your education is left to my discretion, lad. You'll find my system has plenty of room for taking in air. Please, go and enjoy yourself."

I rose, stuffing the book and papers inside my desk in a rush. It wasn't as though I preferred history to running out of doors. "Thank you, Master Humphries. Also, did you say *sisters*?"

"Hm? Something the matter?"

"No, sir. But I only have one sister—Matilda."

Master Humphries waved his hand, dismissing me. My curiosity piqued, I took precautions not to be seen as I walked round the house through the hedge garden. I stopped within an arbor covered in dormant honeysuckle vines to peer at my sister and her playmate. Beyond the arbor, a long stone pavement and three fountains were bathed in bright mid-afternoon sun. I heard the tap-tapping of two pairs of shoes. My sister, Matilda, was playing hop scotch with another little girl her age, someone I didn't recognize.

Emerging from my hiding place, my hands folded behind my back as I'd seen grown-ups do, I met my sister's eye. Matilda's friend was hopping up the numbers, away from us.

"Why aren't you singing, Miss Bancroft!" The little girl giggled, balancing on one foot as she reached for a pebble lying between her shoe and the number nine.

"Ambrose, this is my friend Hattie," Matilda said, making a gesture in the girl's direction. "Hattie, my older brother, Ambrose."

Hattie stumbled off-balance and whirled to look at me. Her eyes widened, and she bobbed in the same jaunty curtsy as one of the chambermaids, a woman whose tight curls always escaped her white cap, much to Tothill's chagrin.

Hattie's bright curls were the same wild gold, and I surmised she must be the servant's daughter. Mother wouldn't approve of Matilda playing with the lower class. I was about to tell my sister as much when Nurse came out of the conservatory with Bennett. He'd been in the kitchen, begging for jam tarts again, from the look of his smudged face and her exasperation.

"Hattie, you and Matilda behave while I pop down to help Cook make your tea," she said.

"Does Mother know *Hattie* is here?" I demanded of Nurse, crossing my arms.

"Yes, Master Ambrose."

Matilda, barely standing higher than my elbows, tugged at my arm, pouting. "Ambrose, why don't you like Hattie? She's ever so pretty. Mother said I need a playmate."

I glanced sidelong at Hattie, who was blowing bubbles and looking over the side of the fountain at the fish. Bennett grabbed hold of one of her golden curls and laughed hysterically at Hattie's grimace. She managed to pry his fist open and free herself, splashing pond water at him. Then she scolded him with a wagging finger and much more confidence than most five-year-olds could be expected to possess. Bennett crowed at her, delighted.

"Servants' children don't know how to behave, Matilda. She's not the sort of playmate I expected," I said in a whisper.

Matilda continued to pout. "Why aren't you studying? Won't Father scold you?"

"Let's catch a fish, Bennett!" Hattie cried, skipping over to pull us along too.

"I don't know," I said.

But Hattie drew Matilda toward the fountain pool anyway. I followed them, intending to put a stop to it should they *actually* step into the water.

But Bennett made faces at me, rolling his eyes at my stiffness. "Ambrose doesn't need to go in the pond. He's already a wet blanket!"

Hattie showed Matilda how to tuck her skirt above her knees, like a washerwoman. They waded into the knee-deep water, calling for Bennett to help them. The fish darted away from their stockinged feet. Bennett was all smiles, teasing them for being too scared of the fish to actually touch one. Even I couldn't help grinning at them.

"Not so!" Hattie squealed, chasing fish from one end of the fountain to another. Matilda laughed but didn't make a serious attempt to seize the fish slipping between her feet.

"Come on, *try*, Mattie!" Hattie exclaimed, catching her breath.

Matilda giggled and waved her arms over the water, encouraging the fish to flee in Hattie's direction. But I knew my sister had no intention of grasping a wet, wriggling fish. Hattie screamed in delight as the half-dozen goldfish shot toward her. The next moment, she'd fallen headlong into the water, dousing my sister and sending a spray of droplets far outside the reach of the fountain pool. It misted down on me and Bennett. He clapped his hands, crowing. The mad dive didn't result in any fish.

Matilda helped Hattie up, getting wetter and wetter in the process. Both girls stumbled out of the fountain and sat on its wall, wringing out their hair. Hattie's ringlets had turned into a haystack. I dabbed the moisture from my face with my handkerchief, then offered it to Matilda. She shook her head.

"I'm too wet for that." Her eyes twinkled. Drops of water sparkled in her dark hair. I'd never seen Matilda having so much fun.

Nurse emerged from the house the next moment, and the girls' laughter was smothered by her scolding. "You'd no business dragging Miss Matilda into the water with you, Hattie. I'm ashamed to say you've proven yourself unfit. You'll not be allowed to play with the Bancroft children after this, I warrant. Now get yourself down into the kitchen and ask Cook to hang your clothes to dry. You're a shameful mess, you are!"

We watched her go. At the door, she looked over her shoulder at us, sniffling a little, as though she hoped we'd entreat Nurse on her behalf. But my sister, Bennett, and I weren't like other children. We knew this brief, unusual mingling with the staff did not happen often.

That evening, my sister fell ill with the first of many fevers. It was blamed on her getting wet, of course. No one seemed to remember Hattie was drenched far more than my sister, without taking harm from it. The only other thing that I remember occurring as a result of this odd interaction was that afterward, Bennett and I called my sister by the nickname Hattie had given her. In the heat of a fleeting, happy moment, my sister, Matilda, had become Mattie.

Smiling softly to myself now, I turn away from my old desk. I still have to find her.

White linen blankets the furniture in my parents' suite. Mother probably instructed Tothill to keep the wing in good order for when I might remarry. I've seen the red notes in Father's ledger about laying aside funds for the "young Bancroft heirs." His hopes, inked in the margins, have never come to fruition. Nor will they. I shut the doors on the west wing and return to the ground floor.

Next, I pass through the moonlit ballroom to the conservatory. My sister sometimes hides here, among the half-dead plants and the hardier, still-green ones that thrive despite being neglected. Gardening was Mother's pastime. Not even Tothill can keep up with the indoor plants, and my sister never took interest in such things. She's not here now.

As I turn to go, I stumble in the dim light on a chair standing against the wall, almost behind the door. It's been here for years. Bumping against it causes me pain deeper than the ache in my struck shin. The sharp agony of memory mixed with regret accosts me there, in the place where I last saw Grandfather alive.

It was the day before Christmas. The candlelit ballroom was decked with holly. Boughs of pine and boxwood and fir lined the buffet and china cabinet. On the refreshment table, a massive centerpiece of greenery and clove-decked oranges dazzled our eyes.

My mother had worked her magic on the house, infusing Linwood's spacious rooms with a warm, comforting atmosphere. We sampled our favorite Christmas dishes and sipped spiced wine, savoring nostalgia and sharing rare laughter. With the wine stirring everyone's spirits, we moved in pairs to the ballroom floor and danced.

It was a small affair—a single cello accompanying a viola and only six pairs of dancers: my tall father, with his shock of black hair, led my mother in her green velvet gown; Mattie, wearing Grandmother's pearls and a flattering dress, flushed crimson beside her besotted partner, Godfrey Foxe; Bennett escorted Mother's second cousin, May, a talkative spinster who loved to pinch his cheeks; two pairs of neighboring nobles and their wives, dear friends of my parents; myself, wearing a gold brocade vest to match my Abigail's shimmering gown. We made the turns with elegance, passing under, around, and among one another in jovial intimacy, utterly ignorant of what was to come.

This memory never comes to me untainted by the events which followed. Even now, my mind's eye focuses on what went unnoticed by everyone that evening, and I recall it in unnatural, vivid detail: Grandfather sitting in the chair next to the ballroom hearth, smiling with a painful tightness. We, who begged him to dance, were oblivious to the grimaces which crossed his face now and again as his heart slowed in his chest. We couldn't have known how soon that tired organ would stand still. Christmas isn't a day one expects to precede a funeral.

I feel utterly spent now as I leave the ballroom and search the remainder of the first floor. No one in the kitchen has seen Mattie. She's not rung for anything all day, though that's not out of the ordinary. Often, when she keeps to her room, moping, she refuses to eat anything. It's one of the many troubling behaviors I fear will prove her undoing.

After wandering all over the house in search of her, I'm haunted by so much remembering it almost hurts to breathe. Briefly, I consider abandoning my search. But my blood is up, and not just from climbing flights of stairs. Worry beats a steady rhythm in my pulse. Rest will be impossible tonight, so long as I'm ignorant of Mattie's whereabouts.

She sometimes walks out of doors at unusual hours, so despite the rumblings of a building storm, I leave the kitchen by the back door and strike out to search the grounds. Weariness blurs my vision, but I'm too frantic to rest for even a moment.

Beyond the shrubbery maze, a gravel path circumvents our small lake. It's a good half-mile walk. By the time I've wound back round toward Linwood Manor, my hands have begun to tingle. Stuffing them into my pockets, I lengthen my stride. The cold night has served to waken me. I feel my senses sharpen in the crisp, moon-soaked air.

The path leads me past the north wing, where the rooms are furnished in brass-gilded Chippendale and outdated textiles. Grandfather bought Linwood from an heirless gentleman over fifty years ago and took up residence in its grandest suite, but the north wing has lain in disuse since his death.

As I pass under its windows, gravel grinds underfoot with an awful clangor. I hurry on, almost at a run. Then something catches my eye, and I slide to a stop. High above my head, in one of the black, mouth-like windows, flickers a yellow light. Craning my neck, I catch sight of a white figure slipping past the frame. It's only there a brief moment before the window is empty again.

I wait, breathless, for the figure to reappear. It's likely Tothill, hunting down a chill draft. More likely her than an apparition. But as the minutes pass and I see no further movements, the deep blackness of the windows begins to bear heavily upon my mind.

Mattie and Bennett went wide-eyed as children when I'd tell chilling tales about the old house being haunted. Making up ghost stories was my prerogative as their eldest brother. But even I never dared wander empty corridors alone. With an immense effort, I turn my back to the windows and race down the loud path. My heart hammers. I take the veranda's marble steps two at a time.

"Mattie, where are you?" I pant, pausing to look out over the desolate, moonlit grounds. "Why do you always disappear when something's wrong?"

CHAPTER 8

Crumbling is not an instant's Act
A fundamental pause
Dilapidation's processes
Are organized Decays—
'Tis first a Cobweb on the Soul
A Cuticle of Dust
A Borer in the Axis
An Elemental Rust—
Ruin is formal—Devil's work
Consecutive and slow—
Fail in an instant, no man did
Slipping—is Crashe's law—

— EMILY DICKINSON

C old to the bone and more tired than I've felt in days, I pass through the sitting room. Candles burn but silence reigns. I peer in at my sister's door. It waits as bereft as before. There remains but one place in the house to look. It's been nagging at me. I turn my feet toward the abandoned north wing as the bells of the grandfather clock echo through the foyer like a gong. *Twelve o'clock.*

The wing is closed off by a set of doors carved with knights and the banners of our family tree. As a child, I was impressed by the carvings, freshly oiled and gleaming in sunlight that streamed through the wing's floor-to-ceiling windows. Grandfather resided there and used his sitting room to entertain political allies and university fellows on rotation.

Now, the doors are cut with deep shadows cast by my lantern. The faces of the knights stare at me, hollow-eyed, with gaping mouths. I pass by this empty wing every day. It seems absurd that the familiar sight of these doors should fill me with such grim unease now.

Reaching for the great brass handle, I recall the ghostly figure I spotted in the wing's windows moments ago.

"Come on, Ambrose," I tell myself. "Mattie's missing. You can't crack now, old fellow."

My hand rests on the knob, turns it. I'm about to push open the door when it falls away. I'm left clutching empty air. Then a chill runs through me.

The door was opened from the inside.

"Wh-who's there?"

A figure draws closer, draped in white. Deep-set eyes fix on me a withering gaze. A ghost?

Then it gives my cheek a slap. "It's only me, Ambrose."

"Mattie?" I gasp, stepping backward.

She pushes past me, heading toward her sitting room. "Were you expecting someone else?"

I swallow back relief, then recall I'm angry with her. I snap the sitting room door shut and pace the room, weighing whether to scold her or ignore her worrisome absence. In the well-lit sitting room, I can more clearly see my sister's face. She's smirking at me from the overstuffed chair by the fire. When I say nothing, she rises and pulls the bell cord.

"Mattie! It's well past midnight," I chide her.

Tothill comes in with tea things, her sharp eyes taking in Mattie's bedraggled hair and dirt-stained travel clothes. Mattie thanks her as though it's four o'clock in the afternoon instead of far past a decent hour of retiring. When our housekeeper has gone, Mattie pours for us. I've been rehearsing rebukes all day, and yet no words will come to mind.

I give up and crumple against the settee, too tired to be angry anymore. Besides, what can I say that hasn't already been said? If Mattie wouldn't listen to any of my scolding in London, how can I expect her to listen to what I have to say now? We've returned to the pain-riddled, sucking mire that is Linwood. After today, I've been weakened by the same slough.

The sound of Mattie's laughter pulls me from my nail-biting.

"Have you been drinking?" I say, peering at her.

"Hardly." She sips her tea, then gives me a genuine smile. Though my misgivings remain, her expression disarms me. I'd forgotten what that sort of smile looks like gracing my sister's face. A smile without trace of care, undaunted by grief, untouched by ghosts.

"Do you intend to give me an explanation? Where've you been today, Mattie?"

"Oh, Ambrose." She sighs, throwing herself back against the overstuffed chair. "You shouldn't have worried. I can see by the pallor of your face it did you no good."

"But you were *gone*." I bristle at her condescension. "Without a word to anyone."

"I'm not a child."

"You've not been well. What am I supposed to assume when you disappear like that—"

"I won't fall into a pond and drown. I won't lose my way on roads I've walked for decades, brother."

It's not her getting lost which haunts me. I control my tone with difficulty. "You shut yourself in your room, refuse to eat, barely sleep ... I know you feel like giving up. But, Mattie, you can't!"

"I'm in no danger in this house."

That last comment doesn't sit right with me. Besides, this is an affront. I'm furious she continues to reject my concern. I've done what she asked and brought us back here, and the defeat I suffered in doing so will only be assuaged if I see it do my sister some good. Looking at her now, I know she's half-starved and bone-tired from our journey. I'm not asking for much. Why can't she just eat a decent meal, wash her face, *talk* to someone? How can Mattie be this stubborn?

"Mattie, are you determined to waste away before my eyes?"

Despite my anger, I can't help the tremble that steals into my voice. I'm ill-equipped to convince her, after what happened in London. The only weapon left to wield against her callousness is pity.

But even this fails me.

"Doesn't Father Amicus say that death is but a momentary separation from the ones we love? If I die, Ambrose, you can just tell yourself everything you've been telling me all these months since Bennett's funeral." She levels me with an even stare, taking my shock in stride. "It doesn't matter if I leave you alone—you'll see me again, after all."

She leans forward, showing her teeth in a wry smile. "We'll see all of them again. It's going to be all right. You're stronger than you think, Ambrose!" Her voice lilts in a mimicry of the many well-meant, ill-chosen condolences hurled at us over the years. "You don't *need* me, and you certainly don't need to cry after I'm gone. What a waste, wallowing in tears like that. It's better to just move on. It's what your family would've wanted ... for you to be happy."

She laughs again, and the coldness of it sends chills down my spine. I'm frozen in my seat, as though I'm watching a screwed-on head slowly unwind itself, dreading the moment it will fall off my sister's narrow shoulders but unable to wrest my eyes from the awful sight.

"Ambrose, I've discovered something special," she says now, more softly, leaning closer to brush her fingers across my furrowed brow. "Linwood Manor has a most delicious secret. Beyond anything *you* can imagine. I hope it will lessen some of your cares as it has eased mine. You must come with me tomorrow and see for yourself."

"A secret? In the north wing?" I repeat.

"Shh." Mattie presses a finger to my lips. "Don't borrow trouble, dear Ambrose."

She lies back in the embrace of her chair, humming a spirited gavotte.

First, smiling and laughing. Now Mattie's got music in her? I don't believe for a moment she's gotten over Bennett's death. The only explanation is that she really must be drunk. That's why she's being so petulant and throwing my words back in my face. She'll be her silent self again tomorrow when she's sober. I must ask Tothill to put a lock on the port.

I know I ought to ask about this secret of hers. I ought to demand an explanation in exchange for bringing her home. But weariness tugs at the corners of my consciousness, begging me to rest. And there's something else I've been meaning to bring up to Mattie. A last plea for her ever-elusive cooperation in making something out of the nothing we have left.

"If you're feeling so improved, why not take up your art here at Linwood?" Mattie bristles, but I plunge headlong into the argument I've been preparing. "I know, I know! It was a mistake to throw you into society before you were ready, and the Academy itself will likely never take you back. But your art isn't just for show, Mattie. You're not some prize mare I want to keep in good form for breeding, no matter how much you malign me with such imaginings. Promise me, at least, that you'll keep painting. You could paint flowers for bedridden invalids and poor orphans. Just hold on to that piece of yourself. Please?"

Mattie sniffs, a sardonic smile on her lips. "If you're hoping the exercise will keep me alive, Ambrose, I'm afraid you'll be disappointed. Death runs in the family."

Shaking my head, I rise to go, but her voice reaches out of the deep shadows she's slumped into. There's a note of regret, which moors me to her side a moment longer.

"I did want to go back to the way things were, Ambrose. I tried. God knows how I tried to get out of bed each day and look you in the eye. But it was no good. Everywhere I went in London, I saw young men in suits. Men with dark hair curling over high collars, just like Bennett's. Boys who laughed as though they're immortal, just as he should've been. I couldn't bear the reminders."

I see him everywhere too, I want to say. But that's not the sort of brother I've been. Mattie's the one who always needed *my* reassurance. I accepted compliments for her in public while she stood beside me, blushing. That was the way we had been. But Mattie is transforming before my eyes, becoming separate, more private. It feels like another loss.

As I pass her chair, I bend and kiss Mattie's forehead. "I know it's hard, but we must go on. At least at Linwood, you won't be able to accuse me of trying to marry you off. There's no one here but us."

Mattie looks long at my face. My weariness and frustration are plain for her to see, but she's untroubled by my mood. Where my displeasure might have once compelled her to apologize profusely, even before she was certain what had caused me offense, she now holds my gaze with cool confidence. That faint smile returns to her lips, like a secret she declines to share.

I take a candlestick and cross the hall to my chamber. Pausing with a hand on my doorknob, I peer into the darkness toward the north wing. It's cloaked in shadows, but I can still make out the carved double doors. We've left them ajar. Mattie's strange pronouncement comes to mind. *Linwood Manor has a secret.*

From the north wing, a voice calls my name. It's not Mattie, and at first, I don't know I'm listening for it. But the eerie silence that follows is deafening. I stand stunned, a drum beating inside my chest. I can't bear to hear it again. But again, it calls.

"AMBROSE ..."

I feel the hair prickle on my neck, and I slip through my bedroom door and snap it closed. I circumvent the room, lighting all twelve candles. But the lack of darkness doesn't calm my thundering heart. Floorboards creak underfoot. I'm continuously glancing over my shoulder. The corners of my room hold a last remnant of shadow, and I have a sneaking suspicion they hide a person too. But no one's there when I look.

I try to regain control. Taking a book to bed, I grasp at the thin hope it will lull my harried mind. As I lie with my eyes fixed on something dry and philosophical, my pulse races on and on. The coverlet jumps with each pound of my heart. My palms are damp. I can barely breathe.

Resolute, I ignore these signs of impending doom. I try to overcome them. But for some hours, raw panic prevents me from falling asleep, though the book's words swim before my weary eyes. Its page is writ with other words than the ones I repeat to myself, a mantra in a hoarse whisper—

"It's not possible. It's not possible!"

In the morning, the fear aroused by the voice in the passage seems utter foolishness. I dress before the mirror, reproaching myself. "You've got to keep yourself together, Ambrose. You're all Mattie has left."

I straighten my blue cravat and stride out of the bedroom, formulating a plan to get my sister to take some air with me while Tothill searches her room for harmful substances. I've not forgotten the missing laudanum bottle and Mattie's propensity for faking illness, nor her propensity for real illness. It's for her own good that I be able to judge which is which, even though it's a trespass on her privacy and likely to be a distasteful enterprise for Tothill as well. But after last night, I'm convinced Mattie is in no condition to manage her own well-being. Less fuss and bother if she doesn't know about it until it's done.

To my surprise, Mattie's at the breakfast table, sipping coffee. She has toast and a soft-boiled egg on her plate. She even asks Tothill to bring up cold ham from the kitchen. Cook has not sent up ham in a long while. There wasn't much point. When Bennett was sick, Mattie and I lacked any appetite for rich food. I sit across from Mattie, stealing glances in her direction over the *Morning Post*. There's color in her cheeks, and the lines of her face are less drawn.

"You seem to be feeling well this morning," I say.

A smile lingers in the corners of her eyes. "Tothill and I were looking at some of the unused rooms this morning. She's suggested we give away some of Grandfather's outdated furniture." Mattie rises to spoon some pudding onto her plate from the buffet. "Did you know there's a boarded-up room in the north wing? I've a mind to make it my new chamber."

"Is that why you've been flitting about that empty old place?"

"Yes. It piqued my curiosity. I swear I've never seen it before."

Mattie's eyes take on a hazy quality. Gathering my wits about me again, I push back the memory of the eerie, half-seen figure in the window. It must have been my sister.

"Well, I'm glad you and Tothill have some useful endeavor in mind. You didn't mention it last night," I say, buttering my toast too thickly. "If you'd tell me what you're thinking, maybe I wouldn't have to nag you so much. You know all I want is for you to be well and happy."

"I'm going to be fine, Ambrose. Stop hen-pecking for once."

My face warms. I'm not used to Mattie's scorn.

Despite the flummox at breakfast, I succeed in giving Tothill her secret task and enticing Mattie to go outside. We walk the grounds, starting with the shrubbery maze and lake on the east side of the house, and continue round the back, along a hedged path flanking the conservatory. After passing its high, beveled windows, we round the corner of the house, and the gravel walk becomes a paved patio. It leads westward a hundred yards, bordered by carefully tended topiaries. In the middle of the pavement rest three separate pools of water, the central one holding dormant lilies. I wonder whether Mattie remembers playing here with Hattie, so long ago.

We speak little. Mattie's always preferred others do the talking. Though the silence once felt awkward, I've learned to weather it. Now it's just us two keeping each other company. When we reach the end of the stone pavement and turn east again, the house casts long shadows across our path. Purplish smoke rises from the kitchen chimneys and brings with it the damp scent of dew laced with pork and baking bread. Apparently, Mattie's appetite at breakfast has inspired Cook to further demonstrations of her culinary skill.

"Shall we walk the lane?" I ask when we turn onto the front lawn. Despite Mattie's silence, I feel more at ease than I've been in a great while. Truth be told, it's easier to deal with my sister in the seclusion and privacy of our country estate. There'll be no gossip here. Winter will pass, and spring will return to these grounds, bringing an invitation my sister may be hard-pressed to resist. We've all the time in the world here, Mattie and me. One day, she'll wake up and feel like living again.

She leaves my side, going to the little rose garden in the midst of the circle drive. Her back is to me, hunching over.

"Mattie?" I say, hovering.

I realize she's shaking. Crying. With growing alarm, I place my hands on her broken, trembling shoulders. Mattie brushes her fingers over a barb-laden stem. Mother had always dead-headed the flowers long before winter, but now the shriveled blossoms hang frozen. Mattie pulls one wrinkled rose close to her face, and something about the way she's crushing the faded blossom appalls me.

"Mattie, are you all right?"

"Neither of us is all right, Ambrose." She clutches the thorny stem till a bead of blood appears. It runs sluggish down her wrist.

"Of course not," I whisper. "But this morning, you seemed much improved. I'm taken aback by this sudden change."

She brings her pierced thumb to her mouth. "Do you suppose any of it meant anything? All those years we lived together?"

"How could you ask that? Of course, it's ..." But the words I hear in church, spoken in Latin, are foreign to my sister. The theological formulas of pain balanced by divine sovereignty feel incompatible with her question.

"You act as though their absence means nothing to you. You seem so *content*. How do you do it? How do you move on so easily?"

I've never heard Mattie speak this way. Taking her hand, the wounded one, I hold it tight. "What do you mean? Of course, I feel their loss as much as you do, Mattie. I just happen to be a little more used to it, I suppose. Life marches on, does it not?"

But my heart squirms. I haven't forgotten anything. I can't forget. I can't let go of any of them. If I'd really moved on, would I still be here at Mattie's side, pleading for her to be well again? Would I be willing to do almost anything to keep her alive?

Mattie's hollow, half-dead eyes meet mine. Her voice rasps from her throat, barely a whisper. "Mother, Father, Bennett ... They're gone. Soon, we'll disappear too. No trace of us will remain. What's the point of living? Of all this pain? How do I stop caring, Ambrose?"

I squeeze Mattie's hand, studying her face. I resent her accusation. I want to argue with her, as I did with Godfrey Foxe. But her quest for meaning is too dangerous to leave unanswered. She's asking the sort of questions we're not supposed to ask. Mother would say, "Doubt does nothing for the soul."

"We've both lost everyone we held dear, except each other," I tell her, firm and authoritative. "That's why you have to let me care for you, Mattie. Don't give in to whatever this is. It'll consume you."

As the words leave my lips, I see her crumbling inside the shell that is her body. It's as though my sister fades away and a gray shadow fills her wilting form. She speaks no more of the pain. But her silence is as loud as screaming.

We traverse the long lane hand in hand. Shadows cross our path, meld together, cover us with darkness. We return with calls of blackbirds and robins overhead, a scraping sound of pebbles underfoot. Linwood Manor rises out of the ground at our path's end, pale in the November gloom.

I find myself glancing again and again at Mattie's face. Doing so is discomfiting. A mere hour has passed, yet lines of sorrow are redrawn across her features. Her skin is ghostly white. Gone is the healthful flush I noted at breakfast. When we enter the foyer and she offers me her cheek in parting, it's cold against my lips. I hug her small, soft shoulders and search her eyes.

"Mattie, let me send for someone. Someone better than me at answering the questions troubling you."

Mattie stares back, emotionless. "Do you mean Father Amicus? The man responsible for burying half our family, who can never resist an opportunity to talk about his favorite dish? Really, Ambrose?"

"Actually, I was thinking of Godfrey Foxe. He'd be happy to see you again, and I'd be glad for an excuse to invite him to Linwood myself. We might renew our friendship with him after ... Well, it's been such a long while."

My sister winces. She shrugs out of my embrace, pressing a hand to her temple.

"He told you, didn't he? You're an idiot, Ambrose. Always plotting and always stupid enough to think I won't see through it. I can't keep letting you do this to me." Her footsteps clip away.

Dear Lord, I find myself thinking toward the paneled ceiling. But I don't even know for what I'm asking.

CHAPTER 9

"Behind Me—dips Eternity—
Before Me—Immortality—
Myself—the Term between—"

— EMILY DICKINSON

The Wilting Woman came to me, smelling of despair. She stepped through my doorway and paced the length of me, squinting at my corners and windows. We had only met once before, and she did not yet know I was always watching her, even beyond these four walls. She still thought she had to come to this room to find me.

After a few minutes, I let her feel my presence, like a shadow moving under the surface of water. She flinched. I saw her glance toward the open door and feared I had alarmed her. I softened my voice and spoke to her from one of the rafters.

"HELLO, AGAIN ..."

She raised her chin, sharp as a dove, wary as a serpent, and gazed into my dim ceiling that reached far above her head. These creatures are so small. But the Wilting Woman was not as small as some who'd visited me. I shrugged into the walls and exuded from them a pleasant scent. I found that something akin to fresh pine pleases these creatures. The Wilting Woman smiled. She stepped to the wall and brushed her fingers against the wood I was wearing.

"I was thinking about what you said last night. I've decided. I'll come and live here, with you. Is that all right?"

"OF COURSE. DID I NOT INVITE YOU?" I said, quite pleased.

"I wanted Ambrose to come too, but my brother and I are at odds right now," she added, apologetic.

"WE HAVE ALL THE TIME IN THE WORLD, DEAR ONE."

She winced, clutching her hands to the bodice of her gown. "Sometimes, we think we have more time than we really do."

"REMEMBER WHAT I TOLD YOU BEFORE? DEATH IS MERELY AN ILLUSION."

She nodded.

"WILL YOU DREAM WITH ME TODAY, SWEET ONE?" I asked her, a little over-eager. "Sweet" is a pet name I usually reserve for those who have known me longer. But the Wilting Woman was desperate for companionship. She accepted the strangeness of me from the start.

"If you will wake me when evening comes," she said, lying down on the bed.

"As you please." My voice carried the tone of smiling. A trick I learned over many decades of friendships with creatures who spoke. Anything is easy if you practice long enough.

CHAPTER 10

I measure every Grief I meet
With narrow, probing, eyes—
I wonder if It weighs like Mine—
Or has an Easier size—
I wonder if They bore it long—
Or did it just begin—
I could not tell the Date of Mine—
It feels so old a pain—
I wonder if it hurts to live—
And if They have to try—
And whether—could They choose between—
It would not be—to die—

— EMILY DICKINSON

I n my defense, I've a very good reason for having forgotten all about my promise to Miss Holm and that poor scally-wag, Tom.

As Tothill shows her into my study late one afternoon after I've had yet another argument with Mattie, I rise from my seat, stiff from staring blankly at the account book for hours on end. Miss Holm gives me a brisk curtsy and sinks onto the very edge of the chair I pull out for her. Tothill slips through the pocket door, leaving it ajar, her sharp eyes taking in everything.

When we're alone, Miss Holm opens and closes her gloved hands over the drawstring purse she's clutching in her lap, dragging her eyes over the room. I don't return to sit behind the desk. Miss Holm and I were once comrades in arms at the societal fray, and I don't wish to weigh our different statuses in the privacy of my own domain. Instead, I bring another armchair and sit on the near side of the desk opposite her, offering an apologetic smile.

"Miss Holm, how delightful to see you again. Though it occurs to me now, I neglected to send Mons. Belot your way. My promise of provision on Tom's behalf was a genuine one; however, the care of my sister has so completely occupied my mind of late, I've been negligent in my duty to you and the boy. I hope you can forgive me?"

Anna Holm's shoulders relax, and she tucks away the little black purse, fixing me with a sad little smirk. "Have you become a mind reader, Lord Bancroft?"

The thought is laughable, but our laughter is not as light as it was on the occasion of our first meeting. I ask after the children at the home—Tom and Finn in particular—and Miss Holm gives me appropriate responses. Still, I feel her coldness keenly. At last, with a heavy sigh, she looks at the darkening window beyond my desk.

"It's growing late, and I'm procrastinating. I'll be frank with you, Lord Bancroft. The home is doing very poorly, especially now it's Christmastide. You'd think the nobility would have loose purse strings this time of year, but everywhere I go, I hear the same thing—'we've our own families to think of,' and 'holiday cheer doesn't come cheap.'"

There is a plaintive plea for help in Miss Holm's expression. "I can barely scrape enough together from what the church provides for our food and fuel to heat the house at night. Will you send me away empty-handed, Lord Bancroft?" I feel her embarrassment, watching her hands clench her plain, black dress. The same dress she's worn on every other occasion, I suspect.

"I'm a proud woman, and it hurts me to be forced to ask help from a stranger," she finishes. "I'd like to be saved the trouble of coming again for a long while, if you've a heart to be generous."

My face feels hot as I go to sit behind Father's desk and draw out a check for my bank. The fault is mine, if anyone's. My forgetfulness, in part, is the cause for Anna Holm having to travel all this way just to beg.

The room is quiet, apart from my pen scratching out a large number on the thin paper of the check. I hand it across the desk to Miss Holm, and she folds it in half, tucking it inside her purse without a glance at the amount. Rising to go, she says, "Thank you, Lord Bancroft."

"Wait," I tell her. "Won't you stay for supper? Donnie will drive you all the way to London if you'd like. You can be home before midnight."

Miss Holm hesitates, her eyebrows drawing close together.

"Please, allow me to make up for my blunder," I explain, opening the door for her.

This supper is nothing like our first meeting. The room is empty apart from we two. I make no explanation for my sister's absence, and Miss Holm is too polite to ask. A storm is breaking outside, and Cook's made a hot pot of lamb and leeks, served alongside her Irish potatoes. But the tense absence of good-natured talk has nothing to do with the weather.

I look to Miss Holm's plate, already half-empty, and force a chuckle. "I'm glad you like it, Miss Holm. Nearly all our staff come from across the Irish Sea, and on nights like this, Cook can't help herself. Most English noblemen would turn up their noses, but I see you aren't put out by such homely fare."

Miss Holm flushes a little. "The good Lord blessed me with a taste for common dishes. Thankfully so, for that's all we can afford."

We finish the meal without further commentary. But when Tothill brings coffee and cake, Miss Holm at last gives me a more willing smile, saying, "I see you are wondering where we've got off on the wrong foot."

"Now who's reading minds?" I smile back, picking at the cake. I don't want this meal to end. I suspect it may be the last time we see each other.

"It was something you said about my Lucia. God knows I'm tempted to bitter resentment where she's concerned. Even after all these years, I can't bear her to be maligned."

I sit straighter, my pulse pounding in my chest. "Miss Holm, I can't bear the thought either! Please, tell me how I offended Miss Lucia. I'm ashamed to admit I don't recall saying anything ... That is, I only meant to compliment you, if I said anything at all."

"I know." She laughs, turning a pitying smile upon me. "But knowing you didn't mean it doesn't take away the sting."

With a long sigh, Miss Holm lifts her coffee and sips. Then, wiping her mouth, she shakes her head. "No, it's not worth dragging up again. I can forgive you, and we ought to put it behind us. You're a good man, in your own way."

Somehow, coming from her, this does not feel like approbation.

"I invited you to stay for supper out of more than just pity," I tell her, laying aside my napkin. "I want to build you a children's home in the countryside here, where they can have clean air and play outside. An old friend once suggested I oughtn't give up my grandfather's dream of preserving the Bancroft name. He said I could remarry, which is something I will never do. He even said I could adopt someone like young Tom, to raise in place of a natural-born heir. But that I cannot do either."

Laughing, I shake my head. "I'd be a terrible father! Instead of singling out some poor soul who wasn't born to a genteel life and doesn't deserve being forced into one, why not adopt a whole school of children? I'll provide everything they need, and the name of Bancroft will fade into obscurity as far as London society is concerned. But even if no one else remembers me, those who come to Eaton to grow up and learn at the feet of the Holm sisters will never forget."

My little speech fills my chest with warmth, and my voice roughens with emotion. Miss Holm at first listens with a furrowed brow, her coldness preventing me from discerning her thoughts. But as I lay my heart bare, feeling my conviction grow that *this* is what I want to do—what I *must* do—Miss Holm responds in kind. She reaches for me, tears trickling down her face. Grasping her strong, warm fingers, I blink back my own.

"Lord Bancroft, I do believe I have no choice but to accept your very kind offer."

"I'm glad to hear it. Though it will take some time to build a proper place, be assured, I'll involve you in all the plans. It's your future and the children's which I'm endeavoring to secure."

"God bless you, sir."

With that out of the way, conversation flows more freely. Miss Holm has decided, it would seem, that I'm not like the other gentry who make empty promises and leave her destitute by the wayside. I ask her about Miss Lucia, careful and polite as I know how to be. Miss Holm is good enough to share a few stories of their childhood.

"Lucia's never going to change," she says, after our good-natured laughter dies away. "That makes me sad sometimes. I'll never watch her marry and have children of her own. We'll never compare tiny noses and curls to hers or catch glimpses of our long-lost mother and father. There are many, many topics on which Lucia and I cannot equitably converse. Her mind is, and ever will be, the mind of my vibrant, carefree, eight-year-old sister.

"In one way, that is a boon for someone like me. I'm always connected to the ten-year-old self I see reflected in Lucia's eyes. I pray I never outgrow my love for her."

The thunder breaking outside adds a somber note to our candlelit conversation. Tothill takes away the coffee and pours us each a glass of port. Miss Holm thanks her, with the comfortable grace of a woman used to passing between classes with the ease of donning and doffing a cloak. When Tothill's gone away again and the grandfather clock chimes ten, I venture into a subject I so desperately wished to avoid earlier in the evening.

"Miss Holm, the night of the Lawrences' party, you said something to me which I believe I've yet to comprehend. At the time, I was attempting to bring my sister, Mattie, back into society. I believed that was best for her. Since we've returned to Linwood, my sister has regressed to the extent I feel at a complete loss. There's nothing I want more than for Mattie to be well again—truly well, in body and mind."

Miss Holm waits while my misery chokes me. Eventually, I swallow hard and add, "You said I ought to listen to her, but if she doesn't confide in me anymore, I don't know how."

Miss Holm leaves me waiting a long moment. I'm sure whatever she might say will help with Mattie, so confident am I of her perceptiveness and empathy.

"There's a great deal more to listening than hearing. I fear in your case, Lord Bancroft, it will take much practice. You seem to be in a hurry." Her gentle smile holds an even gentler rebuke. "Why is that?"

This answer is not at all practical. I feel sharp disappointment. "There's not much time. At least, I feel that way. Because ... because of how the others died. Grandfather died suddenly, from a heart condition we didn't know he had. It was different with the rest of my family ..."

I haven't told her everything. She doesn't know how it all started or how much I wish it had happened the other way round. Even though the candles are burning lower and lower, it feels like Miss Holm is someone who'd sit up with me no matter how long my story takes to tell. I gulp down the remainder of my port and decide I might as well tell her everything.

"My wife's name was Abigail ..."

I'm jolted awake some hours later, sitting at Father's old desk. It takes me a long moment to remember we're not in London anymore. The conversation with Miss Holm comes floating back in disjointed pieces. There's the feeling I've been called. Or was about to fall. My pulse hammers in my chest. The storm still rages outside, and the room is dark. Then I hear Tothill calling for me. Her voice holds an unusual, tremulous urgency.

I burst out into the foyer, my head spinning. "What's happened?"

She's at the top of the stairs, her hands quivering on the banister. Her distressed speech is unintelligible. I take the steps two at a time and seat her on a hall bench. This behavior is unlike our stolid housekeeper. I can hardly keep my own panic at bay.

Tothill draws a shaking breath and points toward the north wing.

"Miss Mattie's gone to bed in that strange room we found, the boarded-up one. I thought—I ..." Tothill inhales with a half-suppressed shriek. Her words echo through the foyer like a child's wail. "I shook her. I even shouted. She can't be woken! It don't look like livin', but she breathes. And I hear her heart patterin' against her ribs."

Tothill's cries continue for several moments as she rocks in her distress, gazing up the hall. "I'm sorry, m'lord. I can't help meself, I'm *that* frightened for her! But she needs you. I—"

I leave Tothill in the hall and run like I've not run in years.

"Mattie!" I charge into the north wing, bellowing. At the far end of the hallway, a long mirror shows me a reflection of myself. I look like a thin, black worm as seen through a telescope.

There's a flash of lightning. Charged air rattles the windowpanes. I notice a fine powder soiling the cuffs of my trousers. A white layer of dust blankets the carpet and hall furniture, and a clean swathe marks a woman's path through it. The trail leads across the hall to one of three doors. Two of the doors I recognize. The one on the left leads to Grandfather's study. The one on the right holds the sitting room where he entertained guests.

If I'm remembering correctly, the two rooms are connected by a door. But now, between them, a third room stands in their way. To this third door the clean trail has led me.

I'm haunted by something Mattie said. *"Linwood Manor has a most delicious secret. Beyond anything you can imagine."*

"Impossible," I whisper, approaching the door.

Opening it, I'm greeted by the scent of pine. Rain patters against a single window in the opposite wall. Beyond lies the slick glass roof of the conservatory. A curtained bed stands in the middle of the room. The surrounding space is cluttered with furniture—a wardrobe, desk, and bookshelf, all arranged in a haphazard manner.

The room is deprived of ornament, except where the bed is concerned. Its hangings are sumptuous red silk, embroidered with gold and silver filigree in a foreign style. Within the outer hangings, sheer silk of red and gold is strung in long sheets. The silks cascade like waterfalls from the edge of the bed, pooling onto the floor. And on it, Mattie's stretched out like a corpse.

"Mattie?" I whisper, stumbling to the bed in the darkness. I take up her hand and shiver, recoiling. It is limp, her fingers ice-cold.

Of late, there are too many things I can't explain. Things I don't understand, that I'm unprepared to protect my sister against. I collapse on my knees next to the bed and grip the coverlet with a shaking fist. There are tears on my cheeks. But my flesh feels heavy and numb, like stone.

"I'm sorry, Mattie," I say, a dread like an anchor in my belly. Too late, I wish to do what I should've done all along. "If you wake up, I promise I'll listen to you this time."

I must send for Dr. Brooks, but I can't look away from her. The room is cloaked in dimness and quiet, like a wake. Outside the window, lightning flashes. A roll of thunder passes over Linwood Manor like a harbinger of death. Only with great difficulty do I tear myself away.

Tothill recovers her iron will as soon as I send Penny for the doctor. She arranges a candlestick and wash basin on one of the dressers and makes silken knots of the bed's curtains to keep them out of the way. Her presence dams up my tears, giving me enough strength to stand at Mattie's bedside. Without exchanging words, we rally to meet whatever this night may bring.

The doctor arrives. Tothill stokes the fire, and I look for a chair to offer him. All the room's furniture is shoved into one corner. A dressing table and stool are crammed behind a massive oak wardrobe. It would take four men to move it. Instead, I go to drag an armchair from the sitting room next door.

As I'm standing in the doorway, I relive the moment I first received Grandfather's summons, when I was sixteen. I'd paused before this room with tingles of excitement and fear coursing through my body. My small hand had turned the knob, and the room had enfolded me with a falling silence, voices of old and young men halting mid-sentence as every eye in the room took my measure. Then Grandfather had spoken, cutting the tension. I'd let the door close behind me, drawn for the first time into that mysterious circle known as "the grown-ups."

Now, white sheets cloak the chairs and smoking tables. They're odd shapes, unrecognizable. I go to the fireside, where Grandfather used to hold forth on his war days. I drag the sheet off his oak smoking chair and smell a hint of tobacco. Hoisting it up, I move instinctively toward the far end of the room where a door used to connect this sitting room with Grandfather's study. But things have changed. I'm facing a solid wall papered with jungle vines.

"Where did it—"

My question is interrupted by Mattie screaming.

CHAPTER 11

"The heart asks Pleasure—first—
And then—excuse from Pain—
And then—those little Anodynes
That deaden suffering—
And then—to go to sleep—
And then—if it should be
The will of it's Inquisitor
The privilege to die—"

— EMILY DICKINSON

I rush through the passage and burst in on Dr. Brooks and Tothill wrestling Mattie in the depths of the great, curtained bed.

"What's happened?"

She looks like a wild thing. Wide-eyed, pale as a ghost, with clammy beads of sweat crowning her brow. Her dark hair clings to her back and arms where the dampness has gathered. She sees me and grabs my arm, digging her fingers into my jacket. She's screaming inarticulately. But from her expression, I understand she's pleading for something.

I sit next to her, with an arm around her shoulders, and turn to Dr. Brooks. "What happened? Why's she like this?"

He throws up his hands. "Lord only knows, Bancroft! She was in a dead sleep a moment ago!"

He attempts to approach her and touch her forehead, but Mattie swipes at him with her fingernails like a cat. Dr. Brooks retreats to a safe distance. "Can you calm her?"

I turn Mattie toward me, gripping her shoulders firmly as she writhes. "Mattie, dear, listen. Dr. Brooks wants to make sure you've not taken ill. Please, Mattie! Let him examine you, and then I'll sit and hear whatever it is you want to say. Remember, I promised. I won't say a word for once. Please, just cooperate this time?"

My words finally reach her. My sister sinks limply against the pillows. Watching Dr. Brooks with half-lidded eyes, she allows him to slip the thermometer between her lips and measure her pulse. The long, silent minutes creep by before the thermometer can be read, and I take a moment to observe her better.

Mattie has a bony look about her, like a small bird when it gets wet and the feathers stick to its body, showing how thin and fragile it really is. She's damp with sweat and smelling like stale linen. I wonder how long it's been since she had a proper wash. Her hair is unkempt and looks slept on. Mother's hair looked that way during her illness, when she was bedridden for months preceding her death.

The memory sends chills down my spine. I pick up Mattie's frail hand, giving it a squeeze. She drags her eyes to my face, staring at me without expression. I've so many questions, but I dare not interrupt the examination.

When Dr. Brooks has finished, I follow him into the passage to hear his assessment. Tothill takes a damp rag to bathe my sister's face, cooing to her as to a small child. I pull the door closed and face the good doctor, with my worries creasing my brow. I'm fearing the worst. Lord knows Dr. Brooks has delivered many instances of bad news to members of my family. If I wasn't so anxious for Mattie's health, I might feel sorry for him.

"How is she, Dr. Brooks?" I wring my hands, hunching over the short man, keen to catch whatever pronouncement will fall from his lips, while dreading it all the same.

The doctor lays a hand on my arm. "No need to worry, Bancroft. There's no sign of fever. She's suffering a severe bout of melancholia, I believe. But following your brother's death, it's to be expected. You and your sister have suffered tremendous loss in recent years."

"You're saying … She's not …" I'm unable to give voice to my greatest fear. Biting the back of my hand, I blink back stinging tears, exhaling a sigh of relief.

"No, no, Lord Bancroft. Your sister is not dying," Dr. Brooks says.

"Thank God." I shudder. "But then, why could we not wake her? She was as still as death itself."

"It may be she was exhausted and in a deep sleep. And sleep is the best thing for those whose hearts are wearier than their bodies can support. Would you like me to stay for a while and ensure the correct dose of morphia is administered?"

"Morphia?"

"You could use a dose or two yourself, Lord Bancroft. It will help the both of you enjoy a sound, restorative sleep at night. I'll give Cook my regimen for a melancholic's diet, and in a few weeks, you'll be feeling right as rain, I warrant."

Although amused by his misinterpretation of my condition —melancholy is a sickness well-known for preying upon the soft and sensitive minds of women, often for no apparent reason—I still cannot quite get over the feeling that something with Mattie is not right.

"*I'm* not ill, Dr. Brooks. Neither am I melancholic! But Mattie—"

Dr. Brooks appears oblivious to my affront. He gives me a polite nod. "Very good, sir. I'll just go speak to Cook, if you'll excuse me. I'm sure your sister wants your company."

The doctor tucks his instruments inside his black bag and shuffles away. The reminder of my promise to Mattie lessens my annoyance at his presumption. I pull Grandfather's oak chair to the head of the bed. Tothill is tidying the room, and my sister is tucked properly under her coverlet, apparently fast asleep.

"Thank you, Tothill," I say with great feeling, when our housekeeper comes to stand beside my chair.

"Forgive me for losin' my composure." We both stare at Mattie for a moment. "She'll be all right, sir. You both will."

I huff. "I don't see why you and Dr. Brooks keep badgering me as though I'm just as ill as Mattie. Anyone can see *she's* the sick one."

Tothill tuts at me. "Beggin' your pardon, but I washed your nappies when you were a wee babe! I know better than to think you're all right, Ambrose." Tothill dips into a shallow curtsy and spins on her heel.

Her lapse in decorum doesn't bother me in the least. She's got every right to speak to me like a child, if anyone has. As she leaves the room, her roused temper sounding in the ring of her heels, it dawns on me that I've often thought of Tothill with the tenderness a man reserves for his mother. I smile, then rub a hand across my aching forehead and close my eyes. I suppose it's possible I've been unwell and too busy to notice.

❧

I've nodded off again, leaning on my hand in Grandfather's chair.

A sharp whisper wakes me. "Ambrose ... Ambrose!"

I jolt upright. Mattie's sitting up in bed, holding a small bottle in one hand, a measuring spoon in the other. I jump to my feet and clutch her shoulders, relieved to see her awake and calm. "Mattie! You're all right, aren't you? Dr. Brooks says you're all right." I look at her more closely, recognizing annoyance in her expression.

"You've jostled me, and now the morphia's spilled on the bed. Sit down, Ambrose."

I sit, then her words sink in, and I snatch the draft away from her.

Mattie squeals. "Ambrose!"

Stepping out of her reach, I clamp the lid on the bottle and secure it and the spoon inside my pocket. Mattie throws herself back against her pillows, growling in frustration. Her balled fists beat the coverlet on either side. I've not seen my sister throw such a tantrum since we were small children.

Sitting on the edge of the mattress, I take one of her hands in both of mine. My shushing only annoys her further. She turns her back to me, sobbing like a petulant child.

"Dear Mattie, what's gotten into you?" I say, in what I imagine to be a patient tone, while stroking her tangled hair.

"Leave me alone, Ambrose! You can't possibly understand." Her voice is muffled by the pillow she's hugging.

"Well, you might try to explain before making that judgment," I say. "I promised to listen."

Mattie sits up, dragging her knees to her chest, keeping out of my reach. She doesn't want to be consoled, it seems. I fold my arms and wait while she studies me with a black expression. At last she speaks, her voice trembling.

"I was going to tell you, Ambrose. When I mentioned Linwood had a secret, do you know what I was going to show you? It was this place." She looks up at the ceiling and around her bed, smiling softly. "Well, sort of. I can't explain it in so many words. I intended to bring you here, to *show* you everything.

"But when we walked in the garden, I remembered how you always ruin things. All I want is to be numb to the pain, as you are. I thought maybe now that we're not in London anymore, you might leave me alone. But then you brought up Godfrey, knowing my history with him, and I realized you'll never stop." Mattie's voice grows tense. "You're always going to be fixated on bringing me to heel."

"I'm sorry you feel—" I begin, forgetting my promise.

"I don't *need* an apology." She presses a hand to her forehead, squeezing her eyes shut. "I understand, I really do! You *think* you're doing what's best for me. It's just, for the first time ever, I truly need you and want you to need me back. After years and years of your meddling, Ambrose, I thought I could count on you to care about me."

"I do care about you, Mattie. Of course I—"

Her eyes meet mine, cold and unforgiving. "You don't. Not really."

I search for adequate justification for my actions. She's only accusing me because she'd rather wallow in despair than move forward. I want to quote scripture on the warring of the spirit against the desires of the flesh. But I don't know the words.

Mattie's eyes are fixed, demanding nothing but acceptance. I swallow my truths, and they taste of ash.

"I'm listening now," I say.

"Then trust me," she says, holding out her hand.

"Where did you get the morphia, Mattie?" I ask, but my resolve is crumbling.

"Dr. Brooks whispers loud enough for the deaf, bless the man. He told Tothill to put a bit in my tea this evening to help me sleep. But I don't want to wait. I picked her pocket—"

"You *stole* it?" Too late, I regret the censure of my tone.

Mattie seizes me by the arm, her voice raised to a hysterical pitch. "Ambrose, I'm warning you. Trust me this once, or I'll never speak to you again! Give me the morphia."

A good brother wouldn't give in. There's something wrong with Mattie, something even the good doctor hasn't discerned. She's gone off in the head, like a character in one of those books set in the Yorkshire moors. Reaching inside my jacket, I pull out the bottle. Mattie snatches it away, unstoppers the neck, and tosses back a swallow before I can blink. Then she carefully pours a spoonful, offering it to me.

"Trust me," she says, her words slurring.

The spoon wavers in her hand. I catch it as she falls back against the pillows, hesitating a mere moment before downing my dose. I stopper the drug and slump into Grandfather's chair. Just as I begin to lose consciousness, I hear the bottle drop with a clatter to the floor and roll, roll, roll ...

CHAPTER 12

And then I heard them lift a Box
And creak across my Soul
With those same Boots of Lead, again,
Then Space—began to toll,
As all the Heavens were a Bell,
And Being, but an Ear,
And I, and Silence, some strange Race,
Wrecked, solitary, here—
And then a Plank in Reason, broke,
And I dropped down, and down—
And hit a World, at every plunge,
And Finished knowing—then—

— EMILY DICKINSON

I feel heavy.

My limbs lie on either side of my torso, made of lead. I can't budge a finger. My eyelids have a sarcophagal weight. My chest barely rises. I long to gasp open-mouthed for air but can't unhinge my jaw. I'll suffocate soon. A red heat is growing behind my skull while air whistles in and out of my nose. Then I feel a light pressure on my chest.

"Ambrose, calm down, dear. You're all right. I'm here."

It's as though her voice is prying up the lid of my coffin. A tiny light appears. Sound pours into my ears. Water, running over rocks. A soft play of the breeze in foliage. The calling of a nightingale. The steady croak of one bullfrog. Behind these, in the far distance, sing the crickets. Light continues to wash over me, bright as day at first, dimming to the softness of starlight.

Above me, Mattie's face is framed by shadowed shapes of tree limbs and silver-bellied poplar leaves dancing in the wind. The night sky is indigo, full of strange constellations. I sit up and make a quick inspection of my limbs. There doesn't appear to be anything the matter with me. The panic retreats, but I'm aware of it throbbing under the surface. I stand to my feet, taking in my surroundings. Mattie clings to me, giggling in delight, dancing on feet that won't stay still.

"Isn't it beautiful here?" she cries.

We're in a forest of poplar, maple, and oak trees. A brook reflects white patches of light from the rising moon. The breeze is playful and warm, the stars twinkling bright enough the ground is completely visible, and there's a spongy floor of grass and moss. An idyllic English picture in every detail.

However, this is *not* England.

"Where are we?" I ask Mattie, whose only answer is to take me by the hand and tug. I follow, and she skips ahead, dancing around the trees. We are both barefooted and wearing some sort of loose, silky clothing.

Treading with ginger steps, I study the ground in fear of tripping over roots or stepping on a thistle. But there appear to be none of these. At length, Mattie grows tired of waiting for me and breaks into a pace more amenable to her excitement. We run through the wood and out into a large meadow profuse with wildflowers. Their scent envelops us like a cloud of intoxicating perfume. My spirits lighten, and I take no more thought for my tender feet.

"This is the secret place I've been dying to show you, Ambrose!" Mattie exclaims, laughing. "You're so old and stodgy. Don't you remember how we used to play in meadows like this one?"

"I remember playing in the garden and conservatory, but—"

Mattie pulls up short, her face drawn in imitation concern. Taking my head in her two hands, she searches my eyes. "Poor dear." She sighs, patting my cheeks. "You've never been a child, have you? The little boy I played with in the creek behind the Eaton post office was beaten out of you long ago. Of course, you don't remember."

"I was never beaten," I counter, affronted.

Mattie waves a hand dismissively. "You were broken all the same. Grandfather's lectures ring in your ears, I can tell. But don't you see, Ambrose? We're free of all that now! Here, in this wondrous place, we can do what we like, be anything we wish, and there's no one to tell us any different."

She races ahead, and I'm forced to break into a run. I don't want to lose her in this place. Despite her airy spirits, I've a vague sense Mattie needs my help, though the reason why eludes me. It's been ages since I ran full out, and for some reason, my knees don't ache as I lengthen my stride to match my sister's. Her peals of delighted laughter echo off a looming structure ahead.

Mattie rushes forward, rapping at a knocker barely visible

in the moonlight. I stand beside her, tipping back my head to take in the immensity of the place. Just as I've decided it bears the shape and height of a tower, a door opens. We are bathed in yellow light.

"Come in, my lady!" says a voice.

Mattie pulls me through the door, and my feet register cold stone before my eyes can adjust to the sudden brightness. I follow her through a hallway to a small closet of sorts. We step inside, and a door closes almost upon my nose. I feel an eerie lurch, my stomach drops, and I totter on my feet.

"Good God—?"

"Excuse me, m'lord, there's no need to curse. It's only an elevation mechanism. EM, we like to call it 'ere."

I look around and see only cream wallpaper dotted with red and white roses. Mattie smiles at me, still holding my hand. I look past her, searching the far corner for the source of the voice, and almost jump out of my skin. A half-sized person with stumpy legs and a bloated, spotted chin is blinking up at me with large yellow eyes. He looks so very frog-like, I'm forced to avert my eyes so as not to offend him by laughing aloud.

"Right, sorry about that," I say, controlling myself with difficulty.

Our arrival, and the stomach-turning lurch it gives me, prevents further awkwardness. Mattie pulls me into the room beyond the EM. Its doors close behind us, with the frog-man still inside, and we are alone. I hesitate in the entryway, which has a black-and-white checkerboard floor. Chess pieces line the walls. Mattie moves into the room beyond, as relaxed as though she were stepping into our old sitting room.

I follow with careful steps. The odd entryway opens onto an oval room. Most of its floor-to-ceiling windows stand open, a breeze stirring their gauzy drapes. Immense sheets of glass form the ceiling, making it look as though the room is suspended in the night sky among the stars themselves.

The furniture is varied—all of a sort I've never before laid eyes on—and arranged about the room like furniture in a child's dollhouse. A white fur rug lies in the center. Next to the rug rests a green velvet couch the length of three settees put together. Mattie reclines on this and pats the cushion seat next to her.

"Come. I'll ring for something to drink. They've got all kinds of delicious things here. What do you fancy?"

I stumble down two shallow steps. There are no candles or lanterns in the room, but it's bathed in the soft moonlight. This place makes me uneasy. It has a peculiar, dream-like quality I find unnerving. The couch is solid enough, though. I sink back, heaving a sigh of weariness. Mattie pats my arm.

"It *is* a strange place, at first. But don't worry. Once you're used to everything, it's marvelous! Watch this."

She reaches into the roomy sleeve of her robe and pulls out a tiny bell. Giving it a sharp ring, she smiles at me in triumph. At the back of the room, a small door opens, and in shuffles another half-sized creature. This time, the woman who appears is almost completely mouse, with gray-and-pink ears, a pointed nose, and whiskers. Only her hands are human. Mattie giggles and jabs me in the ribs.

"Isn't she droll?" she whispers, though I don't doubt the mouse-woman can hear her making fun.

"How can I be of service, my lady?"

I'm astonished to distinguish words in the midst of the mouse's high-pitched squeaking. Mattie raises her eyebrows at me, as though to say, *Isn't she funny?*

"Bring us something to drink and eat. I don't really care what. It's *all* delicious!"

"Yes, my lady, my lord," the mouse says, bowing to us in turn. Then she shuffles back out through the door in the wall, which becomes quite invisible once it snaps closed.

"Now, just sit back and let go of your worry, Ambrose. That's why I brought you here. Not just so you could keep me company. I don't really need you for that, now that I've this place and all my droll little friends. Do you like it here?"

"Where are we?" I ask her a second time. But for some reason, I feel I don't actually care to know the answer. The couch is soft and comforting. The room smells of pine and clean, summer air. I could almost lay my head back and fall asleep. But I'm not the least bit tired, despite running through miles of woodland. Mattie ignores my question, and I let it rest.

"In a bit, I'll show you around. At least, everywhere I've explored. There's much, much more of it, you see. It's incredible! I've been looking forward to discovering it all together, like when we were children. You and I used to be quite close, you know. I miss *that* Ambrose."

"You said something of the sort in the wood a bit ago," I say, taking note of the new warmth of affection filling her gaze. It's been so long since anyone looked at me without a shadow of death and illness in their eyes. "Mattie, have I really changed so much? Am I awful?"

She laughs, tipping back her head. "Oh, Ambrose, you've become almost as awful as Grandfather!"

Slouching in my chair, I long to hide from her, but Mattie scoots closer on the settee and drapes her arm over me, folding me into an embrace. When she's holding me like that, I feel protected from the shame which filled me at her words. I know Mattie's right. The thing I feared when I became Lord Bancroft has come to pass; brought up to always feel inadequate, I stepped into Grandfather's shoes and found they fit just fine.

"I'm sorry," I whisper into her hair.

"Dear, I didn't bring you here to make you apologize," she says, patting my back. "I just want to see you break free of everything, as I am. We can start over, be brother and sister again, like none of that ever happened."

My sister smiles with more warmth than I've seen in her

since Mother died. But instead of reassuring me that Mattie is well, the happiness in her face—the lightness and energy emanating from her whole person—unsettles my sense of rightness. There's more to Mattie than meets the eye, and I suspect not all of it is good.

"Do you remember when you and Bennett took me on safari in the woods behind the hay fields?"

A summer day of pure bliss. Our eyes meet, sharing warmth of heart and the companionship of decades.

"We made you a crown of strawberry leaves with the little white flowers still attached. You looked like a fairy queen," I say, returning her smile. But the memory is also a barb. We weren't the only ones there that day.

Mattie looks away first. "But I'm getting ahead of myself! Before all that, we must wait for your summons," she says, forcing a laugh as she rings her little bell.

"Summons? To what?"

Miss Mouse reenters, bearing a tray as large as herself covered in pastries, chocolates, and several decanters. The goblets and ice cream–laden bowls sparkle as though they're made of diamond. Mattie seizes a spoonful of the cold treat and feeds it to me, while the mouse-woman arranges the rest on a tea table in front of us. I give the room a quick perusal, savoring the delicate cream and the sharp tang of the silver spoon. Where did that table come from?

"Good, isn't it?" Matties asks me.

"The best," I say, my attention riveted to the dessert. "I mean it. Nothing I ever tasted was so good."

"Here, try this." She laughs, picking up a plate of puff pastry filled with jam.

I bite into the flaky crust, and the sensation of the pastry melting between my lips and the cool tartness of the jam seeping into my tongue, like a burst of fresh-picked raspberries, is something I can't enjoy in silence. "Mm!" Crumbs drop from my mouth. "This is *better* than the ice cream."

"Everything is better! You could eat all day here and never get full, and every time you put something new in your mouth, it's miraculous."

"How's that possible?" I ask. But even Mattie knows it's not a real question, more of an exclamation.

"Have a little sip of this," she says, pouring a gold liquid into a crystal glass. "Then you can close your eyes and take a rest."

"I'm not tired, though," I say, taking it up and examining the auriferous drink.

"No, but you might want to forget all the same." Mattie strokes my hair.

I lift the goblet to my lips without hesitation. The potion tastes like pure astral fire. I wipe my mouth on my wrist, and it comes away flaked with gold dust. "Forget what?"

"Your worries, of course." Mattie lifts a second goblet to her mouth.

"Of course," I say and close my eyes.

I am Lord Ambrose, brother of Lady Mattie. We take tea together every morning on the veranda of our own magnificent tower. The veranda overlooks a vast meadow full of the most fragrant poppies, purple ramsons, orchids, and columbine. Beyond, the hunting woods boast the swiftest stags and most cunning foxes a sportsman could desire. And yet, standing above my very own paradise, sipping tea, I can't help but wonder what else is out there, just waiting to be discovered.

"This land is full of delights, sister. We should be off this instant. Let's go further than we've yet been!"

Mattie simpers, setting down her teacup and coming to stand next to me. I turn and give her my full attention. Her new gown complements her well. The fabric is a soft blue and shows off her smooth, pale skin. She's adorned her full, dark curls with a multitude of pearls and stems of baby's breath. My clothing is a woodland theme, greens and browns cut in a noble style, making my slight figure appear more muscular.

"I, too, long to explore the furthest reaches of this great realm, Ambrose. But have patience. First, you must answer your summons."

"Hm?" I feel as though I've forgotten something important, but the impression passes. What a ridiculous thought. Nothing is more important than going further out, seeing everything there's to see, tasting all that can be tasted, enjoying myself to the fullest!

"Are you ready to go now?" Mattie asks.

I give her my arm in answer. We descend the delightful EM operated by the frog-man. He's looking fine today in a tiny pair of yellow dungarees which show off his thick, human feet and sticky frog hands. He doesn't mind my having a good laugh at him.

"You're too kind, m'lord," says he, obliging as ever.

Mattie tugs at my arm, as she always does when she wants me to see something wonderful. We are walking through a rooftop garden. The blue sky above bathes an oblong space with light. Fountains spew streams of water overhead and into pools opposite. Their fine mist fills the air with rainbows. Fruit trees in tiled planters ornament the courtyard. Mattie leads me to the center, to an arbor covered in honeysuckle.

We halt just outside. The vines and flowers are so thick and the shade within so deep, I can barely make out a low couch and, as I surmise, the person we've come to see.

Up until now, we've not met anyone. But when a clash splits the air, I glance over my shoulder, startled by the sudden noise. Just behind us stands a girl who is human, apart from her rabbit ears and rather longer feet than normal. She's holding a miniature gong suspended from a red cord in one hand and a gold mallet in the other. Was she following us all this time?

The rabbit-girl walks around us, silent on her furry pads. She makes a deep curtsy and announces, in a silk-soft voice I can barely hear above the playful fountains, "Your Majesties, may I present Lord Ambrose and Lady Mattie."

I turn toward Mattie in astonishment. She's said nothing about meeting royalty. Mattie's sinking into her grandest, showiest curtsy, and I follow suit, bowing with an elaborate flourish of my hand. When we rise again, the rabbit-girl has gone. There's a long moment of expectancy, during which I feel not quite uncomfortable, but something like it.

Inside the arbor, one of the figures stirs.

"What is it, lady?" The accent is archaic, the tone petulant, but the voice itself has an authority behind it I wouldn't dare question.

Mattie clasps her hands together. There's eagerness in the way she's leaning forward, but she doesn't dare take a step. Her eyes are wide, searching, as though she longs to be given a sight of the person who spoke to her. When she answers him, there's an eager tremble in her voice.

"We received a summons, Your Majesty."

The silence is barely disturbed, but I observe a second figure half-rising within the arbor. The two occupants hold a quiet conference. Then, languidly, a hand parts the ivy curtain. Mattie gasps in delight, plunging into another curtsy.

My own bow is arrested, for my eyes have fallen on a creature of pure appeal. My heart races at the sight of her angelic figure reclining. I worship the roundness of her thigh, adoring the garment which drapes her pleasing curves. Her small foot protruding from her gown makes me feel faint. The elegant bend of her wrist over the edge of her bed has the daintiness of a woodland doe.

Hers is a long face full of pleasing features—red lips, pink-tinged cheeks, blue eyes, and a porcelain-smooth brow. Blond hair of spider-silk fineness streams over her bare shoulders. It's so long it spills over the edge of her couch, reaching the floor. Her picturesque image evaporates all thought from my mind. I am oblivious of the second figure sitting on the couch. That is, until he takes up her hand and places his ruddy lips over it in homage.

Growling, I step forward, prepared to die for her honor or live a murderer of the man who dares touch her.

Mattie places a hand on my arm, saying, "Your Majesties, may I present my brother, Lord Ambrose. How we have longed to meet you!"

"I am King Bonne, and this fair lady is my queen, Beatrix," he with the lips declares. A knave and he knows it, by the crooked smile he offers me. A smile full of devil's mischief, a fitting match for the pair of curved horns atop his curly head.

"We are pleased, so pleased! Thank you for receiving us, Your Majesties," Mattie says.

I wish she would cease her fawning. "I thank you," I say, with another deep bow, tucking away my contempt for now.

"Won't you sit down?" Queen Beatrix motions elegantly to a low couch behind us.

I hadn't noticed it before. What a wonderful hostess is Her Majesty! Mattie and I sit, and there follows a most enjoyable conversation. Enjoyable apart from the participation of King Bonne the Knave. Meanwhile, I've a growing conviction I've seen his impish face somewhere before.

"Are you enjoying yourselves?" Queen Beatrix is saying. "Is the house we provided to your liking, Lady Mattie?"

"Oh, yes, of course. The food is marvelous, the drinks divine! There's nothing lacking, and if I think of anything at all, it simply appears. Your staff are so very obliging."

"They're adorable little things, aren't they?" Bonne says, baring his teeth in another smile.

"Indeed," I say, projecting confidence in my voice to match his. "The only thing we yet require is some mode of transportation. We long to see your realm and discover every wonderful thing there is to know about it, Your Majesties."

"True, there are endless wonders," Queen Beatrix intones in a sleepy, singsong voice. She raises her hand to cover a yawn, and the delicacy of her manner has me in raptures. I catch her eye and give her my most charming smirk. One slender eyebrow lifts above her blue eyes. There's a bemused smile on her lips.

The lilting voice of the knave interrupts our affinity. "I believe there's someone here you'll wish to see more than all the treasures I possess."

"You've found him? Truly, Bonne?"

I glance quickly at my sister, who is rising from her seat in rapture. The king of knaves smirks at Mattie in a way I do not like. But I've not time to discern what interactions have preceded this moment because I'm already falling behind. "Found who?"

Mattie leaves my side with a pained cry, and I look in the direction she's running. A figure is approaching through the garden. He's not like one of the half-sized animal people we've encountered everywhere we go. He's more like Mattie and me than even the King and Queen, in that he's a slight, brown-haired human with pale skin. The only thing he has, which we've been lacking, is an easy smile. I half rise to my feet in utter shock as my sister falls into his arms, crying.

Bennett?

Moving in Mattie's direction, I'm staring, rambling aloud. "It's the morphia ... Of course it is. That can't be Bennett. Bennett's dead. I'm hallucinating ... happens when you take morphia, or so I've heard ..."

CHAPTER 13

"If recollecting were forgetting,
Then I remember not,
And if forgetting, recollecting,
How near I had forgot,
And if to miss, were merry,
And to mourn, were gay,
How very blithe the fingers
That gathered this, today!"

— EMILY DICKINSON

S low, painful realizations wash over me. This isn't real. None of this is real. I've got to get Mattie away.

"Whoa, there," someone snickers in my ear. "That's enough of that."

A rough hand shoves me to the side. I lose my footing. I'm falling, then my face smacks against the floor. Only, it doesn't hurt nearly as much as you'd expect cold marble to hurt. I raise my head to find I've fallen on some sort of spongy, woven floor mats.

A number of these square mats fill the space of a room. It's lit by an oil lamp and bare of furnishings. I sit up, disoriented. The room isn't the only thing that's changed. I'm dressed in my usual suit, my black cravat brushing against my chin. The transition is surreal, like waking from a dream to find I've fallen out of bed.

"Neat trick, huh?" King Bonne gloats, squatting a few feet from me with his irritating, self-important grin.

"Where's Mattie?" I growl, scraping my fingernails against the matted floor, clenching both fists. "Where's my sister? Take me back to her. I swear, I'll—"

"You'll what? Do you dare throw me the gauntlet? I've got more tricks than you can imagine, you skamelar. Here, I'm *king*."

As he speaks to me in this demeaning way, the knave paces the room on light feet. His stance reminds me of a martial arts demonstration I once witnessed. There's not a doubt in my mind: if I provoke him, he'll be on me like a hellion. Folding my legs under me, I prepare to run. But there's no door in the three walls I can see. The fourth is behind me, and I dare not turn my head.

"Your Majesty, I don't know what I've done to offend you, but I beg your forgiveness," I say, half-bowing.

"You lie very churlishly, *Lord Ambrose*." King Bonne stops long enough to throw back his head in laughter.

"I do not like to be mocked," I say, but my mind is at work. What does this fellow want with me? How did we get here in the first place?

Bonne closes the space between us, planting both feet in front of me. He drops to a squat, his eyes level with mine. I expect a blow and raise my arms to defend myself.

The king licks his lips. "I'm not allowed to banish you. And it won't be any fun to torture you. Too much of a weakling. You'd just die on me." He reaches inside my breast pocket and pulls out the jet black locket I keep with me always.

"G-give that back," I say, grasping one edge of it, but Bonne yanks it out of my fingers. He steps away from me, then rounds in one fluid movement, his heel arcing to deliver a powerful kick to my jaw. When I open my eyes, moments later, my vision is blurred. The entire left side of my face feels like fire. I lie on the floor, paralyzed by the throbbing in my head.

"Were you planning to use this to show her *my* version is fake?" King Bonne continues, tossing my trinket up and catching it. "Your sister's imagination will gloss over inconsistencies. She *wants* him to be real."

"An illusion," I say, wincing with the pain. I've so many questions, but I won't be able to voice them in my current state. Raising my hand, I feel with horror how wobbly my jaw is. Without a doubt, Bonne has broken it.

"Yes, an illusion. Unfortunate for you that you saw through it. But no matter! I'll make certain your sister doesn't."

I can't answer him. His pacing is nerve-racking. Every time he comes close to me, I flinch. A frustrated, frightened groan escapes my throat. I try to raise my head, but the pain is excruciating.

Bonne must see the fire of hatred in my eyes. He lunges at me. "Listen, worm. You're not going to muck things up, understand? I'll take you back to your sister as long as you come to heel. You'll tell her nothing. There'll be no mention of illusions or dead brothers."

Bonne tosses the locket toward me. It lands on the mat next to my face. I reach for it with a shaking hand. As my hand closes over the locket, Bonne gives a cruel chuckle. Then, leaping with stag-like agility, he brings his wide, coarse foot down upon my hand. Just before impact, his foot transforms into a cloven hoof.

Crunch.

My inadvertent cry sends hot spasms through my jaw. I wish I would fall unconscious. But the suffering Bonne inflicts balances the fine line between overpowering and what can be endured.

"Even if I can't give you the boot, I can cause you a world of pain," he coos in my ear. "Don't forget that."

Lifting his foot, he crosses to the wall behind me. With great difficulty, I take up the locket with my unbroken hand and slip it into my pocket. King Bonne pulls at the wall, and a panel slides back, opening onto the garden throne room. In the distance, I can see the counterfeit Bennett embracing Mattie as though they'd only just met. I drag myself to my feet and move toward the door. When I reach it, Bonne grabs hold of my lapel.

"Do we have a deal?" he says, flicking my chin. "Protect this secret, and I'll make sure you get what you want."

I nod once. King Bonne shoves me through the doorway, my foot falls on marble, and with an abrupt shift, I'm standing at my sister's side. The pain fades from my jaw, my vision clears, and I can move my fingers. I lift my right hand and place it on the charlatan's shoulder, then place my left on Mattie's. My eyes fill with tears.

Mattie lifts her rapturous face to mine. "I told you it would be all right, didn't I, Ambrose? Bennett's here. Aren't you pleased?"

I see Bonne striding past us, rejoining his queen on their couch.

"It's good to be together," I lie.

◌⁂◌

We share a celebratory feast with the king and queen of this illusory realm. All throughout the meal, I sit in silence, puzzling out who they might really be and what all this might be about. Now I've broken through the magic of this place, I remember where I've seen Bonne's face before. In every detail but the horns, he's the exact image of the sketch in the mysterious journal Father left me.

As we go through the motions of a royal banquet, my resolve grows. Mattie must be rescued from the power of this illusion. In the meantime, I've no idea how to accomplish it. I smile when it's required of me, eating without relish. Just as Bonne said, Mattie imagines anything and everything she likes about the fake Bennett.

He rarely speaks, and when he does, his answers are vague. During dinner, I notice that his eyes, though their shape and expression mimic our dead brother accurately, are a dark gold rather than Bennett's gray. Mattie hasn't noticed. She interprets his words, his expressions even, to mean whatever response most agrees with her opinions.

"Bennett's delighted by the prospect, don't you think, Ambrose?" she says, after insisting we undertake our intended exploration.

This morning, I was burning with the desire to see and taste and enjoy. Mattie appears to be under the same delusion now, convinced there's some marvel waiting to be discovered. She begs Bennett and I to embark with her tomorrow. I nod in agreement, wondering if time even exists in a place like this.

After supper, I feel inordinate stupidity descend upon me.

Blaming the wine, I lounge back in my chair and rest my heavy eyes. I hear Mattie chattering away, the charlatan's vapid replies, and King Bonne holding forth with exuberance. Queen Beatrix has said little over the course of the meal. Now that we've finished eating, I'm curious about Bonne's fair companion. I open my eyes, hoping to determine whether she's an illusion too.

To my surprise, she's still eating. All the dishes have been placed directly in front of her, and Beatrix is methodically finishing them off. With growing alarm, I watch her place an entire chicken leg inside her mouth and yank the bone out bare. Her queenly appearance is lessened by the number of olives she can consume in one minute. She sloshes wine between her lips to wash down whole eggs, half-chewed. I catch myself gawking, my lips curling in disgust, and have to squeeze my eyes shut. How could I have felt an attraction to the wretched creature?

When Queen Beatrix has cleaned every plate, she dabs her mouth with a daintiness that now seems ludicrous. King Bonne bursts into rude laughter.

"The look on the man's face! You'd think she was a sow eating its sucklings, by the look of him," he roars, pounding the table with a fist.

Queen Beatrix blushes and smiles at me demurely. "I have done nothing wrong."

"Come, let us amuse ourselves," Bonne declares, extending a hand to my sister.

I rise and hurry round the table to be next to her, intending to make an excuse and take Mattie back to the tower. But Queen Beatrix slips her hand through my arm and purrs through pursed lips at her brother. "Yes, let's."

Bonne offers an arm to Mattie, and she parades from the dining hall between the knave and counterfeit brother. I don't know which concerns me more. I hurry after, passing under the archway only a stride behind them, but when I emerge from a brief passage into another room, the three of them are nowhere to be seen. Queen Beatrix and I enter a different chamber. I suspect there's a magic about this evil place, letting Bonne manipulate geography to his liking.

"Come, lie with me," Queen Beatrix calls from the center of a round, cushioned bed. She's sprawled across the blush pink velvet like an indolent cat.

I ignore her, distracted by worry. If Mattie is with Bonne and Bennett together, there's little chance of the knave making a fool of her, thank God.

Queen Beatrix sidles next to me, laying her head against my shoulder. Her spun-silk hair falls over the back of my neck, tickling me. I scratch at it.

"But he's not really Bennett," I mutter.

Queen Beatrix sighs petulantly, adjusting her hair so it streams over her shoulder on the side furthest from me. She fumbles with her clothing, muttering. But I've not time to spare listening to her. There's no reason the puppet Bennett would prevent Bonne from making advances on Mattie. She's in danger!

I leap to my feet, scanning the room for an exit. There's no door in sight, even where the archway stood a minute ago. I spin around to demand directions of the pigsty woman, queen though she may be, and I'm blinded by her pale nakedness.

"Great Scott, woman! What've you done with your clothing?" I turn on my heel and slap a hand over my eyes. "Come now, get dressed and show me the door. I must be getting back!"

"Lie with me." This time, there's a tone of annoyance underplaying her words.

"I most certainly will not," I huff, then add, "Your Majesty."

I hear her languid sigh and the shuffle of her bare feet.

"Fine. But as far as my brother's concerned, your deal is still binding."

There's silence. I open my eyes. I've been left alone. "Heavens! Now which way did she go to leave?" I stomp in the direction I'd heard her footsteps receding. "I swear, if I find that Bonne fellow engaged in a similar occupation, I'll strangle him with my bare hands."

CHAPTER 14

"I meant to find Her when I Came—
Death—had the same design—
But the Success—was His—it seems—
And the Discomfit—Mine—
I meant to tell Her how I longed
For this specific time—
But Death had told Her so the first—
And she had fled, with Him—
To wander—now—is my Abode—
To rest—To rest would be
A privilege of Hurricane
To Memory—and Me—"

— EMILY DICKINSON

I walk through a dark tunnel, the ground sloping upward. There's a handful of light at the further end. I hurry toward it, feeling for the wall with my right hand. At the tunnel's mouth, I stumble through a wall of foliage hanging over the doorway. My nerves are jangling as I rip the leafy vines from my arms and head. I hadn't expected to be groped, and the sensation unsettles me.

When I've freed myself, I look around. There's a thick darkness and cloying humidity. The air is filled with night song to the extent I can barely hear my own rapid breathing. I wait with a hand on my side, catching my breath. As my eyes adjust to the dark, I begin to make out the shapes of tall trees. These are not the pleasant, wide-spreading branches of the wood near my sister's tower. This forest is populated by pine, fir, and hemlock. Its ground is rocky, tangled with undergrowth, webbed with creeping vines.

Water rushes somewhere to my left. Stumbling in that direction, I reason that the river or stream should lead me out of this wretched place. Then I'll get advice from a local or find my own bearings. Thinking like this soothes my nerves. I make confident strides over the rough ground until the river appears below me, gushing through a deep ravine. I halt at the edge of the small precipice, wondering where I might find a bridge.

There's a crash and then a growing rustling noise behind me. My skin crawls. Something must be hunting me in the dark. I'm trapped. Sinking to the forest floor, I watch the bushes shake and shudder as it moves closer. A sharp squeal causes me to jump out of my skin, then a small creature darts from the undergrowth not two feet from me, rushing toward the precipice.

"Watch out!" I catch her by the skirt, and she collapses next to me, quivering from head to foot. I feel a deep relief now that my fears are proven groundless. She's a mouse-woman, but not the same one who served us in Mattie's tower. She clutches her chest as though she's in pain. Her black beady eyes are restless, searching the bushes.

"Now, now, you're all right," I say to the little creature, patting her head between her furry ears. She may look mostly mouse, but long, curly locks of human hair grow from her scalp. "Strange little creatures, you are."

Mouse-woman gives a cry and goes stiff. Afraid she's died of terror, I feel under her chin for a pulse. Then I hear a low mewling in the undergrowth. I spot two green lights floating in the dark shrubbery. A clawed paw emerges, followed by a thick cat's ruff and striped, grinning head. The huntress pads out of the bush and then straightens, revealing a pair of human legs.

"Give her back," the cat growls, pacing between the scrub and her quarry as though she doesn't dare come in reach of me.

"Look here, you can't go chasing people about in the dark for fun. You've frightened this poor thing half to death."

"Only half?" the cat hisses. "Back off! She's my prey."

"Prey?" I drag myself to my feet, no longer as frightened as I was.

Seeing me at my full height, the cat shrinks out of sight with a kitten's meow. I hear nothing for several minutes but do not doubt the cat is still nearby. At last, I turn to the mouse-woman and kneel next to her, feeling quite the hero. She's half-raised herself and is no longer deathly still, but her trembling makes it impossible for her to answer the questions I put to her. I pat her head, wondering what is to be done for her.

She makes a sudden move, and my hand falls on air. In horror, I watch her scurry to the edge of the precipice and launch herself over it, into the river. There's a splash, then only the roar of the black, merciless water.

I sit for some minutes, feeling a dread I can't name. But

Mattie's waiting for me, in need of rescue. I get up and slog along the riverbank, through an eternity of darkness, until I find a bridge. The sounds in the forest are terrifying: screams, a chilling maniacal laughter, sobbing.

The bridge is old. Rotting wood falls away in my hand when I grasp the railing. I'm loath to trust it with my weight, so I stand for a while next to it, indecisive. A light approaches from around a bend in the road. As it nears, I hear the familiar creak of wheels over the ground and make out a figure sitting atop a small cart, holding a horsewhip. The cart is pulled by a two-legged donkey holding the shafts with human hands and digging his hooves into the dirt, straining against the cart's weight.

I wave at the carter. He's fully human, from the top of his bald head to his bulbous nose and scruffy beard, especially his beer belly and the black leather boots resting on the toe board. I wave to him as he comes abreast of me, but he merely flicks the whip, a warning to keep back. The downtrodden donkey passes me without pulling his eyes from the road.

"Good sir, I fear that bridge isn't stable," I shout at him as the cart creaks over the first board. "My good man—"

The back of the cart comes into view, and my voice fails me, choked by rising bile. Blood oozes from the box, dripping to the ground, leaving a trail up the road as far as I can see. The carter sits atop a pile of carcasses.

I want to run up to the cart and wrest the whip from the fellow's hand. I want to whip him within an inch of his life, demanding an explanation. I clench my fists and cross the bridge too swiftly to be bothered by the wood groaning underfoot. But as I draw near the cart, I'm able to see it better in the light of a lantern sitting on the box next to its fiendish driver. The bodies are gray, furry donkeys, long-eared and open-mouthed, as though their passing wasn't a gentle one.

"Y-you devil ..." I whisper, but I can't manage more. Anger seethes within me, but it's ineffective. The carter takes no more notice of me than a gnat.

I can't do anything for the poor donkey family now. I turn away from the road and stumble along under the cloaked embrace of the trees. The forest grows noisome around me. Is there no end to this cursed night? Where is the dawn?

Screams split the air nearby. I shudder, shuffling in the opposite direction, only to stumble my way through other grisly scenes.

A man-sized bull mounts a pinned doe.

A quiet orgy between humanoid rats.

A girl-faced fox rips off the head of a rabbit-man.

A praying mantis feasts on a limp lover impaled by her raptorial legs.

This is hell! I scream inwardly. I dare not make a noise as I hurry from one nightmare to the next. Dread sinks into my bones, a certainty that I will not survive this night. Despair erodes my courage until I'm a sweating, whimpering creature fleeing its own shadow. The forest is eternally suspended in night. I would've gone on running and running, until madness took me or a night terror befell me, had not Mattie intervened.

She appears in the path ahead, a figure clothed in faint radiance, like the quiet arrival of dawn. Standing between two towering oaks, she parts the vines that hang like hoary beards from their outstretched branches. I run to her, almost falling into her arms, and she pulls me through into the soft light.

❦

The wood around us is once again the pleasant poplar grove, and I can see Mattie's tower beyond a row of yellow maple trees. The ground is soft. I collapse onto my hands and knees, weeping without shame. This place feels like heaven after the hell I've been through.

Mattie kneels in front of me, and I raise my head to gaze at her. A soft smile lingers near her mouth, though her brows are knitted together in concern for my sorry state. The tenderness in her eyes is an expression I recall from long ago. I cup her face in my hands and beg her, "Mattie, leave with me. Let us not linger a moment more in this evil place!"

Her eyes cloud over, and the line of her mouth hardens. She's again the cold sister in mourning. Behind her, the fake Bennett steps out from among the trees and comes to kneel next to us. He lays a hand on Mattie's shoulder, and she leans into him. All the creases of her face smooth themselves out, and her expression grows peaceful again. She looks at me with pity.

"Why would we want to leave?" She reaches up to stroke the charlatan's smooth cheek. "Everything we could wish for is right here, Ambrose."

I point, with a shaking finger, at the smirking face of the impostor. "Mattie, *that* is not Bennett. He doesn't even have gray eyes, like we do. I don't know what that knave Bonne told you, but it's not true. For that matter, Bonne is lying to you about a lot of things. He doesn't love you, if that's what you think."

"I know he doesn't." Mattie waves her hand at me dismissively. "I don't care. I'm just making a stitch with him."

I sit back, aghast. "Mattie, don't tell me you engaged in"—I lower my voice—"amorous congress?"

Mattie laughs, and the counterfeit joins her with his mocking gold eyes fixed on me. Fury boils in my chest. I leap to my feet and pace in front of them, dragging shaky hands through my hair. This agony is relentless. My heart feels as though it will seize up and stop forever. I clutch at my chest, and my fingers brush against the hard lump in the breast pocket where the locket is hidden.

"Let it go, Ambrose." Mattie sighs, rising with the help of fake Bennett's arm. "You're only upset because I don't let you make decisions for me anymore. This isn't Linwood Manor. You're not *lord* here. I'm much, much more than a sad spinster in this place. Here, I can do anything that pleases me. After all I've suffered, I *deserve* to be happy."

"I-it's not about being a lord, Mattie. It never was. Dammit all, Matilda Anne Bancroft, you are the most irrational, stubborn, rebellious creature I've ever known. I'm trying to *help* you. Why can't you just listen to me?"

My voice rises to a roar, and I charge forward, closing the distance between us until my nose hovers inches from Mattie's hair. The charlatan's golden eyes watch us for three tense seconds. Mattie meets my gaze with guiltless steadiness. Regretting my outburst, I drop my eyes to the grass. My throat constricts. But I refuse to cry in front of her again.

"Mattie, I'm the only one left."

She crosses her arms.

"But if you don't want me, I'll go."

I embrace her, hiding my tears in her hair. There's a soft twitch against my cheek, and I draw back, holding her by the shoulders. Mattie shakes her head at me, unapologetic. Below the hood of her dark hair, I see something white dangling on either side of her neck. I reach out to brush aside her curls.

"Stop blubbering, Ambrose. You're making a fool of yourself," Mattie says, swatting at my hand.

"You've got lamb's ears," I choke. No, this can't be happening. Not to Mattie. Nightmare visions swim before me. Flashes of dismembered prey, blood-soaked carcasses, ravaged creatures with empty, dead eyes.

"There is no escape," a deep voice says.

My head jerks. There's only Mattie with the fake Bennett standing beside her. But the voice doesn't belong to my dead brother. I shudder, backing away.

The frog-man lets me into Mattie's tower without question. For the first time, I don't feel mirth at the sight of his short, hunched figure covered in warts. His yellow dungarees are a damp, stinking remnant of his human need for clothing. Today, the toes on his bare feet look longer than is natural, and the skin of his legs is taking on a yellow-green cast. How long before he's all frog?

The fake Bennett, using someone else's voice, insisted there was no escape. Did he mean escape from the frog's fate, or merely escape from this realm of nightmare and paradise? I make it my aim to find out. If at all possible, I must locate a door back to Linwood Manor.

"I'll take her home by force if I have to," I mutter, stepping from the EM into Mattie's apartment.

It's empty, and unlike my sister, I don't have a silver bell up my sleeve. I walk to the wall where the mouse-woman emerges when she's called for, but there's no crack in the paneling that my fingers can find. I tap the wood with a knuckle. It sounds solid. No one answers. Returning to the settee, I decide to sleep. We came here through sleep, though there was morphia involved in that instance. Perhaps that's the key.

But my mind will not stop running over all that's happened since my arrival in this other place. Hell itself couldn't be nastier. Still, I recall the euphoria which filled me to overflowing that morning when I'd stood on the veranda, dreaming of exploration, discovery, and adventure. For that brief hour, I was in heaven.

"How did I break free of the illusion of this place?" I ask myself, squirming against the back of the couch. I can't seem to get comfortable anymore.

My mind retraces our steps from the apartment, in the EM, out into the royal garden. We'd stood before the king and queen themselves, making obeisances. I'd worshipped the woman, Beatrix, with my heart and eyes, with every sentimental notion of honor I possess. My intentions toward her had been more pure than is natural. It must've been the result of an enchantment. *Is nothing bloody real in this wretched place?*

"That's it!" I slam my fist against the side table, jumping to my feet. "Mattie's under some kind of spell, just as I was. She didn't really *want* to have a brush with the knave. He bewitched her!"

This thought gives me much comfort. I could make a case for Mattie's honor remaining intact so long as her behavior is not truly consensual. If there's a snake loose in the garden, all one has to do is kill it for those under its influence to revert to their senses. I collapse back against the settee with a groan, wringing my hands.

"Just kill King Bonne, eh? Simple as that?" I raise my right hand to rub my jaw. "Just kill the fellow who almost broke my neck with a single kick? I'm done for."

I slide off the couch and crumple against the white fur rug, a puddle of despair. Yanking at my hair, I grit my teeth and recite every curse I know. Despite being in a place of magic and enchantments, I doubt my obscenities will do the knave Bonne any real harm. A thought accosts me. There is one recourse yet untried.

Reaching into a deep pocket of my trousers, I pull out the locket and kneel with my elbows propped on the seat of the couch. It's something like kneeling at church, so I believe it'll suffice. In the whirl of all my strange and obscene encounters in this other place, one thing has kept me grounded—the memory of Bennett. With my head bent over the locket, my fingers caress the familiar, smooth surface. In desperation, I mumble a prayer. It's no prayer ever writ. You wouldn't find it in the gold-lettered, hardbound prayer books of any official church. It's a plea more than anything.

"Let me wake from this nightmare ... Let it all be a dream ...!"

With a rumbling like an earthquake, I am vomited out of the illusory plane. My ears fill with a rushing sound. Blackness envelops me, and I grope the empty space through which I am falling.

CHAPTER 15

What Inn is this
Where for the night
Peculiar Traveler comes?
Who is the Landlord?
Where the maids?
Behold, what curious rooms!
No ruddy fires on the hearth—
No brimming tankards flow.
Necromancer! Landlord!
Who are these below?

— EMILY DICKINSON

I gulp air in one long, shuddering breath.

Rain patters evenly on the windowpane. I bolt upright, Grandfather's chair creaking. Mattie snores softly a few feet away. The fire on the hearth has died down. A heavy darkness broods in the corners of the room. I am not alone.

"Well done, *Lord* Bancroft. Well done."

The deep voice slides along the rafters and sinks into the wooden paneling next to the bed. Heart hammering against my ribs, I move to the edge of my seat, wanting to flee the room. I peer down at the floor and see a huge mouth opening under the bed. It's not really there. It's merely a boyhood nightmare invading my mind. The mouth is followed by snakes wriggling out from under the sheets, face-sized spiders twitching up among the bedposts. These are replaced in rapid succession by horrifying visions of death and decay, of violence practiced on the helpless and innocent and beloved. Heads without eyes, sockets crawling with vermin. Children, bloated and floating face down. The cry of battle. The clash of metal with flesh. Crunch of bone.

All at once, there's stillness. I hold my breath.

"You would be welcome to come and dream with us again. I could give you a kingdom of your own. Mattie will learn her place at last, when your armies stand at King Bonne's gates. Would she listen to her brother then, I wonder?"

I shiver, feeling small. A bitter laugh escapes my lips—nervous tittering, more like.

"That's your scheme, is it?" I say, crouching like a frightened rabbit, ready to spring. "I don't doubt you've tempted countless people with such an invitation. But I've guessed your game, and I know what you are, demon! I know your secrets, even if Mattie doesn't. Illusions of happiness don't reach the soul. She'll still suffer, no matter how many diversions occupy her mind. But I won't give in. I'm going to destroy you and save my sister!"

"Do you really think so?" The voice replies without hesitation. "That's what I like about you and your sister, Lord Bancroft. Your persistence amuses me."

I make a dash for it, expecting vines and snakes to trip up my feet and drag me back into that hellish nightmare. But the voice lets me escape. In the midst of the voice's insinuation about Bonne and Beatrix, I remembered how the knave's devilish face felt strangely familiar, even in the illusory world of that other place. Now, I've recalled where I saw him first—in the pages of the mysterious journal.

Bursting into my room, I hunt through my trunk for it. Once I've found it, I latch the door and light candles at my desk. A scan of the first page is little help with identifying the journal's owner. As I thumb through, the bold handwriting begins to grow more and more illegible. I flip to the back of the book.

There, the last page has a scrawl of letters jumbling together. The man who wrote them seems to have gone senile toward the end. I know it's a man who wrote the entries because he refers to his son in the beginning and mentions his "father's duty" to the young man, Theo.

Taking a new tack, I hold the book by its spine and give the pages a good shake. Loose parchment patters across my desk. Laying the journal aside, I arrange the sheets in a row and examine each with a magnifying glass.

"There's got to be something in here about that other place. What I need is ... a map!" I cry, seizing one of the pages and lifting it to the candlelight.

Rows of parallel lines are separated by small squares and triangles. The bulk of the maze fills the center of the page, but on the right edge, a half-circle is inked all the way to the border, as though the thing it denotes is larger than the map's scale. I stare at its particulars, holding the paper close to my nose. Then I extend my arm and view the whole.

"Why, it's Linwood Manor," I say to myself, miffed. "That's the lake, there. Here's the north wing, the sitting room connected by an inner door with the study, just as I remember. Though, I don't recall there being a second pantry," I murmur, holding my glass over the square labeled *kitchen*. "I'll have to ask Cook about it."

I lean back in my chair, supporting my chin with one fist. I spend several minutes frowning at the striped wallpaper, but my journey to and from that horrible other place has shaken my mental fortitude. There's a puzzle here, and I'm failing to untangle it. Meanwhile, Mattie's well-being is at stake.

Rubbing my eyes, I gather up the loose pages and flip open the journal, intending to tuck them back inside it. There, at the center of the book, lies the graphite sketch depicting Bonne's hateful face. I step back with a cry of alarm, pulling my hand to my chest as though a viper has struck out at me from the page.

Then, leaning closer, I take a good look. The mocking eyes, the mouth shaping a smile that careens between derision and disgust, the curled hair, though lacking devil's horns—all belong to King Bonne the Knave. I slam the journal shut with a shudder. I can feel my blood rushing through my body, pumped by my racing heart. Sweat gathers on my palms, and my fingers tingle. Wrenching myself out of Bonne's terrifying spell, I go to my dresser and change into nightclothes, my numb hands going through the motions of my nightly toilet. My mind mulls over the implication of another human being having encountered King Bonne, returning from that other place to make a sketch of him.

"I must read it from cover to cover, even if it takes me all night," I vow.

Inside an inner cabinet of my wardrobe is a cask of brandy, stashed there for emergencies such as this one. I pull it out and take a swift tug or two, wiping my mouth on my sleeve before replacing the bottle in its hiding place. As I snap the little door closed, I inhale sharply through my nose, then force myself back into the seat at my desk.

Beginning with the first page, I read on and on until I come to something relevant. The candle gutters in a draft that's found its way through the house, and I begin reading aloud, terrified that if I don't, I'll hear a voice calling my name from the hall.

April 12th, 1692.

Wednesday broke clear, and the fields were full of mist. I told Philip it'd be the first and finest day for a hunt this year. My valet always obliges. He readied the horses immediately after breakfast. I made the assumption Theo would accompany me. But my boy declined, saying he was feeling under the weather. I thought nothing of it, though Theo loves a good hunt and we've been cooped up all winter. I went out, shot my pheasants, and came back in time for tea.

"Never thought twice about it, until this morning when Lilly came to call with her aunt, Mrs. Dumfrey. Theo was exchanging letters with sweet Lilly all winter, so I was surprised when he declined to join us in the parlor. When they'd gone—poor Lilly sorely disappointed—I went to see Theo, and the boy was asleep. His hand was ice-cold, his clothing wrinkled as though he'd slept in them, and his room was untidy. I am sending

for the doctor, as he's been complaining of illness and excuses himself from supper without eating much.

"Sounds familiar," I mumble, turning to the next entry, dated May 2 of the same year.

Poor Theo has given me a terrible time of it. The doctor prescribed sea breezes, but I had to make the boy come to Reydon against his will. Now that we're here, I hope his health will improve.

The next several entries describe a fortnight at the seaside town of Reydon, then a visit to the Dumfrey estate, where Theo behaves in such a rude, uncharacteristic manner to young Lilly that his father takes him home at once. I come at last upon an entry describing the author's journey to the other place, on the 26 of July, though it is noted in the margin that the entry was written three days later.

A strange thing occurred when I was sitting beside Theo, who's taken ill with a fever and could not be roused from sleep for two days. I was reading him his favorite book of poems, when I must have fallen asleep. I woke in a forest, next to a large castle boasting numerous turrets, bright banners ...

"Yes, yes, but what of Theo?" I mumble, flipping over page after page, tracing line after line with my finger in search of the name. The author appears to have run off course. He's become quite distracted for someone so intent on his son's health before. "Nymphs of great beauty ... feasting without indigestion ... a moment of euphoria reminding him of a youthful flirtation with opium ... What? Not exactly the preoccupation of a 'dutiful father' as he so calls himself."

At last, the journal records this passage:

> The summer is waning, and my castle is besieged by blood bats, winged creatures with fangs and glowing red eyes. They are a blight on the cattle, and none of my retainers or household servants dare go out of doors after dark. I grow tired of cowering in the castle keep. There's a man to blame, whose reputation I've not dared question before this dark hour—Lord Theophilus Gent of Castle Hammond.

"Ah, so that'll be Theo," I say and breathe a sigh of relief.

> Theophilus Gent is my mortal enemy. These seven months past, he has trampled our fields and taken off our women like a common bandit—

"What? They're enemies now?" I balk, rereading the lines to be sure. "It does say *Theophilus Gent* and not Theo, so perhaps they're not one and the same?"

But a feeling of dread settles into my stomach. I decide to flip ahead to the portrait of Bonne and read the surrounding text. Surely, the old dodger must've found in the king of knaves a more fitting enemy than this Theophilus.

To my horror, my eyes alight on the words—

Like the Greek gods of old, my captain Bonne seized hold of a javelin that had stuck fast in the wood of the door when the castle keep was breached by our foes. Ripping it out with both hands, he turned and launched it through the air toward that monstrous fiend Wolgruff, piercing him through the chest. Wolgruff loosed his hold on my neck, dropping dead at my feet. The timing of it was fortuitous, for at that moment, Theophilus himself was descending upon me with a mighty swing of his mace.

He did not, however, expect to find me ready for him. Thus, I was able to get under his swing with ease, while drawing my dagger, and slew my foe with my own hand.

"No, it can't be," I say, my voice constricting. "It's not the same Theo, surely? But what a coincidence!"

I read on.

Bonne has become like a god to us, and I would worship at his feet if he allowed me. But he is too tender a soul and fond of leaning his head against my breast, like Ganymede in the tales of Zeus. I have spent many an hour perfecting this sketch of his charming face on the following page—

I turn the page, and Bonne's triumphant, mocking face smiles back at me. A chill runs along my spine as I stare into those cunning eyes. I cannot blame the poor soul who penned this journal for falling under his spell. I too was ensorcelled by Queen Beatrix, whose gluttony later repulsed me. What I find most frightening is how easily Bonne's illusions are able to snare persons who stumble into his realm.

"I must go back and wrest Mattie from him. Surely, this journal has some clue, some notion of—" I halt, then flip back to the July 26 entry. "Why, it's *sleep*. We traveled there in sleep, as did this man. And he without morphia." Yet I can't shake the feeling the room itself holds some evil spell, or perhaps harbors a demonic presence. In which case, I could make the thing leave and avoid having to face Bonne where he's stronger than me.

With a howl of glee, I jump up from my desk and run through the house barefoot, unashamed of my state of undress. Slipping past the kitchen, I enter the stable yard and run through sheets of biting rain to the shed where the groundskeeper stores his tools. Careless of any noise I might be making, I wrench the door open. It's dark and I've no light, but I remember well where the item I'm seeking is kept. The massive woodcutter's axe gleams in the dark, waiting for me.

Taking up my weapon with solemn care, I retrace my steps until I stand before the door to the out-of-place room where Mattie is sleeping, gathering my courage. With rapid, whistling breaths through my nose, I stride into the dark. I raise the axe over my head and bring it down into the paneled wall. Chips of wood fly errant and ping against the windowpane. Splinters clatter to the floor. I strike again and again. My cries ring through the rafters.

Laughing, the voice slips away from my blade to an even darker corner of the room. The axe head clunks to rest against the floor. In the storm-scudded moonlight, the room appears ordinary, harmless. Breathing hard, I stumble backward, piercing my foot with a splinter.

"Don't spill your blood so carelessly, mortal. In your world, you only have one life." The voice mocks me, slinking along behind the woodwork. "Unlike in mine, where you have forever."

"Silence, creature of evil," I mutter, swinging my axe again.

"I'm over here," the voice suggests from my left.

I fly at the wall, embedding the blade deep in old paneling, stripping back layers upon layers of veneer and wallpaper and boards, revealing decades—centuries, even—with every stroke. Abruptly, the axe's head plummets through a gaping hole. I fall forward, my knuckles scraping the rough-edged wood and coming away bloody.

Shaking with fear and rage, I tumble back. The axe is sunk deep within the hollow I've opened. I yank at it, but it is wedged firmly in the hole. I get to my feet, plant one bare heel against the wall, and pull. The voice chuckles in amusement, and I realize why too late.

CHAPTER 16

"When I hoped I feared—
Since I hoped I dared
Everywhere alone
As a Church remain—
Spectre cannot harm—
Serpent cannot charm—
He deposes Doom
Who hath suffered him—"

— EMILY
DICKINSON

The axe comes free without warning, sending me skittering back. A nerve-jangling clatter erupts from the dark hole. First, a single board falls loose, then an entire section as tall and broad as a person. Scuttling back, I smack my head against the bedpost, gaping at the secret the wall reveals. Raw terror weakens my grasp of the axe. It falls to the floor with a thud. I can't look away, despite my revulsion.

Two skeletons hang like trophies upon ancient paneling buried deep beneath the skin of this room. Their black eye sockets stare; tiny jaws hang slack with unspoken words. More eloquent than either, their size tells a horrifying tale. The skeletons were once a pair of children.

"Not so intimidating now, are they? Bonne and Beatrix have only ever been children playing at make-believe. Your sister is no different. How do you think her skeleton will look, embedded in these walls?"

Though the room spins, I manage to stumble to the bedside and prop myself next to my sister's sleeping form. I nudge her arm, calling her name. She doesn't respond. I check for her pulse, reaching behind her cloak of dark hair. Thank God, no lamb's ears, at least in this world. She's unnaturally still. Her lack of response only feeds my panic.

"Mattie," I call, shaking her shoulder hard. "Mattie, wake up. You must get away from there! You're not safe!" I shout, shaking her roughly with both hands. My knuckles are still bleeding, leaving dull red stains all over the coverlet. "Mattie, it's all an illusion. You're bewitched!"

They sound like the words of a madman, but the situation is too dire for me to act any other way. On a sudden impulse, I pull my sister into my arms, intending to flee with her, though to what destination I've not a moment to consider. The way her head lolls from side to side makes the air seize in my lungs. She feels ice-cold.

But there's still a pulse. Mattie's not dead. Not yet.

I've got to get her out of here.

A splintering sound cracks like a rifle shot beneath my feet. Floorboards break away. I drop Mattie onto the bed and fall backward. The cry in my throat is cut off by sudden impact with the earth floor of the cellar two stories below. Laughter echoes in my ears as I fall unconscious.

⚜

The landscape of the other place has altered to a degree far exceeding what the passing of a few hours can accommodate. The woods are plowed down and the land piled up. Like the ziggurat of Ur which Loftus uncovered in the Far East, a broad stone stairway leads toward the sky, cresting three battlements standing incrementally higher as you move toward their center. The innermost segment of the city houses a gold-plated palace. Its shining parapets reflect spears of sunlight down upon the city's inhabitants, who surely must feel like insects dwelling below such a majestic edifice.

I'm standing in a road leading to the first and lowest steps of the outer bulwark. For a moment, my arms feel odd, robbed of Mattie's weight, until I recall dropping her. My heart pounds in my ears. Anger has me glaring left to right, intent on discovering my foe and driving it off. But the heat of midday beats down on my sweating head, and the brightness of the sky-climbing road dazzles me. I must have dreamed that terrifying battle.

Numerous people climb up and down, bearing loads in baskets on their heads. None have animal characteristics. This is nothing like the landscape where Mattie lies under a deadly delusion.

I grit my teeth, glaring at the palace as though the intensity of my gaze might melt it. This might not *look* like the other place, but I sense the evil presence filling it, faint like a rotting stench but just as unmistakable. There's nothing for it but to look for Mattie, trusting she's still alive somewhere, waiting to be found.

I raise my foot to the first step, following a shirtless, sweating porter whose muscles bulge under the weight of a roll of woven cloth. The bolt must weigh a good deal, and I've no desire to be flattened under it should the man lose his footing. I skirt around him, mumbling an apology, and hurry upward in my stifling black suit. For some reason, my arrival in the other place has not furnished me with a different set of clothing, nor have I arrived under this place's spell, as I did before.

"A silk robe would be more fitting attire for such exercise," I say, complaining to no one in particular.

My words do not go unheard. Half a dozen of the bare-chested porters crowd around me on the steep stairway, jostling their wares in my face. Most are selling clothing, but some merely take the opportunity to annoy me into purchasing dates, water skins, and golden bangles. I try to shrug them off, but the way forward is impassible. Digging in my pockets, I find a few pennies and a single shilling. The bright colored metal seems to pass for coin, though they compare the copied profiles of Queen Victoria with disgust.

"Debes videre nostrum Regina," one of them says to me.

"You speak *Latin*?" I laugh aloud, then repeat myself in that language.

"Ita est," he says, squinting at me.

Having relieved me of all my money, the merchants move off. I follow them upward, arms full of items. My pennies earned me a large quantity, though I'm not sure what exactly I've purchased.

When I reach the first city ring, drenched in sweat and out of breath, I halt under the shade of a roofed walkway and take stock. Shedding my black coat, I remove the locket from its breast pocket and pull a loose, ankle-length tunic over my head. Stripping requires no small acrobatic skill, but when I'm at last bare down to my skin, I collapse against the wall of a building, sighing in relief. A breeze ruffles my hair. I can feel it drying the moisture coating my skin.

The rest of the items turn out to be more useful than I expected—a pair of leather sandals, a woven belt of gray wool with a clasp, a water skin, and a long scarf I presume is meant as a loincloth. I hold it up between two fingers, grimacing at its length and narrowness.

"I'm blessed if I know how to wear this," I say, wondering whether I should abandon it along with the bangles.

But you never know when something will prove useful, and I've no idea how much it cost me, so I wind it around my waist with the belt, hoping I don't look an utter fool.

"Who knows what comes next? Might as well get moving," I tell myself and step into the hubbub of the crowded, sun-baked streets.

To my left, the stairway continues its ascent toward the second city ring. The palace towers above, nestled among the clouds. Closer to me, houses are grouped around a city well. Aqueducts carry water down into the fountains. Their shallow troughs splash along wide thoroughfares connecting each neighborhood. Children play naked in the water while their mothers beat clothing in the troughs with flayed reeds.

Though this arid city is constructed with clay bricks and ancient-looking earthworks, its technology might rival that of the Roman Empire. In addition to the aqueducts, there are steam-heated bath houses, perfectly level roads paved with stone slabs, and colonnades shading the constant stream of pedestrians. I duck under a colonnade to escape the heat and bump shoulders with the last person I expected to see.

A woman wearing a light blue dress and a white headscarf stares back at me in shock. The moment our eyes meet, I know I've seen her before, and I see the same flash of recognition in her eyes. She seizes my arm, whispering wildly in my ear. Accosted by the tickling sensation of her breath, I shrink back, unable to understand her. Just then, a tall man wearing a whip on his belt steps onto the street. He glances up and down, scratching his black beard, then spots us.

"Beatrix! Woman, come back here," he says in Latin, slamming the door shut behind him.

My memory jogged, I recall our previous interactions. How I was charmed on our first meeting and then repulsed when my enchantment had been broken. Such thoughts occupy the space of a moment, then I shrug her off me, attempting to flee through the crowd.

But Beatrix doesn't obey the bearded giant. She flits toward the courtyard instead, like a bluebird toward the sun. Displeased, the man unwraps his thick bull whip and sends it cracking after her, entangling her feet with practiced ease. Beatrix collapses with a cry. For all her former grace and elegance, she sounds as pitiful as a child throwing a tantrum. She fails to free herself from the cord before the man reaches her. He drags her back toward the house by her hair.

I'm standing at a street corner, peering around it to watch this dramatic exchange. The brute lumbers past my hiding place, taking no more notice of me than he would a donkey.

But Beatrix meets my eyes, forming words amid her whimpering. "Help me!"

"Honestly, I can't," I call after her, apologetic.

"Yes, you can. Just ... push him," she cries between grimaces.

"I'm sorry?" I say, stepping into the street after her, because we're talking in undertones while a crowd of onlookers gathers to see what will become of Beatrix's mad dash.

"Just ... try!" Beatrix squeals, wrenching herself free of the whip's coils and planting her feet in the road. "Help me, and I'll help you find your sister!"

The bearded man is encumbered by Beatrix's struggling, if only for a fraction of a second. I step out, my voice high and strained, and accost him from the distance of several arm lengths. "See here, you can't treat women that way!"

I wave in his direction, lifting my hands and shooing at him. Why I thought doing so would result in anything other than my own painful death, I'll never understand. Yet it is not mine, but his death that occurs. As if commanded by the motion of my hands, three head-sized flagstones uproot themselves from the road and fly directly at the bearded man. The first stone knocks him back against the wall of his house. The second and third plaster it with his blood.

A dead silence falls. I stare in open-mouthed horror at the atrocity I've just committed. But Beatrix laughs maniacally and seizes my hand. Together, we flee before anyone can make sense of it. She seems familiar with the city because, in only five minutes, we've left that neighborhood behind and are climbing a stairway leading up the side of the second ring rampart.

"How did that happen?"

"Magic, witchcraft, fairy-kinship. Call it whatever you like."

"You speak English?" I ask, realizing we've been conversing in my native tongue and not the language of this place all along. "Are you really the same Beatrix as before?"

We reach the top of the stairs, and she lets go of my hand, shoving me against the wall of a house, pinning me to it. I gulp, reminded of her behavior during our last encounter, and attempt to extricate myself from her grasp. I get a pinch in the ribs for my efforts.

"Stay still, imbecile!" she hisses. "The royal guard is passing by."

We wait, and I can hear clinking chainmail and heavy boots clomping over the stone road. Whoever it was continues on, and Beatrix darts out into the street, pulling her head scarf over her hair. Intrigued, I watch her until she catches me with a concentrated frown on my face. She *is* the same woman but lacks the laconic boredom of Queen Beatrix.

"Where's yours?" she asks, glaring.

I pull the cloth from around my waist, smiling sheepishly. "Here it is."

Beatrix wraps it over my head in a turban style that's at once protection from the sun and a nifty disguise.

She leads onward, further into the city. "I know a place we can stay until nightfall."

"What happens at nightfall?" I ask and then turn bright red, accosted by lustful thoughts. "I mean ... That is, I *don't* mean—"

"Don't be an idiot. I've no desire to be reminded of the second occasion a man has scorned me. You have something I want. That's the only reason I'm helping you. Like I said, I know where your sister is. That's why you're here, right?"

It is, but I can't help wondering how Beatrix knows this. I keep silent, mulling over the possible reasons she might be out on the streets of this strange city, suffering at the behest of the bearded brute. It's obvious she and Bonne had a falling out, which might indicate any number of things regarding my sister. Perhaps it's worth my while to cooperate with her a little longer. I doubt she'll tell me anything outright.

"Well, here it is," Beatrix says, stopping at the base of the palace's outer ring wall.

"Here's what?" I stare, puzzled. Before our feet lies a small ditch full of water, and above our heads is nothing but sky and a three-hundred-foot rampart.

"Crawl in." Beatrix smiles crookedly, indicating the drainage shaft.

"Of course," I groan, and I follow her inside.

For some reason, Beatrix expects me to improve our situation as we squat over stale water inside the cramped drain outlet. There's just enough room for two people to crouch with their feet planted on either side of the ditch. Crossing our arms over our knees, we argue in whispers, falling silent each time the thudding boots of guards pass outside.

"I don't understand why you're being pigheaded about this," she hisses in my ear. "I bet you're just as uncomfortable as I, and we've got hours to go before night falls."

"Woman, what am I supposed to do?" I say, scowling at her.

"You know—poof—magic. You did it before without even thinking. Whatever you can imagine will appear, as long as you want it enough. Now, get us some more space. And a couch to sit on would be nice."

"A couch? Make some space?" I say, surprise causing me to raise my voice.

Beatrix shoves me with her shoulder and glares until I continue in a whisper.

"What I did before was an accident. I don't have the slightest clue how those rocks took off flying. Could have been anyone, for all you know."

"Common people don't do magic, you skamelar." Beatrix jabs me in the ribs with a long nail. "They're all puppets. Not like us."

"Then why can't you do magic?" I huff, edging away from her claws.

Beatrix doesn't answer for a long moment. "I was banished. Thuris is pleased with his new pet, more pleased than he ever was with Bonne and me. He does whatever the Magna Regina asks." She shakes her head bitterly. "They took my magic. Tossed me out at the mercy of Thuris's puppets."

"Who's Thuris?" I ask.

"Careful, if we talk about him too much, he might start to pay attention," she says, shuddering. "Let's just say, he's the one who brings people here."

The voice from the room, then. "I would've thought all this witchcraft or poppycock a few days ago. My eyes disbelieve what I see, but the fact remains. Such a world as this one exists."

"And here"—Beatrix grins at me—"you can do magic."

I inhale deeply. "Very well. I'll give it a go. But don't blame me if something bad happens."

Extending my hands, eyes closed, I picture the floor sinking underneath us and expanding in every direction, forming a gourd-shaped cave. I blink them open, and there we are. Beatrix and I stand in the bowl of my excavation, with water pouring down from the drain above us, pooling at our feet.

"Quick, make the water continue its usual course. Somebody outside is sure to notice if the aquifer runs dry," Beatrix tells me, her voice echoing. "Besides, it'll drown us."

It's ridiculous, but the first thing that comes to mind is to lift the water. The impossibility of it doesn't occur to me until after it's already done. "Odd," I say, staring at the band of water passing overhead without anything supporting it.

"Not odd, just magic." Beatrix laughs. "You'll get used to it."

My next endeavors produce far more elegant results. The cave reshapes itself into a small room with four walls, a level floor, and steps leading up to the entrance of the drain shaft. Inside, a couch rests against one wall, with a small table and bench opposite. A minuscule pot-belly stove glows at the center of the room. It doesn't create enough smoke to choke us. Nor would anyone outside guess someone was living underground by the faint smell of burning wood chips emanating from our hideout.

"Lovely!" Beatrix sinks onto the couch, pulling her feet up under her dress. "A bite to eat wouldn't hurt, and some wine."

"Do you have money? I'm afraid I spent all my pennies."

She stares at me. "Didn't I say you can have anything you can imagine? Anything means *anything*."

"Right."

This is all a bit childish, but I'm hungry too, so I put my imagination to work. Roast chicken, a loaf of oven-warm bread, and a slab of rich cheese appear on the table, complete with plates, cutlery, and a tall bottle of wine. A crystal glass appears in my hand as I reach for the drink. I pour Beatrix some and wait while she serves herself from the plates. Only, she doesn't use a plate. She huddles in the armchair next to the feast and digs in, cutting bites for herself from the chicken's back with her knife. Biting mouthfuls from the cheese and bread, she washes each unceremoniously down her throat with wine, finishing the bottle in a few minutes. I'd forgotten she was a glutton.

Sitting on the bench, I produce my own plate of food and a glass of brandy. I hesitate. Do I toast her health, bless the meal, or just start eating?

"We give thanks," I say out of habit, intending to conclude the brief blessing with my usual "Amen." But a clatter interrupts me. Beatrix has shot to her feet, clutching the knife in her hand, regarding me with wide, angry eyes.

"Don't you dare say it," she whispers.

I open my mouth, and then she's standing over me. Seizing the hair on the back of my head, Beatrix places her knife against my outstretched neck.

"Religious practice, petitions of any kind, and the names of ... of divinity ... are forbidden in this realm. He who brought you here will know where we are the moment you speak such things. You'll be hunted, and I'll be left powerless again."

I raise my hands, nodding to show I understand. I dare not speak.

"Good," Beatrix says, shoving me away. "Don't forget it."

She returns to her place, tearing into the last of the loaf with gusto. "What are you going to do when you find your sister?" she asks, eyeing me sidelong.

"Do you know a way out of this realm? I'm going to take her back where we came from."

Beatrix shifts in her seat, patting the couch around her as though she's lost something. Noting the bottle of wine at her side has run dry, she drops it to the floor and springs up, her hand extending toward me. "I'll tell you what I know for another bottle. Malbec this time, if you please."

With a long sigh, I produce the requested item. Beatrix snatches it, then glares at me. "It's too small!"

Shrugging, I return to my meal. "Tell me or don't. I'm determined to save Mattie. If you won't help me, I'll figure it out myself."

"I admire your obstinance, but"—Beatrix plops onto the bench beside me, throwing her supple arm over my shoulders —"what if she won't go with you?"

This question *has* troubled me ever since my return to the other place. Looking at Beatrix, I'm suddenly aware the answer is right in front of me.

"She doesn't have magic, does she? Not like I do."

Beatrix raises an eyebrow. "No, she gets my brother to do her bidding."

"Why is that?"

Beatrix leans back on her elbows. "So, if she doesn't want to go with you, you'll just take her by force? Neither Bonne nor *the other one* will let you have her so easily, you know. And they've an army to call upon, if they're not feeling up to crushing your measly attempt themselves."

"It won't matter," I tell her, holding her gaze. "I'll save Mattie no matter what."

Beatrix laughs. "You'd do anything for her, wouldn't you?

Anything but what she asks. You're not much different from my brother, after all."

"That knave?" I cough, unable to stomach the picture of Bonne as a protective older brother to this woman. Even if they are siblings, he's nothing like me.

"You both believe you can't be wrong." Beatrix sighs. "Just like now. You can't see the similarities between you and Bonne because you've become set on a certain idea and anything that contradicts your perspective you discard as irrelevant."

Beatrix doesn't tell me where I can find the way out of Thuris's realm. Perhaps she doesn't even know. After this interchange, I'm not sure I want her meddling in my sister's and my affairs. The former queen sinks into a dark mood, nursing her bottle of Malbec, and ignores me entirely.

CHAPTER 17

This is the Hour of Lead—
Remembered, if outlived,
As Freezing persons, recollect the Snow—
First—Chill—then Stupor—then the letting go—

— EMILY DICKINSON

As evening falls outside our hiding place, the city Beatrix calls Basilis comes alive. She's fallen asleep on her couch, curled up around the near-empty bottle. Seeing her face relax so vulnerably, I'm reminded of her words from earlier: *"You can have anything you can imagine ... Anything means anything."*

My stomach is filled with butterflies, but I close my eyes anyway. The image comes readily to mind, despite my guilty conscience. There's so much wrong with what I'm doing right now, but my longing to see, to touch, to *be with* is too strong to resist.

My voice is a whisper. "Abigail."

And then she's there. I feel her sink onto the couch beside me, running her slender arm over my shoulders and tucking her left hand with the ruby wedding ring over my beating heart. The scent of her is unbearably sweet and almost forgotten. Her downy hair brushes my tear-wet cheek. Opening my eyes, I embrace again my dear, dead wife, Abigail. She tilts her chin, gazing up at me with the hint of a smile. Her skin is smooth, still twenty-two and wearing the same white nightgown she wore on the night she died. I've conjured a ghost.

Then Beatrix rolls over, falling off the edge of her couch with a muffled cry. My arms fold over air. My replica of Abigail has vanished. I bury my head in my hands, stuffing down bile in my throat. What am I even doing? I've come here for Mattie, to find her and the way back home. There's nothing for me here which can dull the pain of my ceaseless cycle of loss. Shaking my head, I look about the room, searching for the direction I've lost. My companion clambers off the floor, stretching and yawning like a cat.

Then she kicks the bottle into a corner and turns on me with a dangerous glint in her eye. "It's time to go."

We sneak inside the palace using a tunnel my magic carves

for us. I work under cover of thundering drums, thudding feet, and chanting voices. I ask Beatrix what's the cause of the cacophony reverberating above our heads, whether there's a pagan festival going on or rioting peasants in the streets, but she only laughs at me. She doesn't forbid my questions, but she doesn't answer them either.

We emerge in a huge, open-air room high above the city. Its roof is supported by row upon row of Grecian pillars on three sides, double doors closing off the further end. Even the dark shoulders of the mountains on the horizon seem dwarfed by this place.

"What is this?" I ask.

"The palace sanctum," Beatrix whispers, shuddering.

Rows of bronze braziers hold low-burning embers, producing the pungent scent of burning fat and dim light. It's without furniture or ornament. A soft glow shines up from the floor a few paces from us. I can feel an intense heat emanating from its mouth. Beatrix clambers out of our makeshift tunnel, pulling me after her by my tunic.

Motioning for silence, she slinks around the nearest pillar. I close off the tunnel, leaving no trace of our arrival. Then I follow, groping my way beyond the light of the oil lamps. A sudden gust of open air sends tingles down to my toes. I feel like I've stepped into the night and am about to fall—as indeed I have. Beatrix snatches my belt and pulls me back from the precipice. I lean against a pillar, my heart pounding.

Seconds tick by, measured by my heaving breaths. I look into the black, empty space below our feet. This side of the palace slides downward at a sharp angle for fathoms, tipping into darkness. I can just make out the innermost city wall hunching near the palace's base.

The second ring of the city, mostly residential, is speckled with pinpricks of light. But the oil lamps keep a feeble defiance against the heaviness of night. Darkness reigns over all.

Between shadowy outlines of buildings, a concentration of small lights is moving, gathering individual dots of yellow from the landscape, drawing them to itself and funneling them together. They merge into a great throng and mount the ziggurat steps, amassing at the base of the palace.

Beatrix pulls me around the pillar to wait in the shadows. A slap of bare feet approaches from the far side of the sanctum. There's a rumbling and creaking of stone. A throne forms and rises to a fearsome height, elevated atop thirteen steep steps. A veiled figure mounts the dais and sits on the throne. She wears robes of gold-spun thread and a white peacock's tail fanning behind her shoulders, making a bold contrast with dark tresses that spill from under her veil.

"Lord Bonne, command them to open the gate. My people await the Blood Harvest," the woman intones without inflection, without warmth.

I'm asking Beatrix, in a whisper, whether this is the Magna Regina, when she seizes my hand and plunges the both of us into the light.

"What are you doing?" I hiss, pulling back.

Beatrix abandons me. She strides past Bonne to the base of the throne. Kneeling, she raises her voice over the distant drums and the thundering voices of those gathering outside the palace sanctum.

"On this, the eve of the Blood Harvest, I have returned. Most just and fair art thou, Magna Regina. It was right of you to banish me, and I only return to make payment for my wrongdoing. I have brought you someone befitting of the Harvest, great queen. Here he is! Your most hated enemy."

Beatrix abases herself before the throne, bowing her fair head before this dark regent. I feel a moment's pity, remembering the languid grace of the Queen Beatrix I first met. But then I notice her hand sweeping wide in my direction. Understanding dawns. She's using me to buy back her magic.

"It is the Magna Regina who decides whom to harvest, sister," Bonne snarls, looming large over Beatrix's prostrated form.

He raises a hand to strike, but an almost imperceptible motion from the Regina stays him. Bonne and Beatrix lift their heads. The drums outside fall silent. The double doors of the sanctum swing open, revealing a throng of torch-bearing city-dwellers. Every ear hangs on the words of their sovereign. Without meaning to, I move a few paces forward, drawn by a wish to glimpse the veiled face. Who is this arbiter of justice? This judge between life and death?

"Come," her commanding voice says to me. With a flick of his wrist, Bonne's magic hurtles me to the top of the dais. I stand within arm's reach of the speaker, the gauze of her veil no longer opaque enough to hide the familiar heart-shaped face, dark curls, and wide, gray eyes of my sister.

"Mattie," I whisper. But she's speaking again, her eyes shifting to those waiting at the foot of her throne.

"You are right, *former* queen," Mattie says. "My enemy must die. But not for the reasons you suppose, nor for the reward you seek."

As her words sink in, I feel as though the world is spinning. It's all I can do to remain standing. The dizzying height makes me sick to my stomach. There is nowhere to run.

Mattie gives Bonne a nod of approval, and a terrible, agonized scream wrenches its way from Beatrix's lungs in spurts. I dare not turn and look at what is becoming of her. Meanwhile, the Magna Regina lifts her veil, locking eyes with me. She's cradling a small creature against her bosom, which at first looks like illustrations in my encyclopedia of a tropical iguana, until I notice the thing has minuscule wings. Its legs are far too tiny to be of any use in crawling, and its long, serpentine tail wraps up and around the queen's neck. The creature fixes me with cunning, golden eyes I recognize.

"This is Thuris, Ambrose. I don't believe you've met."

"No, we have," I say, swallowing hard, thinking of the fake Bennett and of the mocking voice in the room.

Mattie simpers, and I know at once she's enjoying my intimidation. Dread causes my stomach to clench, but I meet my sister's gaze. I can find no hint of affection or pity in her face. Would she really kill me?

This is wrong. "Mattie," I whisper, hoarse.

"I am no longer that pitiful person, thanks to Thuris. I ought to thank you as well. If you hadn't been so keen on managing my inevitable decline, I might never have had the courage to break free of the little cage that was my whole world. Now, I'm queen in a world of my own making. Here, Ambrose, I'm creator and judge. I hold the power of life and death in my hands. I am the Magna Regina."

Beatrix's screams subside, and I hear Bonne's wicked laughter. He whistles, calling down a great number of birds of prey. An eagle swoops past, stirring Mattie's veil and my hair with its wings. Mattie lifts Thuris to her shoulder. The lizard slinks behind her neck and nestles against her. Is this small creature really at the root of all this evil? Is this the owner of the mocking voice I heard in that room? The one who showed me the terrible fate of Beatrix and Bonne's child-sized bones? If it is, my sister is under a terrible delusion. One that may lead to her damnation.

"You're not," I say, dragging my eyes from the worm's captivating gaze.

"Excuse me?" She snorts, reaching for a jewel-crusted dagger that ornaments her thigh.

"You're not anything or anyone but Mattie, my little sister. And I've come to save you."

Fingering the blade between her face and mine, she smirks at me. "I know. That's the problem, you see. So long as you're here, with your anxieties and insecurities writ across your dear face, I'm unable to forget. I'm unable to be the Magna Regina."

Mattie's hand traces worry lines that have etched themselves into my brow. She brushes aside a wayward strand of my hair. Her cool touch is tender. But there's something in her expression, in the sickly turn of her mouth, that betrays what's coming for me. Mattie grabs a handful of my robe, and as she tugs me closer, she sinks the dagger into the flesh just below my breastbone.

I hear the squelch of my own blood as she turns it, carving a circle. My heart keeps a feverish beat, a futile attempt at clinging to life.

Mattie catches me as I fall, blood gurgling from my mouth. "You know, Ambrose, death offers perspective. In that great, silly old house, I was always being controlled—first by Grandfather and his eternally withheld approval, then by you, with your shackles of concern. I never would've been able to free myself without first losing everything." She lowers me to the edge of the dais, my head cradled against her elbow. Two salt-laden drops land in my mouth, mingling with my life blood.

It hurts. Not the wound, not even this ultimate betrayal. What hurts more than anything I've felt in my life, even taking all my losses into account, is this one thing: Mattie's accusation rings true. I denied it before, but now I can't help but admit I've been hell-bent on giving her a happiness she never wanted.

Placing her brow against mine, she whispers, "I had to send Bennett away, too, in the end. I tried my hardest, but I lost my ability to believe he'd come back to me. Even in Thuris's paradise, grief was devouring me."

I can feel my life seeping away as I study her face. If this is what she wants, then why does she have to look so sad? I've tried to help her without giving a moment's thought to what she might want. Maybe Mattie doesn't know what she wants either. Even as I fade, I gather the last of my strength to plead with her.

"Come back with me ..." I want a second chance. But I've no more breath for promises, that this time it'll be different, that I want to do better.

Mattie stares back for a long moment. At last, she speaks, stroking my forehead. "It's hard for you to accept I don't need you anymore, isn't it? But you'll be all right without me, Ambrose. You've always been able to put troubling feelings behind you."

She releases me, returning to her throne. My head lolls back and hangs over the steps. The strange sanctuary of death is filling with the torch-bearing throng. Before the countless bodies reach the foot of the dais, I locate Bonne. He's upside down, leering at the red thread of my blood trickling down the steps in his direction. At his feet is the mangled figure of his sister, paralyzed in wide-eyed horror as the eagles and hawks and carrion birds shred away her flesh with their beaks.

The room blurs. Darkness creeps in at the edges of my vision. I feel my heart stop, and the pressure of a held breath burns in my lungs. My head is throbbing.

With my eyes squeezed shut, I think an image and hear Mattie and Bonne gasp in surprise. Bonne's murderous birds explode into a profusion of feathers. They float down and settle over the body of Beatrix as it's brought back to wholeness. I hear her flight, the mottled gray-and-brown wings of her devourers transformed into her deliverance. I hope this picture will convince Mattie to fly away with me.

With one last gasp, my half-choked lungs seizing up as I inhale, I raise my eyes to my sister. But Beatrix's escape has done nothing to sway Mattie. The throng of her subjugates await her judgment. A pair of children approach the chasm at the base of her throne—a girl and a boy. With a wave of her hand, the Magna Regina chooses. "Harvest him."

Bonne strides forward and gives the boy a push. The child falls screaming through the open shaft in the floor. Then, silence—

And for me, a sleep like death.

Awareness comes to me in a slow, slogging dance with pain. I open my eyes, only to be pierced by dim candlelight. I raise a stiff hand to my throbbing head. But that discomfort is overwhelmed by the stabbing pain in my ribs. My arm drops to the coverlet. I groan between clenched teeth. In the middle of this fresh wash of pain, recollection of the preceding days dawns upon me. I can see Mattie lying in the sleep stupor, at the mercy of the fiend Thuris. I can hear its inhuman voice, mocking me. Then the events which transpired in the other place flash through my mind in vivid detail, until I'm lying in a pool of my own blood, put to death for my many sins.

I mumble my sister's name, cracking my eyelids apart despite the explosion of pain in my head. Tothill's face overshadows mine. She leans close, squinting at me. She looks worried, and I wonder if she's discovered the wreck I made of the room where Mattie's lying.

"It's all right. There, there now. Calm yourself, sir," she says, patting my hand and feeling my forehead. Her touch is soothing.

"Mattie ...?" I mumble, my mouth so dry it hurts to speak.

"We found you in the cellar, unconscious, bleeding from your head. Gave Cook quite a start, to be sure. Dr. Brooks says you've broken two ribs, falling through the floorboards as you did. Donnie's gone to fetch a builder, to see if the hole can't be patched, but the doctor advises against movin' Mattie to another room."

"You … you must," I manage to say, squeezing my eyes against the pain.

"Dear lad, you're hurtin' yourself speakin'. Rest now. We'll take care of you and your sister, we will."

I try to shake my head, and it's too much. I black out.

CHAPTER 18

Death is a Dialogue between
The Spirit and the Dust.
"Dissolve" says Death, The Spirit "Sir
I have another Trust"—
Death doubts it—
Argues from the Ground—
The Spirit turns away
Just laying off for evidence
An Overcoat of Clay.

— EMILY DICKINSON

"**L**ORD BANCROFT. YOU'RE STILL ALIVE," Thuris's voice jeers from the darkness.

I can't move. A corner of my rational mind reminds me this is only a dream. Whatever Thuris is, it can't hurt me in the confines of my own mind. But this doesn't feel like a dream. It feels like an invasion.

Louder than the remnant of calm, cold logic, a pandemonium of panic is rattling around in my head. This space holds the real me. I've always been alone here. The world at large, other people's decisions, impulses arising from want and need —all of it happened outside this quiet, familiar place. Nothing outside of my mental faculties could touch the *me* inside here. Only the death of my beloved wife could penetrate this place with what Mattie calls "troubling feelings."

But now there's someone in here with me. There's not enough space. This vehicle is careening out of control, two drivers fighting to wrest the reigns from the hands of the other. One of us will have to be expelled, or this fragile mind of mine will crack right through.

"YOU UNDERESTIMATED ME," the voice continues. "YOU THOUGHT I WAS HIDING THERE, IN THAT SMALL ROOM. YOU MISTOOK ME FOR A MONSTER YOU COULD KILL. YOU'VE SEEN A MERE FRACTION OF MY POWER, THE BAREST HINT OF WHAT I HAVE TO OFFER."

"I've seen enough," I say through gritted teeth, shaking my head as though I'll free myself that way. "You destroy everything you touch."

Thuris's low, self-assured laugh reverberates through my brain. It feels like my skin's being turned inside out. "TELL ME, WHAT DOES A MAN LIKE YOU WANT? TELL ME, AND I WILL GIVE IT TO YOU. HOLD NOTHING BACK."

"I want you to leave us alone!"

"YOUR SISTER IS HAPPY. SHE WANTS WHAT YOUR WORLD

DENIES HER, THINGS YOU SAY SHE OUGHT NOT DESIRE. YOU WOULD CHOOSE TO MAKE HER UNHAPPY, OVER EVERYTHING ELSE?"

The words fall over me like a noose, binding me, cinching tighter the more I struggle against them. I open my mouth to object. But Mattie's voice is there too, with the memory of her dagger piercing my heart. *"I don't let you make decisions for me anymore ... After all I've suffered, I deserve to be happy ... If you hadn't been so keen on managing my decline ..."*

"What else was I supposed to do?" I whimper.

The voice doesn't answer. Its silence is far more oppressive than its mockery.

"I was the only one left. A brother ... a brother ought to protect his sister. Mattie's too stubborn for her own good. She needed to be ... She needs me."

Thuris circles, waiting to see if I'll free myself from this trap. I've been under a millstone of anxiety. Whether or not I should be wearing it was never something I paused to consider. I bore it gladly, as a necessity, as a breastplate. Now I'm being crushed under it. I was too harsh with Mattie, but how else was I to keep her from destroying herself?

"COME NOW," the voice says, looming over my minuscule corner of reason. "LET'S NOT PLAY GAMES. YOU KNOW THE ONLY WAY YOU CAN MAKE IT UP TO HER, DON'T YOU?"

Retribution had not yet entered my mind. I was preoccupied with guilt.

"LET ME SHOW YOU HOW," the voice presses inward, taking up more space every second.

"No," I cry in a pained whisper. This feels like death.

"LET ME MAKE YOU FEEL BETTER. OR FEEL NOTHING," Thuris insists.

"No," I wheeze, suffocating.

"LET ME IN."

"I'll kill you, Thuris," I manage, feeling myself shrink smaller before its dominating presence. The voice laughs.

"How unfortunate," Thuris says. "I am eternal. I cannot be killed."

CHAPTER 19

There's a certain Slant of light,
Winter Afternoons—
That oppresses, like the Heft
Of Cathedral Tunes—
Heavenly Hurt, it gives us—
We can find no scar,
But internal difference—
Where the Meanings, are—

— EMILY DICKINSON

When I wake, it's Godfrey Foxe's voice I hear. He's standing in the doorway, speaking to someone. Listening with my eyes closed, I realize the sniffling, nasal voice belongs to Tothill.

"Thank you, sir. And thank you for comin' so fast. I don't think I could've held up by meself, with no one else in the house apart from Cook and Donnie."

After a few more exchanges, Godfrey closes the door. I open my eyes and see he's seated in the chair next to my bed. His smile begins in the crow's feet next to his eyes and tugs up his grin in answer. I can't manage a greeting. My head's still pounding, my pulse racing after that disturbing dream. He lays a hand on mine, reassuring me.

"Don't speak. I've been told everything that happened at Linwood these past days." Godfrey's expression darkens. "But there's news you've not yet heard, I'm afraid. The gossip afoot says Linwood itself is cursed. Now most of the staff have taken fright and resigned. I'm sorry to be the bearer of such news, my friend."

"Everything's gone bad all at once," I say, gritting my teeth against the pain. "Why?"

"Well, it's not your fault, if that's what you're wondering."

But it *is* my fault. Every last bit of it.

I fix my eye on him, wishing I could go back to those evenings with him and Bennett. If I'd been more myself, and at the same time less myself, maybe we'd have arrived at this moment better friends. As it is, I don't know how much of my story Godfrey's capable of accepting. His coming is like a windfall and rescue all in one, and yet if he doesn't believe me, it would be torture and my just deserts.

"I should've written after we last parted." Godfrey gives me a self-deprecating smirk. "I was being pigheaded and selfish. I let myself think it was the right thing, hiding my bitterness in my heart, instead of talking to you."

"You're not the selfish one." My voice scrapes between throbs in my temple. I try not to laugh but can't help chuckling painfully. "I could've written too."

Foxe exhales, releasing something between us.

I want to tell him everything. To explain that more's happened between my sister and I than Tothill and Dr. Brooks know. More than what they've told him. After my oppressive dream, my burden of guilt has become too heavy to bear. But talking will be pointless if I faint from the pain. "Bring pen and paper, please?"

"Now, Ambrose," Godfrey begins, but I cut him off by leaning forward and scooting back against the pillows a smidge. I'm not fully sat up, but it's better all the same. Moving makes me dizzy, but I think Dr. Brooks must've given me something for the pain because I don't feel a stabbing in my ribs anymore. I wave at my desk, and he reluctantly obliges.

It's difficult to write when I can't see the words properly. One of my eyes is swollen shut. I scratch out squiggles and pause every few moments to make certain Godfrey is understanding them.

"'Mattie's not well. You were right about me meddling too much,'" he reads, then looks up from the page to reassure me. "Dr. Brooks says melancholia is an understandable response to your manifold losses. He's sure Mattie will recover with rest."

I write fervently, watching him frown as he puzzles out my meaning.

Something happened to us. A dream? Maybe. But it was unnatural.

"Dreams are rather commonplace, Ambrose," he says, but

he shifts his weight in his seat. He keeps his eye on the page as I continue, his hands clasped tight in his lap.

We shared the exact same dream. In it, we met Bennett.

Godfrey goes very still but continues reading my explanation.

Not the real Bennett. It was an illusion. Mattie created an alternate life inside the dream. She doesn't want to wake up. Ever. There's something else too. The dream is caused by an evil creature—a demon, maybe?

Godfrey goes pale, and that's when I know Dr. Brooks said something more to him about my sister's condition. More than he's letting on.

What did Brooks say?

I look at him, and when he does not answer me I underline the question. Twice.

Godfrey shakes his head. "I only just got here. I don't really know—"

"Tell me," I groan.

Godfrey Foxe swallows, looking straight at me, then leans forward. "Dr. Brooks is going to London tonight, to ask a specialist to come. He stopped administering morphia, but he can't wake Mattie. What's worse, he doesn't know why."

I lean my head back, closing my eyes against the pain and

the heaviness and the dread washing over me. I wish I could just forget all of it. But Mattie's lying in that wretched room, in Thuris's power. I'll have to go there again. And yet, I can't face her as though there's nothing between us. It's clear to me now how much I've hurt her. What a fool I've been.

There's one last thing I need to do while Godfrey's with me. "Hear my confession," I ask.

He laughs softly. "Ambrose, you know I'm not that sort of priest. I can ask Father Amicus to come."

"No," I smile, cracking my good eye to look at him. "I need a friend."

Godfrey Foxe folds his hands. He sits silently, holding my gaze. Then he reaches inside his pocket and pulls out his white collar. He snaps it round his neck, inhaling through his nose. Pulling his chair closer, he leans his face near to mine and says, "I'm listening."

CHAPTER 20

What if I say I shall not wait!
What if I burst the fleshly Gate—
And pass Escaped—to thee!
What if I file this mortal—off—
See where it hurt me—That's enough—
And wade in Liberty!

— EMILY DICKINSON

When the Blood Harvest is done and Basilis is entombed in predawn silence, I sit alone, feeling my limbs grow numb with cold. The smell of burning flesh abated hours ago, the heat of my vengeful furnace cooling along with my anger. Somehow, I knew he'd show up again. I'd built this place intending that one day it would be his body I cast to the hungry flame. But when the moment arrived, I'd been too weak, unwilling to listen to his screams. He didn't even flinch when I stabbed him.

My eyes shift to the floor where the knife lies in his pooled blood. The steps are sullied too. I understand now what the fine, red line represents—a river of sacrifice. Ambrose came here to save me but ended up giving in to my will, at long last.

Leaning forward against my hand, I feel another headache coming on.

A soft footfall betrays Bonne's presence.

"What is it?" I say, straightening my spine against the high, smooth back of my throne. Its stone is too cold for my body to warm, even after sitting here for hours. It's as though the thing I built is sapping the life from me.

"I couldn't find her," he says, turning to indicate the view out the monstrous double doors of my palace sanctum. "She's flown over the mountains, I'd wager."

I force myself to stand. The mountains lie across the horizon like two black pythons sleeping off a meal. On my shoulders, Thuris stirs in his sleep. His small, reptilian head lifts to caress the line of my jaw. Descending, step by step, I fix my eyes on the distant stars. They are what inspired all of this —my rise to power as the Magna Regina, the Blood Harvest to appease an eternity of wrongs, my botched revenge. I wanted to be as cold and unreachable as the stars and as elevated above all the wretched, debauched souls caught in this realm.

My steps falter, halfway from the floor, but Bonne is swift to use his mage-craft and catch up my stumbling feet. With a regal smile, I dip my chin in his direction, slipping out onto the porch without a word. I know what Bonne wants. He'd like me to order him away, to give him liberty to take up his sister's scent and hound her to the far corners of the land. How it must rankle him, knowing I'd rather let Beatrix's escape fester, just to make him squirm. After all, he's a brother too.

"What are you thinking about?" Thuris purrs against my throat.

"I want wings of my own." The words fly from my lips without a moment's thought, followed by the certainty it was a foolish thing to say. Thuris has never once told me what to do. But there were things he approved of, acts previously forbidden which he was delighted to watch me commit, and one unspoken law which I must never break.

"Wings? You have only to ask and Bonne will make them for you." I can sense his unvoiced caution.

"No," I say a bit louder, balling my fists. "I want to leave, Thuris."

"You can't mean that."

"When I came here, all those ages ago, you and Bonne promised I could have everything I might dream of wanting. You promised me forgetfulness, and yet everything here reminds me of *them*. You promised peace, rest, happiness—oh, there was nothing elusive and dear you *didn't* promise me!"

The hysteric edge to my own laughter is frightening. I'm standing here, Ambrose's blood dried along my arms all the way to my elbows, remembering every sin I've committed in pursuit of rest. I've done far more than slay a brother. Yet my hands remain empty. Thuris intends to control me, as all the others did.

"Do you no longer wish to dream with me?"

Glaring out over a dark sea of emptiness, I find the stars beyond the mountains hold no answer for someone like me.

Thuris's realm is all picturesque show, its rotting core carefully tucked beneath the surface. If I remain here, he'll tire of me and throw me to the worms that gnaw their way through the grimy dark.

Creeping over the front of my dress like an insect, Thuris drops heavily to the marble floor, now the size of a large terrier. His serpentine body is growing legs, longer teeth, and predatory talons.

"I ASKED YOU A QUESTION," Thuris snarls. "DO NOT FORGET WHOSE POWER GAVE YOU A THRONE TO SIT ON."

His color shifts in the starlight, ember-red melting into bright orange, then white-hot yellow fading to a deep green. His growing scales take on a metallic sheen, while a low-burning fire illuminates his lizard belly. He shifts his weight, claws cutting deep into the marble floor, and peers down at me with narrowed golden eyes. He means to intimidate me, I suppose.

But I've already made my decision. I stand at the edge of the temple, the dreadful seat of power for a queen who will be forgotten tomorrow, and smile straight into the dragon's teeth. "Even without wings, I can fly."

Snarling, Thuris swells to an even greater size and snatches at me as I cast myself headlong over the sheer drop.

CHAPTER 21

The last Night that She lived
It was a Common Night
Except the Dying—this to Us
Made Nature different

— EMILY
DICKINSON

M orning comes, and I'm ready for it. I push through the pain in my ribs with gritted teeth, shedding my bedclothes. Surprised I can stand without feeling dizzy, I remove the shawl Tothill tucked around my shoulders to keep off draughts. I fold and lay it on the bedside table. For a moment, I look at the chair where Godfrey sat last night, listening to my confession. When I stopped talking, when none of the heaviness remained, it was as though I'd become transparent.

He looked into my soul and spoke words which fit inside all my broken places, like a key in a complex lock.

"You think the pain is too great. That it'll eclipse you. But it actually has the power to transform you. Grief breaks you down to your most elemental parts. It's a little killing, from which you've naturally recoiled. Instead, you must press in. Be reborn."

There's something different about today. I'm missing the Atlas weight on my shoulders, but I feel fragile enough to dissolve. Standing before the mirror, I take stock. My appearance belies the lightness I feel within. The pale, drawn face staring back looks sick. My drooping shoulders and the pain-stricken rise and fall of my chest are incongruous with the spark of hope in my innermost being.

I squint at myself, recognizing nothing of what I see. I'd put up what I thought an impregnable defense against emotion, against loss. But I look haggard, as though a sickness has eaten away at me from the inside, producing this harrowing, ghastly exterior. No wonder Dr. Brooks and Tothill urged me to rest, same as Mattie.

"Who are you?" I ask the man in the mirror. "You're not stodgy, old Ambrose Bancroft, are you? Why, you can't be him. Ambrose never cries."

Touching my face, my fingertips come back trembling and wet.

"That's what made Mattie hate me so," I tell the self I'm meeting for the first time. "I was wooden. As though I hadn't once danced with Abigail. I was stiff, like Grandfather. Even though I *said* I missed them, did I ever allow myself to remember what made me love them in the first place?"

I rest my hand against the glass. We'd always looked similar, but now that I am wan and weak as any invalid, our resemblance is unmistakable. "Dear Bennett, there are too many things about you to recount. I must ask Mattie, if ... if she ever decides to come back. We'll start at the very beginning, and we'll keep on remembering, until there's nothing left to tell."

I hobble into the hall, holding my broken ribs. Movement brings dizziness in waves. I pause at intervals to steady myself. The house is quiet. Donnie's away, taking Dr. Brooks to London. Cook will be at work in the kitchen or the garden. Tothill or Godfrey will be sitting with my sister. More likely, Godfrey's resting in one of the guest rooms after spending long hours with me last night. I haven't the energy to descend to the dining hall, and there's a more pressing matter at hand than my growling stomach.

The north wing's carved double doors stand open. No dust lines the carpet, furniture, and window casements. Tothill must've cleaned them in the fitful hours of our illness, when there was nothing to do other than watch and wait for a change. A sadness fills me at the sight of this clean, grand passage. For whom has it been made thus? Will I keep watch over Mattie until a seamstress is called to make her shroud, as she once said to me in morbid jest? I can no longer ignore the fact that sooner or later, my sister and I will lose one another. It's the inevitable fate of all living.

I gather what strength remains in my legs and walk past Grandfather's study. Seizing hold of the next door handle, I force my skin to touch it, force my body to move, despite knowing a living nightmare waits inside. I swing the door open and stumble forward. My eyes take a moment to adjust to the darkness. Then I see numerous linen sheets holding the shape of solid things. The walls are covered in twisting, supple snakes of green. I'm looking at Grandfather's sitting room. Tucked in the back corner, I make out the dark outline of the pocket door.

"No!"

I stagger to the study. It contains familiar furniture and shelves and books. The connecting door is in the back corner, where it's always been. I crash through the room, heedless of the furniture in my way, and throw aside a heavy curtain hanging over the single window. It overlooks the glass roof of the conservatory. There can be no mistake. The room where Mattie has lain in her unnatural slumber *was* here.

I scream. "How can it be gone? It's a room, for God's sake!" I stumble toward the door. "Godfrey!"

He bursts out of his guest room three doors up the hall. I'm leaning against the study doorframe, and he slips his arm under my shoulder and supports me, half carrying me to a hall bench. My eyes are fixed on the five feet of wall stretching between the open doors of the study and sitting room. There's not enough space between for the room I *know* was there only yesterday. In that other place, plenty of things happened which defied explanation. But this is happening *here*, in the real world.

"It's not possible," I say, shaking my head. "Where's it gone?"

I cast my eyes up and down the passage. My head spins. I'm rocking back and forth, hugging my aching ribs. I become gradually aware Godfrey's been speaking to me without my hearing him.

"Ambrose ... Ambrose! Ambrose, what's the matter?"

I meet his eye. "Mattie's gone. It took her."

He looks toward the study, a cloud of sorrow mixed with confusion passing behind his eyes. Then he turns to me. "You shouldn't be out of bed yet." Giving me his support, Godfrey guides me out of the north wing. "I'll find her, trust me. Let's just get you—"

But I won't allow myself to be dragged back to bed. I wrench free of him and stagger downstairs into the foyer. Cook is in the dining room and bobs her head around the doorway when she hears me coming.

"Father Foxe, you're up early ..." Her smile disappears when she sees me. "Oh, m'lord! Beg pardon. I thought—"

"Tell me something, madam." I push past her, collapsing into a dining chair.

"Why, yes, sir. If I know it, I'll tell you anythin,' sir."

Godfrey Foxe enters after me and exchanges a glance with Cook.

"Does Linwood Manor have two pantries?" I ask, thinking of the map in the journal.

"Pantries, m'lord?"

I nod and regret it. The room swims. But it's better than speaking. My ribs feel as though they'll come right off. Breathing doubles me over in pain. I rest my head on my arm.

Cook cries in alarm, "No sir! There ain't."

"Ambrose, you ought to go back to bed." Godfrey's voice hovers over my head, but the throbbing between my ears almost drowns it out. My pulse beats a drum of dread.

She's gone. She's gone. She's gone ...

And ...

The worst has happened. I'm left alone.

Godfrey half drags, half carries me. There are red and black explosions behind my eyelids. A rush of blood roars in my ears. At some point, I crumple against the hall rug. Shoulders spasming violently, relentless sobs robbing me of breath. Godfrey Foxe might be sitting next to me; he might be running downstairs for help. All I know, all I hear, all I see is one life-encompassing thing—the dark, gaping mouth that is unbearable loss. Weeping, I lie in the middle of Linwood Manor at the mercy of a voracious grief.

I comprehend little of what follows.

Bedridden, I live in an agonizing state of mental and physical anguish. Godfrey remains for many days, a ministering presence at my bedside. But eventually, things must return to their normal course. The words I used to comfort Mattie return with a bitter bite to them—life marches on. Godfrey returns to Oxford. Tothill, Donnie, and Cook move about Linwood as they've always done. Spring returns to the manor house.

Constantly, a maw of pain sucks at my mind. I sleep much, and my broken bones gradually heal. But every morning, I open my eyes on a new day and spend the entirety of it flinching from one unanswerable truth. Mattie is finally, truly lost to me.

CHAPTER 22

"A wounded Deer—leaps highest—
I've heard the Hunter tell—
'Tis but the extasy of death—
And then the Brake is still!
The smitten Rock that gushes!
The trampled Steel that springs!
A Cheek is always redder
Just where the Hectic stings!
Mirth is the mail of Anguish—
In which it cautious Arm,
Lest Anybody spy the blood
And "you're hurt" exclaim!"

— EMILY DICKINSON

E nveloped in burning heat, I become aware that my entire body is covered by hot sand. I sit up, choking on the grains that coat the insides of my mouth. Shading my eyes against the powerful glare of a gigantic sun overhead, I struggle to stand. The heat saps all moisture. It radiates off the sandy ground. My exposed skin is being scalded. My arms are still covered in Ambrose's blood. I'm dying of thirst. Breaking my neck on the city streets would've been a far easier death than perishing in this wilderness. But even though he's nowhere in sight, I doubt Thuris is done with me yet.

This vast plain is an arid, waterless grassland. Ambrose's *Encyclopedia Britannica* had an illustration of this type of terrain —an African veldt. Though, the only reason I took note of the name was because Bennett teased our older brother mercilessly for trying to pronounce both *d* and *t*. His agonized embarrassment was both painful and hilarious to watch.

An unbroken horizon stretches in all directions, and the sun is at its zenith overhead. I start walking. My queenly robes of silk cling to my sweating skin, and the heavy jewelry on my neck and arms begins to heat to a scalding degree. I cast off my ornaments, breaking the delicate chains and tossing away arm bands crusted with jewels.

As I walk, the stillness of the place begins to feel ominous. What I know of Africa would lead me to expect even as arid a place as this to teem with wildlife. This place is barren. Too quiet. Surely, Thuris is near.

"Come out, why don't you? You know I don't fear you, Thuris," I lie.

"You should," he purrs from the chest-high grass.

"Who is Thuris of the other place? A mere spirit of ill-will, haunting an old house and pretending to rule a world of his making. I know exactly who you are, you pitiful creature." I laugh, spinning round to see if he's crept up behind me. My voice holds a bitter tone. "I know you because I've become just like you."

"Foolish girl, you know me as I present myself to you— a maker of worlds, dreams, and nightmares. But this is only the inside of my belly. My true nature is the same as starlight, as cold as the endless night sky, as all-consuming as the fire of burning giants."

As he speaks, Thuris circles me. He's taking pleasure in prolonging this slaughter. I'm the prey, and my whole body recoils from this fate.

"You're unnatural," I growl at Thuris.

"Nature is a word you use for things you understand. No, I am not part of your so-called natural world. I transcend it as time transcends your puny mortality."

"Being immortal hasn't made you any wiser, old one. You're just as much a fool as I, if you believe holding people captive is a power worth boasting about. You might not have death hanging over you, but your time will come. In all your ages and ages of devouring, have you forgotten to be afraid?"

"Afraid of what? You?" Thuris's laugh is gravel scraping deep from a lion's throat. He emerges from the grass to my right, his tawny golden hide rippling with powerful muscle, his golden eyes full of ancient cruelty.

I try not to show fear, smiling back at him with tight lips. My whole body wants to flinch away as he steps closer, close enough I can feel the warm breath emanating from his stinking, dripping jaws. For some reason, this form is a far more sinister one than the dragon.

I shake my head, almost imperceptibly. "In all the time we've spent together, I've learned you have one weakness. Despite your god-like arrogance, you *do* have a sense of the cosmic hierarchy. And you're not very high up on it, are you, Thuris?"

His rumbling amusement unsettles me. I watch the lion shrink back into the shifting golden grass, vanishing like salt in sifting sand.

"Run, little mouse," he purrs, suddenly behind me. "Run."

I know it's pointless, but my body surges forward. Instinct for survival outstrips my thinking mind, driving me into a headlong pursuit of the sliver of a chance I might not be caught. I dare not imagine what will happen to me when I am.

Waves of heat cascade over me. The sun's setting behind my back, and I squint at the horizon ahead, wondering if those are green treetops I see beyond this wilderness or storm clouds. I believe I'm being pursued, but I hear nothing at all. Then, when my lungs are burning and I can run no further, a movement in the grass stops me short. My cramping muscles shudder, and I'm frozen in place. Wherever I look, there's nothing. At least, nothing I can see.

Pressing forward, one stiff step at a time, my awareness heightens. Grass rustles. I see darting, creeping glints of yellow. My eyes flit from one side to the other, but always, the thing has gone. Flashes of color—yellow, gold, tawny brown—make my lungs seize in bouts of panic. It might just be grass.

I glance over my shoulder as I run and almost fall, stumbling into an earthen bowl that was once a murky watering hole. Beyond the dusty rim of the bowl, the sky burns red in the west, with great streaks of gold and orange and pink, like claw marks dragging across the blue. When I turn round again, a startled yelp leaps from my throat.

At the crest of the bowl, two yards from where I stand, a lion crouches in the grass. Its black claws grip the curved rim of dirt, muscles gathered to spring. Two more lions creep out from the shadows on either side of me. I hear the rumbling snarl of a fourth behind. Four? How are there four? But this is Thuris's realm, and I suppose he can do as he likes.

"You and I are not the same, my sweet. You are right to

FEAR ME. I BROUGHT YOU HERE FOR MY ENTERTAINMENT, AND YOU HAVE PROVEN YOURSELF A SOURCE OF DISAPPOINTMENT. BUT WORRY NOT. IT SO HAPPENS, I'M VERY GOOD AT GETTING EXACTLY WHAT I WANT!"

Thuris's maw lifts to the sky in uproarious laughter. It breaks upon my ears like a clap of thunder, knocking me onto my back. The four lions leap as one. My flesh is ripped from my bones. The red sky mirrors red sand.

And yet I live.

I lie across the lion's jaw in such agony I can no longer form thought. Its teeth sink into my back, preparing to snap me in two. If I were the sort of person who prayed, I might know words powerful enough to ward off this fiend. But I turned my back on God when we buried Mother. For all my posturing, I'm powerless, and Thuris knows it.

"LET'S PLAY," the demon purrs, then he bites down.

CHAPTER 23

Each that we lose takes part of us;
A crescent still abides,
Which like the moon, some turbid night,
Is summoned by the tides.

— EMILY DICKINSON

"There've been enough Bancroft funerals," I tell Father Amicus. "Besides, Mattie's not dead." *Not exactly,* I want to add. But her disappearance feels like the same thing.

I sit up in bed, wearing a loose jacket over my nightdress in a show of decency I only perform on Tuesday afternoons, when the village priest comes by on his rounds. He spends a half hour describing for my benefit the changes Eaton has undergone in the last month.

Saint Anne's Home for Children was brought out of the city slum into temporary housing in January. Since then, Anna Holm has overseen the construction of the new house and grounds, stables and outbuildings, largely without my involvement.

Eaton's a hive of gossip on a good day, and Father Amicus has plenty of material with which to fill the space of thirty minutes. But today, I'm not in the mood to humor him. I *want* him to take offense. And I hope he won't ever come back.

"But Lord Bancroft, the coroner has been asking me—"

"If you've something you need taken care of, please contact Monsieur Belot directly, Father. Such things are in his capable hands now. I am convalescing, meanwhile."

Father Amicus smiles, tilting his head in that pitying way of his. "What would Miss Bancroft have wanted, I wonder? Would she not have wished for the rites to be read over her final resting place?"

This is a point of tension for the priest. Amicus must feel his duty to his parish is on the line. He's concerned with pews, with headstones, with sacrament. How can I make him understand? Mattie's not dead.

What's happening to her is far worse.

"It wouldn't do her any good," I whisper before I can stop myself. I've been staring at my clenched fists, but now I drag my gaze upward to look Father Amicus in the eye. "Mattie's lost. She gave herself over to fornication, to murder. Her heart is bent on sin, in thought if not in actual deed. You don't know what she was like this past winter."

The priest lays his hand over my fists. "God is merciful."

I shake my head. "If that's true, why did He take them all, one by one? Why am I still here? Where's the mercy in that?"

Ever since my confession to Godfrey and my subsequent plunge into this pit of despair, my emotions have been raw and on the surface of every interaction. Like wild horses put too green into a harness, they drag me from the height of wrath to the furthest reaches of loneliness, through blazing longing into a cold, numbing bitterness.

I wait for Amicus to answer. The priest sits back in his chair, folding his hands over his round belly. His small, blue eyes are studying the play of light across the far side of my bedroom. Spring's come in earnest, and Tothill insists on keeping my windows open for the air, despite how I complain the birdsong gives me headaches. No one listens to me in this house anymore. It's like they're all waiting for me to roll over and die as well.

"I don't want to live like this," I tell Father Amicus, my lips curling into a snarl. "Until God sees fit to make me understand why my family was plagued with tragedy—cursed, more like— I won't pretend nothing out of the ordinary has occurred. I won't go through with the usual tradition. I refuse to bury my sister."

"If it pains you so, I won't bring up the funeral again, m'lord. I beg your pardon." I watch Father Amicus pull himself to his feet, a smile affixed to his face. He sighs and raises a hand to bless me. The words fall over my stiff figure like water over stone. Then the floorboards creak, the door clicks shut, and only the trill of robin redbreast trespasses upon my solitude.

When four o'clock rolls round, my solicitor comes calling. Monsieur Belot is a man of few words. At least, he's a man of few English words. He takes tea with me without speaking of anything apart from the weather. He's brought a stack of documents from Saint Anne's. My tea cup and biscuit sit on the bedside table, untouched, while I peruse them.

"I see the home's been awarded a grant. Very good," I say, setting the papers aside. "I want you to procure a cook for them. Someone young so they'll be able to rely on her services for a good while."

"Yes, sir."

"Very good," I repeat myself, handing the papers to Belot.

He sets them on his lap and pulls another document from his leather satchel. It's a thick stack of long-leaf legal paper.

I frown. "What's this?"

"Your will, Lord Bancroft."

"I know it's a will, Belot. What's it doing here?"

Monsieur Belot sets his tea cup on the table beside him. He pulls out his spectacles, balances them on the pinched tip of his nose, and lifts a leaf from the stack of papers in his bag. "This is the death certificate I was given by the coroner. It states Matilda Bancroft has been presumed dead, but you should also expect the coroner's officer to ask after her disappearance, my lord. I suggest you and I go over the particulars of your will, especially in regard to your sister."

"But Mattie's the benefactor of my will, and after her, Saint Anne's. I don't see what any of this has to do with the coroner."

"He will want to know why you aren't changing your will, now that she's—"

"It's fine as it is. I don't wish to discuss it further, monsieur."

"The will contradicts the registry of death, presenting legal problems. Rest the matter for a week or so. But I urge you to redraft the document soon." He tucks his spectacles inside his breast pocket, fixing an expression of condolence on his stolid face. "I have to advise you, as your solicitor. I understand this is difficult, Lord Bancroft."

I don't think you do, I think, but I say nothing.

Belot takes my silence in stride. A quiet man himself, he makes no further comment but gathers up the papers and lines his satchel with them. At the door, he mumbles what might be a polite good day, but even that sentiment is reviled by my inner critic.

My days have long ceased to be good! I want to shout at his back.

The door closes. I am alone.

⬥

But only for the space of an hour. Misery likes company, I suppose. Tothill hovers near my bedroom door, blushing in a manner I find most unlike her.

"Come now, what is it?" I sigh.

"A visitor, sir," Tothill manages in a conspiratorial whisper. "A *woman.*"

"Oh, is that it? You're concerned for the impropriety of my receiving a female visitor in my bedroom? No matter. Is it Miss Anna Holm?"

Tothill's eyes blink three times in succession. "Yes, sir. You're going to receive her? A woman?"

"Why, you're a woman, Tothill. You haven't any objection to bringing us tea, in my bedroom?"

"No, indeed, sir!" Tothill huffs and shuffles out.

I've had a lengthy correspondence with Miss Anna Holm while the plans were being laid for Saint Anne's. She's been an invaluable source of practical wisdom, ensuring we did not put the schoolroom too close to the kitchen, or the lavatory too far from the furnace. She enters my bedroom without any apparent discomfort, and Tothill serves us tea.

"Won't you stay?" I ask my housekeeper, when she's finished laying out cucumber sandwiches on the bedside table.

Tothill obliges, pulling my desk chair alongside the high-backed armchair Miss Holm is occupying. The two women and I sit for some minutes as the afternoon sun reddens the floor-boards and steam curls up from the porcelain. I notice Miss Holm is no longer in full mourning attire. I want to speak to her about it—about the loss of a loved one and the strange passage of time despite their absence—but I fear such questions will weaken my shoddy defenses. I won't weep in their company.

"The story in the village is that you've suffered a bad fall, Lord Bancroft," Miss Holm says at last, her light blue eyes watching me carefully. "It might be wrong to ask about it, but I understand your sister is missing as well. How I wish I'd been able to meet her! Offering condolences seems the barest of comforts, but I came anyway. I know firsthand how painful it is for folk to act as though nothing's happened. Sometimes, the loneliness which follows is more acute a pain than the bereave-ment itself."

It's as though she's guessed my mind. But she's wrong about Mattie. They all are. But how can I expect anyone to understand?

"It's difficult to admit how great my loss truly is," I say and let it rest at that.

"And tempting to pretend to be strong." Miss Holm nods.

Tothill sneaks a handkerchief from her sleeve and dabs at her eyes. I'm reminded of how like family she's become. My losses are hers as well.

"Does it get any easier?" I ask, embarrassed by a break in my voice.

Miss Holm's sad smile fills her face with crinkles. She shakes her head slowly. "Not easier. But familiar. One day, you realize you're still alive and that means there's much you have yet to give, to be given, to suffer, and to rejoice in. It feels wrong that life goes on. But that's just because we get stuck in our pain. The true wrong is anyone dying in the first place."

Tothill nods vigorously. "Aye, merciful Lord knows we feel it in our bones how wrong death is. Christ felt the same and wept as we do."

Anna Holm places a hand over hers.

"How did you ..." But my words falter as I wonder if it's wrong to want to move on. How can I ask such a thing? Thankfully, Miss Holm doesn't hear the choked beginning of my question. Tothill squeezes the widow's hand in return, smiling through her tears. Bitterly, I'm grateful at least one of us finds comfort in Anna Holm's words.

⁂

Evening draws on. The sun sets on the opposite side of the house from my room, making the afternoon light dull and cheerless, growing dimmer each moment. At last, I hear the clock in the hall chime six. Tothill will be coming in with my supper soon. I don't eat much, of course. I'm often in too much physical pain for food to be appealing.

Dr. Brooks says the relentless ache in my ribcage is a good sign—my bones are growing back together—but their glacial progress is far more excruciating than the pain I experienced that first delirious week after my "accident." Some nights, it's more than I can bear.

Tothill seems to sense my mood. She usually makes cheerful comments as she waits to take the tray away. Her presence makes it awkward for me to eat nothing. Tonight, however, the silence is unbroken. I slurp a little broth, and it doesn't make my stomach turn. I drain my glass of wine. Tothill refills it with a tense smile pasted on her thin, spiderweb lips. She sits in the armchair next to the bed, folding and refolding the napkin.

I lift the tray from my lap, and she takes it from me. I can't ask her if everything's all right. Nothing is. "Tothill, do you wish to say something?"

She sniffles, blinking back tears. "Oh!" she cries, tensing her shoulders. "It hurts me to see you so, sir! That's all."

"I'm getting better." I want to paint a brighter picture for her sake, but we both know my body's recovery isn't what's troubling her. "I'll be able to walk around the house soon."

"Yes, Lord Bancroft. You will."

She goes. I wish I could ease her discomfort. But I soon forget all about it.

Every night for the past three months of my convalescence, a feeling has come over me with the darkening of the room. As the shadows from the window lengthen, it creeps upon me. It is like fear, in that it makes my heart race and my throat constrict, but its source is more lethargic than panic. The feeling is a weight, like a suffocating boulder made of coarse wool, or a cloying stench invading my nostrils. It's inescapable and yet offers no clear threat. Nor do I understand it enough to discern its remedy.

As Tothill's heels click down the foyer stairs, the darkness falls. I lie in bed, paralyzed, haunted by a dull ache of physical pain, my mind squirming. There must be a way out of this. I can't bear another long stretch of hopeless hours. I won't lie here, waiting for dawn to break fear's stranglehold.

"Thuris," I pant, panic driving my heart rate through the roof. "Thuris! I know you can hear me, dammit!"

The heaviness bears down on me like gravity. My chest rises and falls with extreme difficulty. But I can feel a presence. Thuris is here.

"Thuris, let me go back. Let me see my sister, one more time."

"Why should I, little lord?"

"If I can see her and speak to her, I promise I'll let you in. You can have me."

"Really?" the voice exults, circling me in the darkness. "I don't believe you. Swear it on something precious. Not your god."

I didn't expect this. What can the fiend be trying to get out of me?

"I swear on Linwood Manor, on all my earthly wealth, prestige, the title Grandfather bought, the reputation he spent his life building for us Bancrofts—I swear on everything I possess. I have nothing else!"

"Worthless."

I know this already. Without children to leave my name to, what is a title? Without a family to shelter in it, what is a home? But I'm not ready to admit defeat. My mind scrambles for leverage, but as always with Thuris, I've no influence.

"What, then?" I ask in exasperation.

"Unfortunately, I am no longer interested in having you. There is so much to do, now that your precious Mattie is done playing her games. You'll have to wait till I have time to listen to your pitiful whining." Thuris slithers away before I can recover from the sheer terror of this pronouncement.

"Dear God, no," I rasp, my chest heaving. "No, Mattie. You can't give in!"

CHAPTER 24

I can wade Grief—
Whole Pools of it—
I'm used to that—
But the least push of Joy
Breaks up my feet—
And I tip—drunken—
Let no Pebble—smile—
'Twas the New Liquor
That was all!
Power is only Pain—
Stranded—thro' Discipline,
Till Weights—will hang—
Give Balm—to Giants—
And they'll wilt, like Men—
Give Himmaleh—
They'll carry—Him!

— EMILY
DICKINSON

I do not sleep after that, not for four days. I make Tothill promise she won't send for Dr. Brooks, no matter what happens to me. Pacing my room in a cold sweat of pain, I curse at the ceiling and beg to be let alone to die. True to her word, my stolid housekeeper sends for Godfrey Foxe instead.

Godfrey finds me leaning my forehead against the bedroom window, my bottle of brandy in one hand, dressed only in a nightshirt. I stare at the lake with its gravel walk border. The water's surface looks like fire wherever the sun touches it, and I can't shake the feeling that if I could manage to sneak past the remaining staff, I could disappear in the baptism of that flame.

"You fool," Godfrey says at my elbow before I'm even aware he's come in. "I'm getting you outside. There's something you need to see."

He dresses me himself, kneeling in front of my armchair to tug socks onto my barebones feet. I look like a skeleton and feel just as lifeless. Godfrey hardly hunches under all my weight as he takes me down the stairway and halts before the front door. Tothill's waiting with a blue wool muffler and my hat. Grandfather's cane leans against the door, and Godfrey hands it to me while Tothill wraps the muffler round my neck. Her eyes are watery and red, but she refuses to give up on me, it would seem.

"Thank you, Father," she tells Godfrey.

He supports me all down the lane without saying a word. The further we get from the house, the more my muscles warm to movement. Lying in bed may have left me weak, but my legs haven't forgotten how much I enjoyed a good stroll once upon a time. The linden trees have voices of their own, a gift of the late April breeze. It puts me in mind of the day we buried Bennett. It'd been a raucous day of bright sunlight, the plant life bursting from every corner of this rolling green countryside. It felt like my childhood haunts were laughing in my face while Mattie wept softly at my side.

Godfrey had been there too, longing to slip away and yet too kind to leave us to face the funeral reception alone. A wry smile tugs at the corners of my mouth as Godfrey matches my labored stride. Even then, a year ago, Mattie had begun to change from the shy, submissive young girl who wilted in the glare of anyone's displeasure to the prefigurement of the Magna Regina. I'd been blind not to see I was pushing her away.

"The Bloody Mary of Thuris's realm," I mutter. "Who'd have guessed it would be my sister?"

If my words shock my companion, he gives nothing away. When we reach the end of the lane, Godfrey continues on into the main thoroughfare toward Eaton. He stops to grin at me when I hesitate at the border of Grandfather's estate.

"I'm not done with you yet, Ambrose."

Grunting and reluctant, I hobble over to him. "It's three miles to Eaton Village, if that's where we're going. You know you're going to have to carry me long before we reach it, right?"

Godfrey shakes his head, laughing.

"Just so long as you're adequately prepared for the gossip that'll stir," I huff at him.

It's hotter out here on the open road, beyond the shade of the linden trees. Godfrey offers me his handkerchief when we stop to rest under a sprawling oak. It sits at the center of the crossroads, half a mile from the train station. The lowland dips below our feet, blanketed with wildflowers and fields of winter oats ripening in the sun. Eaton looks like a model town, with its little stone bridge drawing the road over a shallow creek and into the village green.

A red brick post office sits beside the milliner's shop Mother loved to visit. Donnie's favorite haunt, the two-story pub, towers over the slate-roofed train station. No matter how many months or years it's been, Eaton never changes.

"They brought us food, you know," I tell Godfrey, watching

the distant figure of the postman emerge from the post office and trudge across the street, placing letters in boxes. "When Mattie and I were leaving Linwood for good, as I supposed then, Donnie stopped the carriage in the road before we reached the train station. I looked out the window, and there they all were, two hundred odd souls, holding baskets and crocks ... and pies, so many pies."

"I didn't know," Godfrey says. He's leaning back against the ancient trunk, watching me gaze down over the village square.

"You know what they used to call my grandfather, Lord Henry?"

Godfrey shakes his head, bending to pluck a purple clover.

"Batty Bancroft—because he was a boot-maker's son who thought himself made of the stuff of lords." I laugh at the thought. "They probably harbored a grudge because he never hired the Eaton women or boys as scullery maids and stable hands. Maybe they thought he believed himself too good for Eaton. In fact, he once told me he would if he could, to save the expense of finding Londoners, but he was intimidated by the Eaton gossips. He dreaded the thought of all our private affairs being aired from here to town, especially after the train station was constructed."

"That's all?" Godfrey chuckles, and I find myself laughing along with him.

"I suppose he knew he was a hard man as well as we did." The thought sobers me. I've often regretted the characteristics I share with my namesake. If I'd not grown up under his reproachful glare, what sort of man might I have become by my own merit? It has never occurred to me that Grandfather might not have liked who he'd grown up to be either.

Godfrey tosses the clover over his shoulder and takes my arm. "Shall we go on?"

"Not back?" I ask.

"I thought we'd pop in on your children's home, while we're here."

Shaking my head, I smirk at him.

"Your ears are turning red," he says, tugging me out into the road again. "What's that about?"

"I'm embarrassed to be seen with children by you," I reply, dragging my feet as we approach the bridge.

"You already told me you're not good with them. But I hear otherwise from Tothill. She said something about making a bargain with some rascal you found in a London alleyway. Are you going to tell me that story next?"

Flushing even more, I oblige him. We cross the babbling water, pausing to note the teeming silver trout making their way upstream. My story about meeting Tom is interrupted on several occasions by village folk. They have the upper hand on me because they know my name, while I only recognize a handful of faces. Under Godfrey's guidance, we pick our way through the winding streets until we reach a small farmhouse where the children and Holm sisters have been staying until the new buildings are finished.

"Here we are," Godfrey says, holding open the gate while I hobble through.

The front door stands open, but he raps on it anyway, loud enough to draw the attention of anyone in hearing. But we wait a good while before a light, uneven step comes tapping along and Miss Lucia skips into view.

"Oh, the Lord!" she exclaims. "Come in, kind sirs."

"Good morning," Godfrey tells her, smiling.

She energetically indicates the settee, and we sit as she plops down into a wooden chair opposite. She crosses one hand over the other atop her knee, a stiff and practiced pose, and looks down her nose at us. Then, with a spark in her eyes, she purses her lips and says, "Gentlemen, you will please forgive the tragic absence of my sister, Miss Annie

Holm, who is at this very moment *out*. If you please and thank you."

Too late, I realize I ought to have prepared Godfrey for Miss Lucia's peculiar charms. But then I glance at him and see he's not put off in the least. As is his way, he takes Miss Lucia in stride and gives her the whole of his attention. We talk of the ripening oats which she's been hard-pressed to keep the children out of, as well as kidding goats and hatching chicks, the mystery of what makes sun-dried laundry smell so divine, and dozens of other captivating topics, all in rapid succession.

"I had hoped to meet Miss Holm too," Godfrey interjects during a brief pause, offering Lucia a hopeful smile. "Will she return soon?"

"Oh, I don't think so," Lucia says, cocking her head to one side. "Folk in the big house on the hill are sick, and she went to take them pudding. It was an excellent pudding—she let me have a taste before she went."

Chuckling, Godfrey raises a hand as Miss Lucia prepares to launch into further anecdotes. "Do you mean your sister went up to Linwood Manor? How interesting we didn't come across her on our way. Perhaps she took one of the back roads to visit the—"

Laying my hand on his knee, I arrest him before he can inadvertently cause Miss Lucia any embarrassment. "Will you give us a tour, Miss Lucia? I'd like a chat with Tom as well."

Following in Miss Lucia's wake, we are shown from room to room amid a volley of excited talk. Children appear from every direction and follow us like a flock of shy doves, jostling each other for the best view of "the lord" as she continues to call me throughout.

I've not been to Saint Anne's at all since they came from London, and I am struck by the wrongness of that. I don't want to be like most noblemen who'll write a check without ever bothering to learn the names of their beneficiaries. As Godfrey and I are led from the dormitory to the schoolroom, past the lavatories and through the backyard to see the hen house, I find myself searching the faces of the little ones who giggle and hide, peering out at us from every corner. I resolve to learn all their names. What better occupation can a lone, invalid lord make for himself, if he presumes to call himself the caretaker of so many souls?

We eventually make our way round to the kitchen, where a kettle of tea is whistling its boiling song. Miss Lucia cries, "Oh! I forgot Cook asked me to watch the kettle! But that's perfect. Now we can all have tea. Go wash up, children."

Godfrey and I sit at one end of a long table lined with benches. Miss Lucia sets out a dozen mismatched china teacups, a sugar cone, and a clatter of spoons. When all sixteen children have seated themselves along the benches, hands folded in their laps, she hovers from cup to cup, pouring.

Last of all—instead of first, as most folk would've done— she offers a good strong tea to Godfrey and me. He carefully cuts nibs of sugar for the children. Miss Lucia settles herself at the far end of the table and shouts across to us above the happy chirping of all her little chicks.

"Indeed! What brings you to visit us today, *lord*?" It sounds so like a mimicry of something an adult would say, all jumbled out of context, I can't resist smiling. She leans forward with expectation.

"Why, I was in need of good company, Miss Lucia," I say, and the truth of it sinks deep. "I've been in a valley of shadow."

She nods, then quotes from the twenty-third psalm, "'Yea, though I walk through the valley of the shadow of death—'"

"I will fear no evil, for you are with me!" chorus the children in response, laughing.

"Quite right." Godfrey nods at them, grinning. "I suspect you know your catechism as well."

"And twenty-four hymns!" Miss Lucia chimes in.

At that moment, a familiar golden-headed boy heaves awkwardly into the room, dragging a box of coal behind him. A cry of "Tommie!" rises from the tea-takers. He strides over with a bar of soap in his grimy hands, scrubbing away the stains.

"Save any fer me?" He says cheekily, then catches sight of us at the far end of the table. "What now? We've company! Why didn't anybody tell me my godfather was 'ere?"

This sets Godfrey off for good. Sputtering his tea over the table, he shakes for some time behind his cloth napkin, much to Tom's delight. Apparently, the idea of my being any sort of father is amusing. I offer my hand to the boy, once he's doused his hands in a bucket of water and returned to my side. Squinting at me, the old look of cunning comes over his face.

"You near been done in," he says. Then, shooting a glance in Miss Lucia's direction, adds with a solemn bow, "my *lord*."

"Not enough to kill me," I tell him, mentally adding, *Unfortunately*. But my voice catches, and I can't remember all the things I thought it would be nice to ask Tom.

Godfrey comes to my aid, finally recovering his composure. "I hear you were given a gold watch, young man. Do you still have it?"

Tom beams back up at him, digging in his trouser pocket. "'Course I do! I'm still 'ere, ain't I?"

"Very nice," Godfrey says approvingly. "They called the original owner of that watch 'Batty Bancroft,' don't you know?"

Tom and the other children hang on every word as Godfrey spins the tale. Embellishing on Grandfather's eccentric tendencies for the benefit of his young audience, he holds every last one of them enthralled, Miss Lucia included. The lemony, bitter tang of the tea lingers on my tongue, and the scent of rising, yeasty bread is making my stomach rumble. But I don't feel quite myself in this room, where children are laughing at Godfrey's jokes. Children and a young woman like Miss Lucia might overlook my stiffness, but it doesn't make it any easier to navigate a social setting for which I never learned any rules.

"A wonderful idea," Godfrey is saying moments later. "We can walk back together and surprise her."

"What now?" I stammer.

"Miss Lucia was just suggesting we take the children on a stroll up the hill to visit the sick lord ourselves—since he's been left all alone for months on end, and Miss Holm may need our assistance in rousing him from his melancholy."

The squint of his eyes, with crows' feet appearing at the corners, is both intimate and reproachful. He means to push me as far out of my isolation as possible, it would seem. I wonder whether he knows me as well as he believes, or if he'll end up breaking me with this strange healing process of his.

"Why not?" I reply tersely.

Miss Lucia and the children put on their bonnets and caps, bringing along an odd assortment of baskets and dolls, running hoops and balls. Our party marches steadily over the road, surrounded by the earthy scent of hot dust and fresh-cut hay fields. Thankfully, there are many little ones who must be held by the hand and carried at intervals. With Godfrey's assistance, Miss Lucia and her little flock keep a pace I have no trouble matching.

We reach the shaded lane at last.

Godfrey exclaims, "Why, the irises have all come out, haven't they?"

"It's quite a lot for one hillside!" Miss Lucia says, clapping her hands. "Look! Look there, lovelies. Pretty, isn't it?"

We traipse onward. I am surrounded by a bevy of energy and good spirits. Miss Lucia alternates between asking Godfrey a host of questions and admonishing the children to keep to the path. The meadow beyond the linden trees is full of more than irises, though their purple blossoms bend in the breeze, begging to be plucked. A sore temptation for the little ones.

I remember telling my sister, in one of our many arguments, she should paint pictures of wildflowers for the poor, attempting to motivate her to cease moping. It never occurred to me orphan children might enjoy picking the flowers for themselves. I find myself choking out the words, "Please, Miss Lucia, let them run free."

"But won't the master of Linwood have us thrown in jail for trespassing *and* stealing?"

I gather from this comment Lucia Holm harbors a secret wish to flirt with danger. Amused, I tell her, "You should have no trouble with him. The master of Linwood Manor is completely blind, *especially* where women and children are concerned."

Godfrey laughs at me, giving her his nod of approval.

Miss Lucia throws off her bonnet with a squeal of delight. "Children, we may pick all the flowers we can carry!"

Her joyful little flock darts from the cover of the trees like lambs to sweet grass, and soon the hillside below Linwood is decked with their hats and bonnets.

CHAPTER 25

Where I have lost, I softer tread—
I sow sweet flower from garden bed—
I pause above that vanished head
And mourn.
Whom I have lost, I pious guard
From accent harsh, or ruthless word—
Feeling as if their pillow heard,
Though stone!

— EMILY DICKINSON

"I've decided, Godfrey. I can't save Mattie. But I've wronged her, and I must at least try to make amends," I tell him as we reach the midpoint of the ascent, the place where Linwood first becomes visible. My gaze is drawn to the bright cream stones and grandiose windows of the manor. "I'm going to tear it down, stone by stone, until there's nothing left ... or until I find her."

Godfrey places a hand over my shoulder. Staring up through the tunnel of shade, I wonder how much of Mattie there might be left to find. When we reach the rose garden, I collapse onto the moss-covered bench abandoned amid the overgrown, weed-choked canes. In silence, he and I watch the children and Miss Lucia make gradual progress toward the house.

As they approach, Miss Anna Holm rounds the corner of the house, talking with Tothill. Their faces are drawn with worry. I feel regret, not for the last time, on behalf of my steadfast housekeeper. I've caused her so much hardship.

"You know, Godfrey—" I begin but never finish the thought, for the children have begun to sing. Whether by Miss Lucia's encouragement, or simply because of hearts brimming with joy, their voices float up to us on the breeze. The words are old ones, wielding ponderous significance:

"And though this world, with devils filled,
should threaten to undo us,
we will not fear, for God has willed
his truth to triumph through us.
The prince of darkness grim,
we tremble not for him;
his rage we can endure,
for lo! his doom is sure;
one little word shall fell him."

As the children draw closer, cresting the hill with armfuls of lilies, daisies, peonies, irises, and daffodils, their song echoes off the stone face of the great house. With a rumble, something begins to give way. A terrible roar reverberates through the stone and timber.

"What's that?" Godfrey whirls round to stare up at the groaning roof.

Tothill and Anna Holm fly to his side, crying in alarm, "The house! The house!"

Donnie runs round the side of it, waving his arms at us and bellowing, "It's comin' down!"

Alarmed, the others scurry back away from the toppling building. Drawn to my feet, I step closer to the four of them, leaning on Grandfather's crutch. The sound of crashing intensifies as the glass windows splinter, and long fingers of cracking stone work at the walls overhead. Tothill and the Holm sisters shepherd the children out of harm's way.

But my attention is caught. My heart races with a feeling I've never known in my life. Foreseeing the banishment of my untouchable foe, I'm drunk with the thrill of triumph filling me.

Tom sees the danger before anyone else. With the bellowing gusto of a practiced guttersnipe, he barrels into my side, knocking both of us clear of the tiles that have worked their way loose and plummet, shattering where I stood not moments ago. Donnie is there an instant after, dragging the child and I back.

The dust begins to rise from inside the house, then it buckles. Somewhere deep inside, a resounding wail rips from the woodwork and screams its way skyward, like a waterless hurricane. An eerie stillness falls over the place for the space of a breath. Then, all at once, Linwood Manor crashes to the ground.

We shrink back onto the grass, then creep round the crest of the hill to stand in the shady lane.

Tothill crosses herself, trembling from head to foot. "Thank the Lord no one was inside!"

"Not Cook?" I say, ashamed to not have thought of it myself.

Tothill shakes her head. "She's been in need of a holiday for some time. I sent her home this mornin'."

The children sit at our feet, chattering in mild interest about an event of biblical proportions as though it were an everyday occurrence. Miss Lucia, just as unperturbed, crouches and shows them how to make flower crowns. Miss Anna Holm studies my ashen face, while Donnie pats Tothill's back, his arm wrapped around her quivering shoulders. Godfrey is staring at me, his expression the question Anna Holm voices. "What was that?"

I know one look at my face betrays the fact I know the answer. "A cry of defeat from someone who isn't used to losing," I tell them with conviction. In the face of a power seemingly small, an older power has crumbled. Linwood Manor crumbled with it.

"Mercy!" Tothill says when the cloud of dust settles and we can at last see the ruin.

"This must be Lord Christ's doing," Godfrey says, grinning. "Marvelous, innit?"

"I was already intending to tear the place down." I smirk at him. But then my smile disappears.

"Ambrose, what's wrong?" Godfrey asks, his smile fading.

Now Thuris has fled, what has become of the strange, vanished room? Surely, wherever Thuris hid it away, it too has crumbled into a heap of broken stone.

With a tightness growing in my chest, I turn to the shaken group. "Tothill, Miss Holm, do you know where we might find the builder, Master Gates? Donnie, go down to the village and send out telegrams. We'll get as many men here as possible. We must search for Mattie in the rubble. I know it doesn't make much sense, but I know she's there somewhere!"

Tothill wavers on her feet, doubtful. Miss Holm holds her thin shoulders, steadying her.

I meet her eye and then look to Godfrey. "I know it's hard to believe, but after all the strange things which have occurred, may I ask you simply to trust me? All of you?"

Without need for more discussion, the steady gaze of each of them assures me. Donnie sprints to the stables, and Godfrey gives my shoulder a reassuring squeeze. I turn to look at the mountain of rubble which stands between us and Mattie. It's true, I can't save her. But we who love Mattie will be unable to rest until we know her fate for certain.

In very little time, my world has become something unrecognizable. I don't know what will happen. However, I am bitterly familiar with this feeling of dread.

🪷

Unfortunately, the fall of Linwood Manor occurred during the height of spring harvest, and the builders can't come immediately. Donnie, Godfrey, Tothill, and I set to work at once. Anna Holm brings food at intervals after she and Lucia take the children home. It's a long day and an even longer night before a wagon pulls into the circle drive, full of the men I've hired.

Tothill puts down the basket of stones she's gathering and sprints across the muddy yard, avoiding puddles. It rained a great deal overnight. I watch her go from behind a shoulder-height pile of rubble. Despite my weakened condition, I've been making slow progress from where the outer wall once stood, turning over Linwood's crumbling stones in search of my sister.

"Mr. Gates, good mornin'," I hear Tothill greeting the wagon driver. Her voice is too chipper. She's worried for me and exhausted enough for two of us.

Gates stares. He drags his eyes from the mountain of rubble to look the small Irish-woman square in the face. "Don't you stand there actin' like nothin's happened, Margaret Tothill! There's a ruin behind you. A ruin what Lord Bancroft hired me to haul away without a word of explanation!"

"That's so."

"Well," Gates plods on, "are you goin' to tell me what happened?"

Tothill slaps her hands on her hips, pursing her lips. "Did m'lord hire you to gawk, or did he hire you to work?"

"Speakin' of—where is Lord Bancroft?" Mr. Gates counters, a little crossly.

"He'll be here, by and by. He'll no more care to stand answering all your questions than I do!"

Turning on her heel, Tothill walks back through the yard, adding as she passes me, "He's no idea what folk've been through in this house, that Mr. Gates! If he'd the least hint of it, he'd think 'twas right and good the place has fallen down. Might even call it providential."

I smile at her, too weary to say anything. After Mr. Gates arrived, I sank onto one of the larger beams and haven't been able to drag myself to my feet again. Tutting with a worried frown, Tothill comes over and feels my forehead.

"You're burnin' up, sir! Let Donnie take you back down to the inn. It won't do any good, your goin' on and on without food or rest like this."

"Dear Tothill," I tell her, "I wish you'd never come to Linwood Manor. You don't deserve to suffer so much on behalf of us Bancrofts. What good have we ever done for you?"

"Now listen you here, Ambrose, and listen well," Tothill says sternly, taking out her handkerchief and dabbing my sweat-soaked brow. "The love someone else has for you, it's not your responsibility to earn it or deserve it. And no matter what you think to the contrary, I'll never regret lovin' you. Even if you are the only one I have left. Even if I lose you too."

Taking my face in her hands, she places a kiss on my forehead and makes me look her in the eye. "You're worth it, laddie."

"But you saw how much I tormented my sister ... You saw everything, Tothill! How can you say that to me?"

Tothill's eyes well with tears. She gives my cheek a firm pat. "You only did that because you loved her. Given a second chance, do you suppose anything will have changed? We do the best that we can."

She releases me and goes to tell Donnie to bring the carriage, though I've not given her permission to send me to bed. Shaking my head, I stumble forward, holding myself up by gripping the beams and stones of the ruin. My hands are bloody, the skin torn to shreds and bandaged with strips of Tothill's apron. It's hard to tell whether they smart from the blisters or the dozens of splinters that pierced me as I moved beams and shattered wood paneling.

Even after hours of relentless searching, we've yet to make much progress. I can hear the guttural grunts of Donnie and Godfrey working nearby. Tothill can't lift much, but she carries off the smaller rubble, which would trip us up as we dig. She brings water and food, though we can hardly bear pausing to rest. None of us can sleep more than a few hours at a time. The thought that Mattie might be trapped under the house keeps all of us working like madmen beyond reach of physical pain.

We are covered, head to foot, in dust and ashes. Deep in the belly of the rubble, a fire is burning, choking the air around the ruin and raining grey flakes on our heads. My mind flinches from the thought that the fire might reach my sister before we do. Godfrey suggested we begin digging on the east side of the house, where our living chambers were, and hope for the best.

But his sunken eyes and ceaseless motion belie the encouragement he uses to buoy the rest of us. Almost more than my own, his longing to succeed against all odds is driving him to the brink of what is physically possible. Perhaps he is hoping for another miracle.

"Ah, there you are, Lord Bancroft," Gates says and stops short when I drag myself out from under the house's shadow and into the sunlight. The master builder hurries forward and takes my arm, noticing before I do that I'm about to fall.

"You there, bring water!" he shouts to one of the men unloading tools and ropes from the wagon.

In a moment, they've carried me to a shadier spot and wet my lips with a canteen of water mixed with light beer. I grimace at its lukewarmness, but Mr. Gates continues to proffer it until I sputter at him, "I'm fine! Indeed, I can take no more, Mr. Gates."

"My Lord Bancroft, what's happened here?" he says, waving his men off to their work.

"I can't explain, nor can I expect you to believe me, good sir." I wonder what nickname the village folk might find for me when the truth of the matter finally comes out. But a sharp pain in my side wipes the smile from my face. Gates leans forward, listening to my heart, and then gingerly presses on my ribs where I'm clutching my shirt.

Another spear of pain shoots through me like a dagger. My breath comes in short, agonizing gasps.

"I'm afraid that's a broken rib, if I've ever seen one. And in my line o' work, I've seen plenty," Gates says, sucking his teeth.

"It had healed," I groan but am unable to speak further. A searing heat blooms over my whole chest. I'm blinded by the intensity of it.

"Broken ribs are tricky like that," Gates says. "Plenty o' my men return to work sooner than they ought—afraid their families will starve otherwise—only to rebreak the bone with too much labor."

In my pain-fogged stupor, I hear the carriage and familiar gait of our horses approaching. Donnie's boots thud to the ground near me, and the two men lift me into the carriage.

Tothill hovers nearby. A cool rag is placed over my eyes. "There, there. You'll be all right."

The jostling of the carriage is too much for me. Through fluttering eyelids, I see the first of Grandfather's trees pass by the open window. Then a dead faint relieves me of having to endure the rest of our short journey.

CHAPTER 26

Adrift! A little boat adrift!
And night is coming down!
Will no one guide a little boat
Unto the nearest town?
So sailors say—on yesterday—
Just as the dusk was brown
One little boat gave up it's strife
And gurgled down and down.
So angels say—on yesterday—
Just as the dawn was red
One little boat—o'respent with gales—
Retrimmed it's masts—reduced it's sails—
And shot—exultant on!

— EMILY DICKINSON

From a distance which feels a fathom deep, from a darkness which enfolds me like an ink-stained sea, I hear him calling my name. It's a name I've not heard in such a long, long time that I've almost forgotten I belong to it. Other names, accompanied with torturous barbs, have plagued my waking moments.

"MY SWEET. FOOLISH GIRL. DARLING PLAYTHING."

Thuris has never tired of toying with me. I lost myself in that mad whirlpool which sucked me of all reason, tossed like a ragdoll from stage to stage to act out Thuris's twisted fantasies.

Until there comes a stillness like death. And I am glad to sink into something like rest. For the first time, I can feel all my bones in the waking world and know myself to be home again, no longer trapped in that other place. Thuris himself is a distant memory. I wait, the moisture sapping slow and stealthily from my flesh, my chest barely rising and falling inside the dark space. My coffin? My harried mind falls quiet, lulled by a numb sense of waiting. To disappear into nothing, I hope.

But then, the call comes. It reminds me who I am, where I am, and what has come before. And with a wash of light and a waft of fresh air, the lid is lifted. I emerge, a skeletal ghost of my past self, and *remember* all my regret.

"Noooooo!" The cry wrenches from my throat, my guttural scream scattering the onlookers like a flock of frightened sheep.

Godfrey holds me tight. I try to fight him off, to scrabble my way back inside my coffin, back to that sleeping death which brought me peace. I can't bear the reminders that now flash before my eyes. Last of all, worst of all my sins, I watch my own hands plunge a dagger into my brother's chest. Last of my kin, slain by my hand.

His bloodstains have coated my arms and hands ever since.

But I lift them now, turning them over and over, and I'm

shocked to see the white, clean flesh. Was it all a dream? Does it count if you murder someone over and over again in your heart but never actually sever the cord binding them to life?

And then that name falls softly against my cheek, where Godfrey's wet face is pressing kisses.

"Miss Bancroft! Miss Bancroft!" He shudders, gratitude and relief filling his voice like a broken dam.

For one fleeting moment, I'm pure-hearted enough to think *I don't deserve such a good man, not anymore*—but only for that moment. Then, craning around to reach, I clutch him about the neck and fill his mouth with kisses. I'm thankful, so thankful, it's Godfrey who's brought me back.

CHAPTER 27

"Tis good—the looking back on Grief—
To re-endure a Day—
We thought the mighty Funeral—
Of all conceived Joy—
To recollect how Busy Grass
Did meddle—one by one—
Till all the Grief with Summer—waved
And none could see the stone.
And though the Wo you have Today
Be larger—As the Sea
Exceeds it's unremembered Drop—
They're Water—equally—"

— EMILY DICKINSON

"They've found her. She's alive. Your sister was found alive ..."

Tothill continues speaking, Donnie and Miss Holm filling in details here and there as the story unfolds. I hear none of it. Four more days have come and gone since I was brought to Eaton's quaint little inn and put on bed rest, half-blind and unable to speak for shortness of breath. Dr. Brooks came at once, administered opioids, and sat by my bedside through the long days and nights. I spent them alternating between a deep slumber and mind-breaking hallucinations.

"Godfrey's with her," Tothill says before the room falls silent.

They're waiting for me to say something. I'm barely lucid, but my vision has improved now that the headaches and pain in my chest have been tamed by Brook's dosing. I look long at these few friends, common as orange ditch lilies, who've endured a cataclysm of change in the course of their devotion to my family. They're inestimably dear, proven by fire.

Miss Holm's arms are wrapped around her waist, as though she feels out of place here. She probably doesn't remember all the bouquets of truth she's offered me over the few months of our acquaintance. Her words were always attractively arranged and presented with unconscious grace, penetrating my callous defenses. She might never know how much of a heart's balm they were to me. Now's not the time to tell her, though perhaps such a time will come.

Donnie is covered in soot, and dirt cakes his hairy, exposed arms where he's left his shirtsleeves rolled back. The dark circles under his eyes match Tothill's. I imagine neither of them have left the manor ruin for all these days, sleeping in the stables and rising early to work themselves to the bone. All on behalf of two pitiful souls who can't do a bloody thing for themselves. And never could.

Tothill's years are beginning to show too. Gray hairs curl from both her temples, making her wise, pointed face look even more catlike than usual. She's stronger than she used to be. There's no handkerchief in her hand now, though her eyes still see all there is to see of me in a glance. With a thin line to her lips, she nods in approval. She already knows what I'll say and what it costs me to say it.

"Let Godfrey take her back to Oxford with him," I manage, stringing the words together in short bursts. "Did she ... How was she?"

Tothill shakes her head, and Donnie averts his eyes. It is Miss Holm who first forms an answer, drawing closer to lay her hand reassuringly over mine.

"She was not in her right mind, that much was certain. When she emerged, your sister was frantic, acting as though there were something repulsive touching her skin that she wanted to get off. Godfrey took her out of the box he found her in and held her for a long time to prevent her from harming herself.

"She lifted her hands up in front of her face, turning them over and over. It calmed her. Perhaps she saw whatever it was she feared had gone."

"Are you sure you don't want to see her, m'lord?" Tothill asks.

"I think it's best I let her go," I try to explain. "If Mattie saw me now, it would bring to mind sorrows too great for her to bear." Besides, I can't bring myself to tell them, but what Tothill said about love is right. If I were to see Mattie again, wouldn't I just return to old habits?

It's likely I'll never know what terrible fate befell her after Thuris refused me. But even if nothing else is certain, I know deep in my aching bones that Mattie doesn't need me. She's never needed my sort of love, or my protection.

"Godfrey will take care of her," I rasp out. After all, wasn't he the first to love her enough to let her go?

This feeling welling up in my chest, the tightness of my throat and tears pricking at my eyes, was once a foreign phenomenon. I duped myself for years into believing I'd closed off my heart, that I needed only a controlled, productive mind to survive the aching loneliness left behind by those I lost. Now grief is too familiar. I don't want to be numb. But neither am I prepared for all the many forms loss can take.

Late one afternoon in August, the summer heat finally drives Saint Anne's children indoors after months of swimming and picnics in the shade. They aren't used to being cooped up. Nor are they delighted to learn Miss Anna and her sister have been for a great while intending to give everyone a thorough scrub with rag and bristle brush before the kitchen fire. One by one, they're taken away from the front parlor to have their wash, while the rest sit in rapt attention at the feet of Miss Holm's frequent guest.

I am now known to them as "Mister Lord" by Miss Lucia's christening. With the passing of time, my bones have healed of their own accord. Tothill endured my complaining as she weaned me off the opioids with saintly long-suffering. We've taken up residence in Eaton, much to the astonishment of the townsfolk.

When Mr. Gates asked whether any of the stone salvaged from the Linwood ruin ought to be used to build me another fine house on the estate grounds, I raised my voice in answer, hoping to settle the matter once and for all.

"Not at all, sir. Grandfather hated being called 'Batty Bancroft' by you village folk, you know. He was more afraid of the Eaton gossips than a pox. But I say, call me batty and anything else that pleases. I'll be your neighbor now so you can gossip about me all you like."

The Linwood stone and timber were auctioned off to fund the children's home, and Mr. Gates expects it will be ready for them to relocate before the first frost.

Sitting in the middle of her flock, reading a picture book with a child on each knee, I am struck by how odd a person I've become in so little time. But the months since Mattie's rescue have crawled by with the weight of eons.

Miss Holm returns from the kitchen with her sleeves rolled above her elbows. Her apron is spattered with water and soap bubbles, her hair falling out from the bun atop her head in playful tendrils. If her face looks a little reddened, I suppose it's from the heat and not the tender picture I make, surrounded by her young charges.

"Lord Bancroft, I'd no idea you were stopping by for tea today. What a pleasant surprise," she says, pressing her hair back into order with damp fingers.

"Ah, well, I was given a note. Here." I pull it from my breast pocket and hand it to her. "It looks to be in Miss Lucia's handwriting."

"*May I request your company for an evening stroll by the clover field? M. A. H.,*" Miss Holm reads aloud, eliciting a chorus of giggles from the little girls in company. Blushing, she tuts at them, handing the note back to me. "You're correct about Lucia being the author. Dear me, I beg your pardon."

"On the contrary, I think it's a wonderful notion. I'm ashamed not to have thought of it myself," I tell her, gently shifting the children from my lap to the floor.

Tom, the last of the bathers, comes into the room with Miss Lucia and gives me an irritated eye-roll. "Just have done an' get married, already!"

"Tommie, you rascal!" Miss Lucia says, as if she is horrified. "You can't say such things outright." Then she adds in a loud whisper, "You have to let them figure it out on their own, or they'll think it's a bad idea."

After this sage pronouncement, Miss Holm seems just as eager to be out of the sitting room as I am. We don hat and bonnet and make our way through the shady apple orchard behind the farmhouse. Bees buzz in the treetops, seeking out the white blossoms. We pass through the humid, sticky grove and descend into the clover field. At the far edge, a narrow footpath runs alongside a forest-flanked creek.

"Tom seems to be doing well," I tell her.

Ever since I began coming for afternoon visits, much of our conversations concern the doings of the home children. It's a wonder I once thought not being good with children a suitable excuse for holding myself above the interests and affairs of innocents such as young Tom. Of late, whenever he comes to me with a line of worry between his brows, I find it quite satisfying to tease it out of him, coming to understand better and better how his canny little mind works.

"Miss Holm, have you ever wondered what sort of person you might've been had you not had Miss Lucia for a sister?" I ask, thinking how like Bennett I've become, with Tom's and my philosophizing.

"Oh, I think of that all the time!" She laughs, then glances at me with concern. "Do you miss her? Your sister?"

"I was thinking of Bennett, actually."

But her question brings to mind a fresher wound than my brother's death. Ever since Mattie was rescued from Linwood's ruin, I haven't been able to think of her at all. My mind flinches away as the memory of things we said and did only a short while ago torments my conscience beyond bearing. Confessing my sins to Godfrey may have absolved me of guilt, but the consequences of my actions will forever mark my sister, and there's nothing I can do to ease her suffering.

"You know, Lord Bancroft, you've changed," Miss Holm

says, breaking upon my reverie. "When I met you at the Lawrences', I thought you a most naive young man. That impression was confirmed by our conversation at Linwood, when you told me your family's tragic history. In your narrative, you placed yourself at the center of the family conflict and seemed to take it personally each time one of those you loved left you behind. As though they'd meant to bereave you, and their dying was something of a personal injury.

"Now, you don't seem like the same man preoccupied with his own affairs. You look after us all far more carefully than a financial benefactor."

As we walk, Miss Holm's long skirt brushes the plump, purple heads of clover bending across our path. The afternoon birdsong has a sleepy note to it, as though the robins and star-lings are too warm to make much of an effort. I find myself turning her words over in my mind. I've a strong feeling Miss Holm has asked me a question.

"I don't feel different," I tell her, searching for the truth. "To be honest, I don't feel anything at all. I'm like an empty box full of things I'd rather not take out and look at anymore. When I first met you, I was running from grief. When I surrendered to my sorrow, it was as though all of me was consumed. I've nothing left, certainly nothing to offer, other than what remains of my wealth."

Miss Holm's hand applies light pressure on my forearm, pulling me up short. I've been staring at the packed dirt of our path, idly curious about the imprints of wildlife and partly exposed root systems. Lifting my eyes, I find her sky-blue ones hold an expanse's worth of empathy. She's always been able to say so much with so few words. It's as though she sees into my soul and is pleading with me, *That's not true!*

Our path winds on through maples and pines which clump together on the bank of the rushing creek. The sinking sun filters through their boughs with amber fingers that hold dancing clusters of mayflies. A cicada takes up his rasping call.

"I suppose there are little things that have changed, mostly due to meeting you, Miss Holm. Without the children to distract me from my cares, I might've faded into a sad, old grump long ago. And then, the valuable advice you've given me on more than one occasion has been a priceless boon. I don't think you realize how thankful I am ... In fact, our friendship has been my one ray of hope on this long road of recovery. I don't just mean from the injury—there are wounds upon my mind which will forever remain, like scars."

We stop under the canopy of a wide-reaching oak, the ground under our feet crunching with thousands of dropped acorns. I look at Miss Holm's face, uplifted to peer into the canopy. Hers is a quiet sort of beauty. The kind of fairness that's at once a physical and spiritual meeting, an incarnate soul.

"You know, when I lost Mattie, I also lost someone who might've become my dearest friend," I tell her, thinking of Godfrey Foxe. We write, and he keeps me informed about my sister's progress, but it's never going to be the same now I must stay away.

Miss Holm purses her lips, studying me. "Are you lonely?"

Again, a question I've not asked, and one which pierces to the heart of the matter. "If I am, it's better than being alone."

She smiles, understanding at once the way a person can feel keen loneliness in a crowd—of rowdy children, for instance. But this same loneliness is far more bearable than the intrusion of unwanted memories that flood my mind when I'm by myself. Perhaps Anna Holm seeks a similar refuge, in making herself mother to Saint Anne's.

"Is that wrong of me?" I ask her.

She shakes her head. "We need each other; that is the fundamental truth of humankind."

"Mattie didn't need me." I turn one of the fingered leaves of the oak tree over in my hand. The breeze tousles my hair, mercifully drying the tears pooling at the corners of my eyes.

"If I may," Miss Holm says, taking my hand in both of hers, "I think your Mattie needed more of you than you wanted to give."

A bitterness rising in my throat prevents me from speaking. The oak canopy stirs, its ancient leaves speaking with a wind-birthed whisper.

"Is that why God's taken everything from me? To punish me for holding back?"

I take the soft, care-worn hand of this eternally kind woman in my own, stepping closer to fold her hands against my chest. In the meeting of two souls, our eyes speak a thousand words for the half dozen that find their way to our lips. Within the privacy of that sheltering tree, Miss Holm and I keep counsel for some minutes without speaking.

Then, as frogs nestling in the muddy creek bank begin to sing, we turn back the way we came.

"I won't ask of you more than this," I tell her, standing on the porch at the back of her quiet house. The children will be at their supper by now. "I fear what might happen if you become too dear to me."

Her smile is sad, and there's a reproachful look about her eyes. But when she speaks, any rebuke is understated, and her words are far more gracious than I deserve.

"Dear Lord Bancroft, I wish you could trust, despite all you've been through, that whatever good comes your way isn't on loan. Neither is it earned. I believe, if we have a happiness, it's because there's someone who's delighted to see us happy."

"As always, you've a charmed view of this world, Miss Holm. Thank you for walking with me. Truly, and thank you for the steadfastness of your friendship."

Bowing over her hand but not daring to kiss it, I take my leave.

It's October when I return to Bennett's graveside for the first time since his funeral. The leaves rain down gold and red, stirring about my feet as I walk the long line of Bancroft headstones. Each name evokes a face in vivid detail. Henry Lloyd Bancroft. Francis Henry Bancroft. Helen M. Bancroft. And next to the empty plot which will one day bear my name, Abigail Ruth Bancroft. I find Bennett's half-buried in the brown, decaying hands of oaks and maples, and I kneel to brush them aside.

Bennett Allen Bancroft.

There was a time when I kneeled at Abigail's grave, day after day, weeping. Despite what anyone said to me, I couldn't tear myself away. Now I intend to linger only a moment. I place the last of the roses from Mother's garden atop her headstone, brush a squirrel's picnic off Father's, kiss my fingers and run them along the stone of my dear wife, and then come to stand at last before the one with Grandfather's name. Thick moss grows atop the wind-eaten headstone. I wonder how long it'll take for the lichen to cover all our names, once I'm gone.

The nearby woods smell of musk and fungi, and somewhere far off, well-seasoned logs are burning. In the village, harvest festivities will be underway within the fortnight. For Londoners, high-society balls and soirees will begin in earnest, gathering the marriageable young and the venerable old from all corners of the nation.

At the new Saint Anne's, a bonfire and pie contest are being planned for the night of All Saints' Day. I feel an inward revulsion that life marches on, whether I like it to or not. But of late, I find myself thinking of Mattie much in the same vein as the rest of my long-lost loved ones. It feels strange not to find her name here, among all my dead. Strange, and relieving.

Turning to go, I hunch my shoulders, burying my face in my

coat. I decided to shave my beard recently, to amuse the children, and I'm not used to how cold I'm left without it. That is probably why, when I pass a pair of walkers on the cemetery's gravel path, I do not recognize them.

"Ambrose, is that you?"

In all my wild imaginings, I never pictured myself and Mattie reuniting here. Because, despite all my doomsday assertions to the contrary, some part of me still held fast to hope, believing we might one day be able to see each other again.

I crane my neck round, half-hiding behind my shoulder to mitigate the disappointment I expect to feel should I realize I'm only daydreaming. But Mattie's standing in the path next to Godfrey Foxe. Just as real as any of the Eaton folk who call me by name, never minding I'm a lord and a Bancroft to boot.

She's wearing a pair of trousers that balloon around her knees, like one of the suffragettes the *Morning Post* is busy declaiming of late. Her hair is curled and tied with a floral kerchief under her chin, her healthful complexion tinged with pink from the exercise of walking. She and Godfrey are wearing riding boots, and his gloves are tucked into his jacket pocket. Taking all this in, I remember he sent me a note some time ago, asking if it would be all right for the two of them to visit the graves.

"I-I'm sorry, I don't mean to intrude," I stammer, backing away and shuffling up the path toward the little iron gate.

My heart hammers in my chest, and I find myself grinning like an absolute fool. But I can't help it. Mattie looked so well. And so very at ease, standing with Godfrey at her side. As though she's found, at long last, a place where she can be happy.

I enter Eaton Village, striding with all my might up the rutted, rain-washed road. Tothill will be out shopping for our supper this time of day. Donnie's taken a job at Saint Anne's, keeping their coal in supply and tending the farm animals that provide the children fresh milk, eggs, and bacon. The clock on Father Amicus's little bell tower chimes three as I'm fumbling my key in the lock. I don't realize, until I've bitten back a curse or two, that the reason I'm having difficulty with it is because I'm blinded by my crying.

I let the key fall, clattering against the stone walk. My head rests against my raised arm, the door supporting me as I hide my face and let out sob after shuddering sob.

I'd no idea I missed her so much.

"Ambrose," her voice says again, and a light touch on my shoulder convinces me I'm not imagining things. But I can't meet her eye. She doesn't deserve to read in my face all the many reminders of our shared history. I'll never let myself cause her pain like that again.

"Ambrose, will you keep yourself from me, even now?"

She has every right to rebuke me. I shake my head, trying to regain my composure and failing to do more than inhale great, ragged breaths broken by weeping. Mattie slips her arms around me, squeezing me tight. I hear the little wooden gate clack shut, and I know Godfrey's here too. It seems fitting he should bear witness to this, though I've no inkling of what is about to happen.

Will I turn around, only to see disappointment in my sister's face? Will she scream at me for abandoning her, and rightly so? Will she ask me why I never wrote to ask her forgiveness, or why I couldn't bring myself to attend her and Godfrey's wedding?

Before any of my manifold fears can come to pass, Mattie's voice banishes them all, filled with an emotion I can't mistake for anything but tenderness.

"Ambrose, I wanted to give you some time, and I didn't intend to visit so soon—but I can't stay away any longer. I really, really want my brother back!"

Of all the things she might've said to me, this is not what I expected. Gathering my courage, I turn and lean back against the door, holding my aching side. Mattie steps back with a pained smile, tears running freely down her cheeks. She seems suddenly shy and leans back against Godfrey's chest. My old friend—not just Bennett's—has that knowing glimmer in his eye. He smiles at me, like he did the day he dragged me out of Linwood to remind me I belonged to the living, the day Thuris fled for good.

And then I can't keep from laughing. Enormous relief and a strange sense of becoming seep through my broken, weary body. After mourning, it seems, a new daybreak cannot fail to come.

EPILOGUE

"Since then—'tis Centuries—and yet
Feels shorter than the Day
I first surmised the Horses' Heads
Were toward Eternity—"

— EMILY DICKINSON

When April comes round again, the folk of Eaton Village gather on the spacious lawn behind the new Saint Anne's. Its construction was finished too close to winter to have an outdoor festival. But now the snows have melted, and spring's warmth has returned, and the village folk are putting on an elaborate picnic in celebration of Eaton's home for children. For after all we've been through together, the village has extended once again a heart full of hospitality and adopted my pet project as their own.

They've set up an outdoor kitchen under an awning. Tables covered in sky-blue linen are crowded with pies, roast fowl, and all varieties of sweets. The children buzz like bees from field to table and back again, picking flowers from the one and snatching cookies from the other. The women gather in groups, gossiping, as is the Eaton way. A few pretend they aren't watching their men show off, but most give rowdy appraisal of the feats-of-strength contests in voices pitched to carry.

"Lord Bancroft, I see you've recovered from your injuries."

I turn to find Monsieur Belot and extend my hand to him. It no longer feels like a foreign gesture to grip hands, though Mons. Belot appears to suffer a minor affront when I do so.

"Just sir, monsieur," I tell him. "After today, I won't even be that."

Mons. Belot coughs. "Is there somewhere we can sit? I have your will and the deed of the property, as well as the bills of sale prepared."

"Yes, I was told Tothill prepared something," I trail off, scanning the village folk for a sign of my housekeeper. "But I don't see her."

"That's because I'm right under your nose, as usual." Tothill chuckles, shuffling round to hand me a bowl of cool lemon custard. She offers one to the solicitor as well, but Mons. Belot shakes his head.

We follow her to a festival tent furnished for our comfort. Sitting at a white table, I begin to go through the legal requirements for giving away all my earthly possessions. If my grandfather had lived to see this day, he'd have run me through with the imitation saber our Bancroft ancestor was supposed to have wrested from the hands of a Sultan. Another one of his sitting room stories, calculated to give the Bancroft name an air of ancient respectability.

But I've no qualms about this decision. With a few strokes of my pen, I undo his life's labors, sinking what remains of our prestige back down to the class from which young Henry Bancroft came.

"Now that's done," I say, ignoring the somberness of Mons. Belot's expression, "you must stay and enjoy the festivities. I hear there's more than custard coming, by and by."

Rising from his chair, he clears his throat. "My train leaves at three, I'm afraid. I'll be returning to London at once, sir."

I extend my hand to him again. "It's been an unpleasant and brief position for someone of your expertise, monsieur. I appreciate all you've done for my family."

After Belot takes his leave, I sit a moment under the tent, staring at the pen and empty table. I've made plans up until this juncture. Going forward, there are no longer any expectations for me to fulfill, no rules by which to abide. I don't even know the name for the feeling rising inside me. A buzzing of insects and distant laughter of children sharpen into one clear call, beckoning me out.

Beyond the tent, the children lift a cheer, drawing my eyes in the direction they're running. The lightness filling my chest bubbles over into laughter. For there, across the lawn, parting the way through the merry-makers, Mattie is riding atop a shaggy-coated donkey. Donnie has the animal by its lead, beaming back over his shoulder at my sister. All the children skip round them, catching at flower petals Mattie's tossing to the breeze. She has a basket full of them, and her laughter rings out above little ones calling, "Me! To me!"

"Have you thought about what comes next?" Godfrey asks, ambling up beside me.

I watch my sister slide off, her basket empty, and lift two little girls onto the donkey's back. They form a small parade, skipping in circles on the green while young Tom plays a pennywhistle tune. Eaton folk mill about here and there, faces bearing names I've only recently learned, stories I hope to learn soon.

The Holm sisters, who've come to be like family, stand arm in arm, clapping their hands to the music. Miss Lucia draws her sister into a country version of the gavotte. Miss Holm flushes in embarrassment but dances along anyway.

"How do I know, Godfrey? It feels too daring to try and be happy after all that's happened. I don't even think I deserve it." I shrug, feeling disjointed from the gaiety happening before me. Despite the fact it's happening because I decided to let go of everything.

"You don't have to deserve it," Godfrey tells me.

"But it's—"

"Ambrose!" Godfrey chides, bumping my shoulder with his. "You'll probably be happy without meaning to, perhaps in a very short while."

I follow his gaze and see Anna breaking away from her little sister's frolicking. She's red and out of breath, her hair falling loose from her braid. She looks around and finds me, smiling in that charming, thoughtful way of hers. I duck my head, my face growing warm.

Godfrey laughs. "Don't ask what you have to lose, my friend. Ask yourself, who do you have to love?"

He leaves my side, spinning on his heel to grin lopsided at me as he walks backward. Then he sprints to his wife, scooping her into his arms with such abandon that Mattie laughs and kisses him. Averting my eyes, heat tinging my ears for the second time this evening, I begin to shuffle in among the village folk. Their mirth is contagious, and I've become more light-hearted than I would've thought possible. It's a night I know I'll never forget. It'll be one of those memories that linger, long after the lively figures who play a part in it have gone.

THE END

ACKNOWLEDGMENTS

Ambrose's story came out of a season of depression, when I was learning how to grieve deep losses of my own. Without the compassionate support of family, friends, and health professionals, this book would never have come into the world. Creating *A Voracious Grief* was a lot like birthing a child—and I know a bit about that, having five of my own—and just like any labor of love, I needed a team of people supporting me.

First, I want to acknowledge the fact that Jeffrey is the ideal husband for a creative personality like mine! He genuinely enjoyed hearing about my multitude of story ideas while bemoaning the fact that I never finished anything. Without piling on shame, he gently challenged me to go for that elusive goal post of completing a manuscript. After my fantasy novel's first draft rolled out, then the second, then the third, fourth, and fifth, Jeffrey was never too busy or too over it to sit down and let me read him my latest work. By the time *this* novel entered its final drafting stage, Jeffrey had become a pro at bouncing back and forth ideas about character development, plot twists, and the delicate balance of understated vs. overstated themes. His perspective as a deep-thinking reader was invaluable. Above and beyond all of this, being a self-published author requires a heavy dose of business know-how, and Jeffrey has been an amazing partner in transforming my writing hobby into a professional career.

Secondly, there are a number of friends—artists and otherwise—who provided much-needed encouragement along the way. Kate Wood, my best friend and confidante, is one of the few people who loves to hear me gush about my latest writing news. Jacinta Meredith, fellow writer and pen pal, was someone I could always "talk shop" with as we both worked on revisions. Ray Foy, my most thorough, constructive beta reader, provided clarity after my first draft left me feeling a little lost. And to all my friends at the SCWA COLA III writer's group—thank you for all your helpful advice about improving my voice and grammar, structure and pacing. I've learned a lot from each one of you!

Thirdly, I honestly believe I am a writer because dozens of men and women have gone before me, doing the incredible labor of bringing their own stories into this world. The books I grew up reading had a deep impact on my personal development. More recently, reading several women authors persuaded me to pursue my dream of writing books. I now have a taste for the amount of dedication, stubbornness, endurance, and courage it takes to do this work. I feel I'd be remiss not naming the authors who inspire me: Laura E. Weymouth, Helena Sorensen, Alison Croggon, and Madeleine L'Engle—your books were well worth all they cost you. Thank you.

Lastly, I'd like to acknowledge and thank my editor, Amber Helt, over at Rooted in Writing. Amber and her team took a fair book idea and provided the knowledge, motivation, and direction I needed to take my story deeper, creating something I feel captures to a far greater extent what I'd envisioned for it from the start. I couldn't ask for a better team. Thank you all so much!

I'd also like to thank the artist, Silvyu, who created the book cover. It certainly takes a whole mess of people to put everything together. I appreciate how things turned out.

Ambrose's story has just begun, but there's a lot you still don't know about him.

AVAILABLE FROM LAMH BOOKS

An anthology of short stories about the Bancroft family, including Beatrix and Bonne's chilling origin story.

www.LindseyLamh.com

ABOUT THE AUTHOR

Lindsey Lamh is the author of dark stories shot through with hope. Chronic pain and seasons of depression have given Lindsey a deep respect for those who endure seemingly endless suffering. Her books wrestle with the purpose of pain and acknowledge that traumas can threaten our desire to continue living. Lindsey doesn't hesitate to ask the questions you're not supposed to ask, to give voice to the doubts which arise in the midst of darkness. Her books bring you to places where evil is overthrown, introducing characters who fight monsters and demons but who are a lot like the person you see reflected in the mirror.

Subscribe for her publishing newsletter to hear about upcoming books.

www.LindseyLamh.com